STORM'S REVENGE

AMELIA STORM SERIES: BOOK NINE

MARY STONE
AMY WILSON

DESCRIPTION

Revenge is sweet. But justice is sweeter.

Seven months ago, one of the FBI's own went missing without a trace. The forensic analyst was smart and beautiful, and she had been dating Joseph Larson...the same man who'd been working with the Chicago PD to investigate the young woman's missing persons case. The same man who'd just been forced to resign from the Bureau.

Something's terribly wrong, FBI Special Agent Amelia Storm knows it in her gut. But knowing and proving are two very different things.

When Special Agent Journey Russo blows into the office implicating Larson in her sister's disappearance, Amelia is even more certain that the disgraced ex-agent is involved. The question is how.

As Amelia and her partner investigate, she and Zane quickly realize that Larson has woven a twisted web of deceit that encompasses mafia influence and political sway. Worse, the truth behind the analyst's disappearance is darker than anything they could have imagined.

Amelia is determined to find the young woman and ensure Joseph Larson gets what he deserves—a miserable life in an eight-by-ten cell. But Larson is just as determined to see Amelia dead.

From the wickedly dark minds of Mary Stone and Amy Wilson comes Storm's Revenge, book nine of the Amelia Storm Series, where you'll think twice about who you trust.

1

One more.

With her palms flat against the floor, Michelle Timmer straightened her back, gritted her teeth, and lowered herself until her chin met the cool tile. Muscles in her arms and chest burned like they'd been set ablaze, but she powered through the pain to push her body back up to its raised position.

Done. For now.

Letting out an explosive breath, she shoved backward until she was resting on her knees. Workouts had never been a regular part of her life *before*, but now, they were all she could do to keep from losing her mind. From losing all hope and sinking into a pit of despair as black and thick as tar.

Michelle now understood why prisoners incarcerated throughout the world turned to exercise. She had no other form of distraction—no television, no books, not even a ray of sunlight. There were no other prisoners with whom to associate. Aside from the men who'd taken her, Michelle had barely glimpsed another human being since she'd been imprisoned by these terrible men.

Despite the beads of sweat still forming on her skin, a shiver raced down her spine as she recalled her last night of freedom...

A humid summer breeze rolled off Lake Michigan, whispering past Michelle as she climbed out of the passenger's side of Joseph Larson's sedan. Her heels clicked against the asphalt, and she smoothed the front of her lace-trimmed cocktail dress.

With a career as an FBI forensic analyst, Michelle's opportunities to dress up were few and far between. Sure, she had to look professional when she testified in a trial, but the courtrooms of Cook County, Illinois weren't the prime location to show off a new pair of heels or a designer party dress.

Michelle was far from a fashion icon, but even the geeks in the forensic lab enjoyed a black-tie event from time to time.

Looking back, she wanted to kick herself for worrying about such unimportant issues. Her clothing mattered little now. Neither did her memories, but that didn't stop them from coming...

As Joseph circled around the front of the car and hooked his arm in hers, she made her best effort at an enamored smile. Joseph returned one of his patented grins—the type that softened his face but didn't completely eliminate the menacing edge in his pale blue eyes.

Or maybe Michelle had simply begun to view him differently ever since she spotted another woman's nude photos on his phone. He'd been a mixture of surprised and angry. "Are we exclusive?" The question had been filled with bitterness. "You sure haven't acted as if you wanted anything more solid than we have now."

Gaslighting.

Michelle understood the term, but when the covert manipulation had been turned on her, she found herself doubting everything...even her own feelings.

In the week following her messy discovery, Joseph had

done something she'd never expected from a tenured FBI agent. He'd begged and pleaded for her forgiveness.

Before then, Michelle hadn't been sure the man reciprocated the feelings she thought she'd had for him. Apparently, her assumption had been incorrect.

Or had it?

There was part of the situation that made no sense to Michelle. This man had been so aloof, almost to the point of apathetic, and suddenly, he was plagued by dreams of the two of them together?

Then again, he was a man. As an ex-military FBI agent in the Bureau's Organized Crime Division, Joseph Larson wasn't the type to familiarize himself with his own emotions. Michelle tried to give the men in her life the benefit of the doubt when it came to stereotypical masculine faults, but more often than not, she was disappointed.

Joseph was no exception.

Under normal circumstances, Michelle would have told him to get bent. But in the last couple weeks of their so-called relationship, she'd picked up on a few oddities. Phone calls he'd receive in the middle of the night that didn't quite correlate to a case he was working. Michelle wasn't a field agent, but she understood enough of the Bureau's processes to glean that part of Joseph's explanations were…off.

Word of a rat in the Organized Crime Division, or in an adjacent department, had filtered down to Michelle and her colleagues in the forensic lab. According to the rumors, a rogue agent had provided information about an undercover operation during the investigation of a mob-run sex trafficking ring.

As luck would have it, the timeline of Joseph's strange behavior correlated directly to the big case.

Michelle had gone back and forth with herself for weeks. She'd even attempted to get ahold of her sister to ask for help, but Journey Russo was on an undercover assignment for the FBI in Las Vegas.

Without Journey to point her in the right direction, Michelle was on her own. She'd tried to ignore the suspicions burrowing into the back of her mind, but she'd done a piss-poor job.

If Joseph was the FBI's rat, and if Michelle had suspicions but didn't act on them, then what did that make her? Some kind of accomplice?

At the same time, she wasn't confident enough in her assumptions to go to the field office's Special Agent in Charge, Jasmine Keaton.

She needed more information. So, when Joseph had come begging and pleading for her to take him back, she'd obliged. If she could do more snooping, then maybe she could get something solid enough to bring to the SAC. Or, more likely, she'd allay her concerns by affirming to herself that Joseph was just a womanizing prick. Chances were, his late-night phone calls had to do with him banging another chick and not ratting out the Organized Crime Division of the FBI.

What had she been thinking? Even then, she'd known she was acting a fool. There was a chance Joseph had been sincere when he'd pled for her forgiveness, but deep down, Michelle doubted it. Since she'd supposedly forgiven him, he'd forever view her as a doormat.

All because she...what? Thought her boyfriend was a corrupt federal agent? Thought Joseph was in bed with the Italian mob?

She'd been watching too much television, or maybe she didn't have enough excitement in her life, and she was vying for a little intrigue.

"Stop it." Her sharp words echoed in her tiny cabin as she castigated herself for the thousandth time. She softened her tone. "There's no way you could have predicted this happening."

It was true, but that knowledge didn't make her current situation any easier to face.

Sitting on the floor in the lotus position, Michelle worked to cleanse her mind of the racing thoughts that wanted to consume it. Since her captivity, she'd forced herself to workout every day and meditate even more often. When she escaped—and she *would* escape—she needed to be both physically and mentally fit. She refused to crumble because of these men.

"Breathe in…" Inhaling deeply, she mentally counted to seven before holding the breath. "And out…" The air whistled through her lips, the only music she'd heard in…

How long?

Michelle didn't know, but it felt like forever.

As she attempted to deepen her meditative state, she struggled not to let her mind slip back to that long ago summer night…

As Michelle and Joseph boarded a large, luxury yacht decked out with string lights, neatly set tables, and well-dressed men and women, Michelle wished she was at home.

This was a stupid endeavor. There were people at the FBI who knew Joseph better than she did. People trained for these kinds of things. She should have left this detective shit to them. After all, they had badges and guns. Michelle had…

"Agent Larson, there you are!" A man's excited greeting ripped her from her regrets and worry.

Turning her attention to the speaker, Michelle painted another smile on her lips. The black-tie event was a small fundraiser to solicit donations for one of the city's hospitals. Joseph claimed a couple of his oldest friends would be in attendance, and he was eager to introduce her to them.

In hindsight, Michelle realized how ominous the explanation really was.

When she'd met the pale green gaze of a tall, impeccably dressed man in his late-forties or early-fifties, Michelle had no idea whose hand she was about to shake. In that moment, on the deck of a luxury yacht docked on Lake Michigan, she didn't realize she was exchanging pleasantries with a monster.

Over the next god knew how many months, she'd learn the depths of Brian Kolthoff's depravity.

She should have turned and run off the yacht or claimed she was ill so she could go home. Anything to get her away from those psychopaths...

"You must be Michelle. I'm glad to finally put a face to a name. I'm Brian Kolthoff, one of Joseph's friends. We go...way back."

The man's name was vaguely familiar, like a tickle in the back of Michelle's head. She couldn't place it right away, so she ignored the thought.

"It's so nice to meet you." Michelle clasped Brian's hand in a firm, confident shake, offering him a smile that was largely feigned. *"I haven't really met any of Joseph's friends, so I'm glad I was able to tag along with him tonight."* She was impressed at her ability to remain polite and cordial despite her nerves.

Joseph turned to Brian with a wide grin. A wolf's grin, though she hadn't realized it at the time. *"We appreciate the invitation."*

"Of course." Brian waved a hand to a bar located near the entrance to the yacht's second level. *"Please, go grab yourselves a drink. We'll have food brought out soon."*

Michelle's stomach grumbled quietly at the thought of eating. She wasn't sure if her nerves would allow her to shovel down a full meal, but she could go for some finger foods. If she didn't, then the alcohol from her drink would hit her hard. Being wasted around Joseph and his friends was among the last things she wanted.

Side by side, she and Joseph made their way to the bar. As they waited for their drinks, Michelle glanced around the deck, her eyes widening for a beat as she spotted a pair of vaguely familiar faces. Senator Stan Young and his wife, Cynthia.

The sight of the Illinois senator and his wife was enough to put to bed the worst of Michelle's fears. Surely, if Joseph was up to no good, he wouldn't associate with friends of a senator, would he? Corruption couldn't possibly run that deep—not all the way to the senate.

"What a complete dumbass I was."

Rubbing her eyes with the heels of her hands, Michelle pushed aside the memory as well as the self-flagellation that came so quickly when she thought of how naive she'd been. She'd thought through that night at least a hundred times by now. She'd analyzed every interaction, though there hadn't been many. While she'd been busy gawking at the sight of Senator Young, Joseph must have slipped a drug into her drink.

The last memory of the party was of the rich wooden surface of the bar as she tucked her head into the crook of her elbow and passed out.

When she woke, she was in a room almost identical to where she was now. She'd been alone, but not for long.

Nausea churned in her gut as she recalled Joseph Larson's face as he'd walked through the heavy door. The mask he'd worn for all the months she'd known him had fallen away, revealing who she now realized was the real monster behind the façade he presented to the world.

His pale blue eyes had been lit with a sentiment that went beyond lust. It was a predatory hunger. Like Larson was a vampire and Michelle was about to become his meal.

No, that wasn't quite right. Larson was far worse than a vampire. He was closer to a demon, some sort of demented hell spawn that could only draw pleasure from forcing women to bend to its will.

She closed her hands into fists and turned her attention to the room, knowing her mind wouldn't settle enough to meditate right now.

The space wasn't a room so much as a cell. With four beige, unadorned walls, a bed, a stainless-steel sink and toilet, and a door locked tighter than Fort Knox, the resemblance to a prison was uncanny. She'd memorized every square inch of the cell, having searched fruitlessly for a structural weakness she could exploit.

To her dismay, she wasn't Andy in *The Shawshank Redemption*. She couldn't chisel a hole in the wall of her cell and cover it with a poster of a pinup girl.

If she tried, Brian Kolthoff would know. Stan Young would know. Joseph Larson would know. Kolthoff paid close attention to the state of Michelle's room. Any abnormality would set his hackles on end, and then he'd be on her, attacking her, beating her senseless like he was some rabid dog.

She touched the fresh scar behind her ear. It wouldn't be the first time.

How long have I even been here? Six months? A year?

Not that she knew where *here* was. She'd gathered she wasn't on solid ground and that she was aboard a seafaring vessel of some kind. However, the knowledge only made her conundrum worse. Three-fourths of the planet was ocean, meaning Michelle could be almost anywhere. She'd identified a few patterns to help narrow down her location, but there were only so many aspects of the environment she could piece together while in this windowless cell.

Based on the regularity of storms, Michelle assumed she was somewhere around the East Coast—the Pacific wasn't quite as volatile as the Atlantic. The lack of humidity in the air led her to believe she wasn't in the tropics, either.

Pushing to her feet, Michelle went to the sink. After wiping off her sweaty skin with a washcloth, she changed into a fresh t-shirt and shorts. Well, not fresh as in they'd just been pulled from the dryer, but fresher than the tank top and shorts she wore during her prison workouts. Unless she was exercising, the chill of the room typically permeated her skin, muscles, and all the way down to the marrow in her bones.

She sat cross-legged in the center of her bed, tugging a thin blanket up over her lap. With a sigh, she flipped over her only pillow.

The sense of relief she felt upon gazing down at a crudely illustrated face she'd drawn so long ago would have been embarrassing if she was anywhere else in the world.

But she wasn't. She was here, in this beige, windowless hell, and she'd do whatever it took to come out alive on the other side. Not just alive, but *sane* as well. Michelle knew from her Yale education that the greatest risk to a person in solitary confinement was, put simply, losing their marbles. Humans were social creatures, and without some sort of companion, their cognitive functions suffered greatly.

Tom Hanks had Wilson the volleyball, and Michelle had Laurie the pillow.

"I had a good workout today. I did three more reps per set than yesterday. I think I'm getting stronger. You know, I used to hate working out. I'd have to bribe myself to go to the gym or even to go for a run around my neighborhood. But now," Michelle sighed, fidgeting with a piece of her faded auburn hair, "it's the only thing I can do that reminds me I'm still alive."

Why do you even want to be alive?

The question invaded her head like it had been spoken aloud by a stranger. Her logical mind knew there was no one in the room but her. There were no cameras, no hidden mics. Michelle had checked. There were just four barren walls and a metal door. Still, the knowledge did little to quell her body's visceral response.

Stomach twisting itself into knots, Michelle tightened her grasp on the blanket and inhaled deeply. A hot strand of anger unfurled beside the rush of anxiety. "I'm not going to die in here. I won't give those sons of bitches the satisfaction."

You've come within an inch of death once already. Who's to say the next time won't be your last?

"I don't know." She pinched the bridge of her nose, a headache building behind her eyes. "I don't know why Senator…why Stan Young told Kolthoff to leave me alone. At first, I thought it might've been because the senator had a conscience buried somewhere in his head, but…"

She left the thought unfinished. Neither her brain nor Laurie chimed in.

"No." She rolled the thin fabric between her fingers and dragged in a long breath. "That's not why Stan told Kolthoff and Larson to leave me alone. If he actually had a conscience, he'd have pulled me out of here. He wouldn't have ordered Kolthoff to keep me alive after Kolthoff had almost killed me."

She'd long refused to think of Brian or Joseph by their first names. They didn't deserve that amount of intimacy. Not after they'd…

On cue, an ache radiated outward from the site of the wound behind her ear. Tears sprang to her eyes at the sudden stinging pain, but she squeezed them closed and brushed them away.

Medicine hadn't been her specialty in graduate school, but she knew how serious and long-lasting head injuries could be. When Kolthoff had smashed her skull into the floor, Michelle had watched her life flash before her eyes.

Part of her had been relieved at the idea that she might die. She'd suffered so many assaults at Kolthoff and Larson's hands, she couldn't imagine how she'd ever go back to normal if she broke free.

There is no "normal" where you're going.

Michelle licked her lips, glancing to her only companion as the pain in her head diffused into a dull ache. Before she could respond, a metallic *click-clack* sounded from the door. In reality, the noise was quiet, but to Michelle, the lock disengaging was like the cocking of a gun.

Flipping over the pillow to conceal the face of her only friend in this place, Michelle folded her hands on her lap, closed her eyes, and pretended to be in the midst of meditation. Mentally, she crossed her fingers in the hope that the visitor was Kolthoff's head of security. Whenever he brought her a meal or herded her to the shower, he at least kept his mouth shut.

As the door creaked open, she made a show of blinking to reorient herself. Blood thundered in her ears, the volume increasing as Brian Kolthoff emerged.

His pale green eyes inspected the room, searching for any abnormality that might indicate she'd tried to break free.

He'd find nothing. Michelle wasn't that stupid. Even if she Shawshanked her way out of this place, where would she go then? They were on some sort of seafaring vessel, and she wasn't a fish.

Of course, she'd rather die trying to swim away than let this man kill her.

Kolthoff's gaze settled on Michelle as he set a plastic container of food on a small table beside the door. Like everything else, the table was bolted to the floor, completely immovable without a set of power tools.

Michelle prayed to any god who would listen, begging them to make Kolthoff leave before he opened his mouth, or worse. He hadn't touched her since Stan had ordered him and Larson to keep their hands off her, but she could never be sure how long the men would obey the senator.

Especially after her last encounter with Stan Young.

Cocking his head to the side, Kolthoff crossed both arms over his white dress shirt. "You know, I really should have bashed your head in harder. The only reason I didn't was because I figured I'd get another opportunity. I didn't expect Stan to jump in and save your ass."

The man's tone was cool and casual, like he was discussing the weather or a ball game, not how he'd nearly splattered Michelle's brains across the floor.

Terrified to her very core, Michelle resisted the urge to dive behind the bed as Kolthoff drew closer. She'd been at this prick's mercy for god knew how long, and she'd given in to plenty of displays of fear before.

But the bastard got off on it. Her terror and suffering gave this psychopath a hard-on.

She wouldn't give him the pleasure anymore. For whatever reason, Senator Stan Young had ordered Kolthoff to keep his hands off her.

Rather than cower behind the flimsy bed, she met those eerie, pale green eyes with her back straight and her expression carefully blank. Kolthoff dropped down to his haunches in front of Michelle's pathetic excuse for a bed, his gaze unwavering. Like one of those angels from *Doctor Who*.

Without warning, his arm snapped forward with the speed of a venomous snake. His rough grip clamped onto her chin, holding her face like a vise.

Seconds dragged by as if she'd stepped through a portal into a vastly slower universe.

Stan's order still stood, didn't it? Her last interaction with the senator had been...less than kind. Had he changed his mind? Had he ordered Kolthoff to kill her?

"I can feel your pulse. I know how scared you are right now." A lazy smile crawled to his lips, self-satisfaction radiating off his body in waves. "Oh, how I miss all the fun we used to have. It's just like Stan to claim the best plaything for himself. But I'll be honest. The last few times I've spoken to him, he didn't seem all that thrilled about your continued existence. If you ask me, I think he just wants to kill you himself."

Michelle resisted the urge to rip herself out of Kolthoff's grasp. He already had some inclination of how much he got under her skin, and she didn't want to give him even more evidence of how desperately he terrified her.

"Just know this, my sweet little sin." He tightened his grip until Michelle wondered if his fingers would leave marks. "If you try anything, I *am* permitted to kill you. If you think you're going to try to run away like you did the last time we moved you, I will make your life for all these months look like a pleasant vacation."

How many months had it been? And what in the hell could possibly make being repeatedly raped and beaten seem like a vacation? This man was evil incarnate.

Bile surged up her throat as he leaned in to brush his lips against her ear. She wished desperately she could transform into a werewolf to rip this man's head from his shoulders.

"I'll tell you a secret. I hope you do it. I hope you try to pull some *Mission Impossible* shit to break out of here, and I hope I catch you." With a low chuckle, he gave a condescending pat to her cheek and rose to his full height.

Michelle wanted to throw up, but only if she could drown this asshole in the vomit. It was no less than he deserved.

Kolthoff could make his ominous warnings. He could continue to try to intimidate her, but it mattered little. The next time an opportunity presented itself to escape, she'd take it, no matter the stakes.

Or she'd die trying.

Death—even hell, or the devil himself—couldn't possibly be worse than staying here.

2

As Special Agent Amelia Storm closed the door of the small incident room, her mind was still reeling from the announcement she'd just received. Turning to her frequent case partner in the FBI's Organized Crime Division, Special Agent Zane Palmer, she squared her shoulders and made her best effort to wipe the dumbfounded look off her face. Amelia and Zane weren't only partners at the Chicago Bureau, but in the last couple months, they'd also become partners outside the office.

A measure of amusement danced in the back of her head as she recalled the first time she'd made the cheesy observation to Zane. He'd flung an arm over his eyes, slumped so far down in his seat he'd almost plopped onto the floor, and groaned. Loudly. Puns and dad jokes were the lowest form of humor, but that had never stopped Amelia.

She brushed away the musing but was grateful for the shot of normalcy. Zane had blown into the incident room proclaiming Michelle Timmer's sister—a special agent from the Violent Crime Division in the Bureau's Las Vegas Field Office—was here looking for clues regarding Michelle's whereabouts. Since then, Amelia couldn't help but feel like the hallways of the ten-story FBI building had been replaced with the corridors of a funhouse.

For a beat, Amelia had been convinced Zane was pulling a prank on her and the Assistant U.S. Attorney, but Zane wasn't much of a prankster. Virtually all his pranks were reserved for Amelia's cat, a long-haired calico named Hup.

"Michelle Timmer's sister is here to talk to us?" Amelia's voice was barely above a conspiratorial whisper. "The same Michelle Timmer who was dating Joseph Larson before she disappeared? The Michelle who Larson *lied* about dating, at least to me? That Michelle Timmer, right?"

Zane offered a half-smile as if to let her know they were both on the same page—surprised but prepared. They were always prepared. "Yeah, that Michelle Timmer. Michelle's sister is in a meeting room on the first floor. I already shot an email to SAC Keaton. Spencer Corsaw is down there with her right now, but they're waiting for us before they start going through anything major."

Goose bumps prickled the back of Amelia's neck. Ever since she'd first dug into Michelle Timmer six months earlier, she'd had a nagging suspicion there was more to her story.

Michelle had held a position as a forensic analyst in the Chicago Field Office before she'd disappeared. Why on earth would a woman who'd graduated Yale at the top of her class vanish when she had such a promising career ahead of her?

Simple. She wouldn't.

Though Amelia had found no evidence to link Michelle's disappearance to her then-boyfriend, former Special Agent Joseph Larson, Amelia's gut told her the connection wasn't a coincidence.

Joseph was a rat, a chauvinist piece of shit, and a liar. After the prick had tried to blackmail Amelia into screwing him, she'd known what she had to do. A man like that didn't randomly decide to rape one of his coworkers. He had a history of that behavior, and Amelia had taken it upon herself to unearth the old skeletons.

Excavating Joseph's secrets and discovering his long-standing friendship with Brian Kolthoff hadn't been an easy endeavor. However, with Amelia and Zane's efforts, they'd provided SAC Keaton with enough information to force Joseph to resign from his position as an FBI special agent.

Even that hadn't been a slam dunk. If it wasn't for Zane's CIA connections, who knew how long it would've taken to get Joseph out of the Bureau.

On paper, Zane had worked for the Federal Bureau of Investigation for the vast majority of his adult life, from age twenty-one until now, at thirty-four. However, by Amelia's best guess, the official records had been forged by the CIA itself. Including one's tenure as a covert operative on a resumé wasn't exactly how the CIA preferred to operate.

Zane hadn't revealed any of the gory details of his time with the Agency, but he'd confirmed he *had* worked for the CIA. Amelia wasn't sure how long he'd been with them, but his stint had lasted long enough to yield him a reliable contact who'd come through with video footage of Joseph Larson fraternizing with his old friend, Brian Kolthoff.

The video surveillance had corroborated a couple photos Amelia had received from the man who could best be described as her informant. Alex Passarelli, a capo in one of the city's two major Italian crime families, would cut out his own tongue before he'd let himself be labeled an informant, but Amelia wasn't sure what else to call him.

A friend? Her high school sweetheart? Both titles were accurate, but they didn't sound great on paper.

The end result was what mattered. With the CIA's footage to corroborate Alex's paparazzo-style photos, Joseph had been forced out of the FBI. Joseph's friendship with Brian Kolthoff—the man who'd been the prime suspect in Amelia's first major case in the Chicago Field Office—had compromised the integrity of the investigation and had called into question whether Joseph could be trusted at all.

Joseph and Brian's alliances with organized crime were a damned mess. A twisted, interconnected web of mafia influence bleeding over into the political landscape not just of Chicago but the entire state of Illinois and the federal government as well.

To say Joseph had friends in low and high places would be an understatement. Hell, Joseph had existed simultaneously in the lowest low and the highest high. His position as a federal agent had given Kolthoff and their other criminal counterparts god knows how many advantages over the years.

Amelia wouldn't, *couldn't*, underestimate Joseph. The man was a sleaze, but he was smart, and he was manipulative. Dealing with Larson was like playing a game of chess. Amelia had to think two, three, or even four moves ahead.

Taking Joseph's gun and badge was a start, but it wasn't enough. The bastard needed to spend the rest of his life in an eight-by-ten cell, under constant threat of being beaten to death by some of the same criminals he'd put away during his tenure with the Bureau.

Renewed determination rolled over Amelia as she and Zane approached the elevator. Maybe, with the help of Michelle's sister, Joseph would finally get what he deserved.

Neither Amelia nor Zane spoke for the remainder of their short journey to the first-floor meeting room. As eager as Amelia was to learn more about Michelle's FBI agent sister, she didn't want to try to speculate on the situation. She'd prefer to let Michelle's sister fill in the details.

Pausing in front of a door labeled "1-C," Zane lifted an

eyebrow as his gray eyes shifted to Amelia's. His sandy hair was brushed forward, styled as neatly as ever. Along with his tailored Tom Ford suit, expensive watch, and lean, muscular frame, he could have passed for a CEO or a wealthy banker, maybe even a Wall Street day trader.

He could have chosen any of those occupations and likely succeeded. His mother was a fabulously successful hedge fund manager, but like her son, she'd wanted to do some good in the world, so she'd left the world of finance. Wealth clouded the judgment of many people, but the Palmers had their priorities straight.

Amelia nodded, and Zane shoved open the door. Blinds were half-drawn over the expansive window on the far end of the room, blocking out the brightest part of the midday sun.

Spencer Corsaw leaned against the edge of a whiteboard, his black suit nearly as impeccable as Zane's. Months ago, the Supervisory Special Agent of the Organized Crime Division had announced his plan to step down from his leadership position. Either Spencer had changed his mind, or the Special Agent in Charge, Jasmine Keaton, hadn't settled on a suitable replacement yet.

The SSA's Italian heritage was plainly visible in his brown gaze, tan complexion, and slicked-back ebony hair. Amelia wondered how many mafia-related undercover operations Spencer had conducted in his tenure with the FBI. She knew painfully little about the man who'd been her boss since she'd transferred to the Chicago Field Office nearly a year ago.

Spencer wasn't the person Amelia and Zane were here to meet, though.

An unfamiliar woman rose from where she'd been seated at the oval table in the center of the room. The knit sweater she'd layered over a pastel blue button-down, chevron scarf, and charcoal slacks could have been stolen straight from

Amelia's own closet—simple, comfortable, but professional, and even a little stylish.

Spencer straightened and gestured to the woman. "Palmer, Storm, this is Special Agent Journey Russo from the Las Vegas Field Office. Journey, these are agents Amelia Storm and Zane Palmer. I'm sure you can figure out which is which."

Journey Russo humored Spencer with a soft chuckle. "Please, call me Journey."

Ignoring Spencer's attempt at humor, Amelia extended a hand. "Afternoon, Journey. I hope the cold hasn't been too jarring."

The agent's indigo eyes moved from Amelia to Zane as she accepted their handshakes. "A little, but it's nothing I can't handle. I...*we* grew up in Pennsylvania. Michelle and I."

"Which is why you're here, for Michelle."

Journey blew out a breath and pushed her dark shoulder-length hair back from her face. "Yes, my sister."

Amelia wanted to delve straight into their collective suspicions about Joseph Larson, but at the same time, she reminded herself to keep an open mind. Besides, the two women looked nothing alike. Genes could split in interesting ways in families, but Amelia needed to make sure Journey Russo was as close to Michelle Timmer as she claimed to be.

"Pardon me for being intrusive, but you and Michelle don't...um..."

"Look alike?" Journey smiled, but the grin fell away too quickly, worry taking its place. "We get that all the time, for good reason. We actually aren't related at all. My grandparents raised me and a slew of foster children." The smile returned, almost reaching her blue eyes this time. "Michelle was special, and when she came to live with us, she never left. My grandparents adopted us both, but Michelle wanted to keep her last name in honor of her parents, who died when she was little."

The story warmed Amelia's heart, cementing her desire even more to bring Michelle home. "So, she really is your sister."

Journey's eyes glistened. "Yes, she is. I may have Italian roots, and she might be as Irish as they come, but we're sisters in every way that matters."

Amelia reached over and squeezed her hand. "Then let's get to work on bringing her back to you. Tell me everything you know."

"Okay." Journey returned to her seat, followed by Spencer and Zane. "Michelle worked in this field office before she… disappeared, and she was dating an agent from the Organized Crime Division here." Her mouth was a hard line as she glanced to the door. "Where is he? I'd like to speak to him directly."

Amelia's eyebrow arched. Journey was truly in the dark. "He's not here. He was recently relieved of his position."

For a split second, Journey's dark blue eyes widened, though she was quick to wipe the surprise off her face. "He was *fired*? What for? When? Has he been charged with anything?"

As much as Amelia wished she could say yes, she shook her head slightly. "No, we didn't have enough to charge him."

Spencer cleared his throat, and the room's attention shifted to him. "None of this leaves the room. SAC Keaton and I are keeping the details about Joseph Larson under wraps, just in case there was anyone else in this office who might've been affiliated with him. Officially, he resigned. In reality, he was forced to resign due to his relationship with a suspect in a previous investigation."

From there, Spencer walked Journey through the Leila Jackson investigation—including their suspicions that Joseph had worked with the Leóne family to compromise an under-cover venture.

By the time he'd finished, anger sparked in Journey's gaze. "This can't be a coincidence. Joseph Larson was dating my sister at the time of that investigation. She disappeared in July, a little less than a month after your office closed the Leila Jackson case, didn't she?"

"As far as we can tell, yes." Zane leaned back in his chair, tapping an index finger against the table. "Michelle's case has been primarily worked by the Chicago P.D. so far. Agent... sorry...*civilian* Joseph Larson claimed he helped the CPD, but if you want my opinion, he only did that to make himself look good."

Since Michelle hadn't actually been involved in the Leila Jackson case, Amelia hadn't given much real consideration to the idea that the two events might be connected. She'd considered the possibility, but that was the extent of it.

Journey flattened her palms on the table and took in a deep breath. "I don't think it's a coincidence, and I'll tell you why. I talked to Michelle right before I went on my most recent assignment, and one of the topics of conversation was the guy she was seeing, Joseph Larson."

The concept of a casual conversation about Joseph was such a foreign concept to Amelia that her knee-jerk reaction was to think Journey was messing with them. She pushed aside the inane thought as the agent continued.

"She told me she was interested in him, possibly even in becoming more serious. I think more than anything, she was grateful to be with someone who understood what a career in the Bureau is like. I wouldn't say she was smitten or anything, but she was...intrigued by him, I guess. They'd become intimate, but she couldn't tell if he wanted more than that." Journey averted her eyes, and it took Amelia a second to realize the woman was experiencing a moment of powerful regret.

So far, Amelia liked Journey Russo. Though she was instinctually compelled to provide reassurance, she stopped herself. She didn't know the rest of Journey and Michelle's story.

Journey scratched her temple and sighed. "She was in the middle of telling me about Joseph Larson when I got a phone call from my SSA. It was about my newest assignment, which was a deep undercover investigation into a cult out in rural Pennsylvania. The Philly Field Office wanted someone who was a local, and the Las Vegas SAC recommended me since that's where I grew up."

The puzzle pieces clicked into place in Amelia's head. Journey regretted not listening more closely to her sister's rundown of Joseph Larson because she'd been preoccupied with work. A pang of sympathy stabbed at Amelia as she considered her own sister, Lainey Storm.

Lainey was a heroin addict, and Amelia carried a large part of the blame for her sister's current position in life. After being caught with drugs at the Milwaukee airport, Lainey had been arrested by the Drug Enforcement Agency. Amelia could have used her position as an FBI special agent to seek leniency for her sister, but she hadn't.

If Amelia had stayed in Chicago instead of fleeing the city, the state, and then the entire country after being threatened by Alex Passarelli's father, Luca, maybe Lainey's fate would have been different. But back then, Amelia had been an eighteen-year-old girl with stars in her eyes, and Luca Passarelli had been a hulking mafia capo. She'd have been hard-pressed to find someone in Chicago who *wasn't* frightened of Luca.

In her family's pitiable financial state, Amelia had only one option to get far away from Chicago and the Passarelli family—join the military. She'd walked through the doors of a local recruiter's office, and for ten years, she hadn't looked back.

She could definitely relate to Journey.

Amelia's chair squeaked as she straightened and folded her hands atop the table. They could deal with the emotional fallout from Michelle's disappearance later. Right now, she wanted to learn more about what had happened to the forensic analyst. "Did you hear from Michelle again after that?"

Journey pushed a piece of dark, shoulder-length hair out of her face. "Yes…once."

A bolt of anticipation rushed through Amelia's veins. She'd expected the answer to be a resounding no. "What did she say? Anything about Larson?"

"Yes." Journey's remorse was abruptly replaced by determination as she unlocked her cell. "She sent me a message on an app we used to use in lieu of texting. It's more secure, or at least that's their selling point. Here it is." She slid the device across the table to Amelia. "I didn't even see it until I got back from deep undercover last week."

Hey, Journey. I know you're busy working right now, but I wanted to send this message because I know you'll see it eventually. Remember that guy I was "dating," Joseph Larson? Well, long story short, I've started to think he's up to some shady shit. I dumped him, but he's been up my ass for the last week. I'm going to go with him to some fundraiser event tonight, and I'm going to try to learn more about what he's up to. I'll keep you posted.

The message was dated July 11.

The taste on Amelia's tongue turned sour. She slid the phone to Zane, and his dark expression soon mirrored her own.

Anxiety played at the edges of Amelia's nerves like a harp. She already knew the answer to her next question, but she was compelled to ask anyway. "Did she send you any other messages? Anything to follow that up or elaborate?"

Journey scooped up her phone and shook her head. "No. That's it. That's the last message, call, email, or anything I received from Michelle. Since I returned from Pennsylvania, I've tried to get ahold of her every way I could, but..."

She trailed off, leaving Amelia with another ache of sympathy.

"There've been a couple social media posts made on her account." Zane was back to drumming his fingers, as he often did when he was lost in thought. "And the CPD's case file noted that a suitcase and some clothes were gone from Michelle's apartment."

A crease formed between Journey's eyebrows. "How did they know that?"

Zane's fingers halted mid-tap. "Joseph Larson told them. They showed him photos from her apartment, and he claimed a suitcase was missing."

Anger unfurled in Amelia's chest like a living flame. Everything always came back to Joseph Larson. In her gut, Amelia knew he'd twisted and manipulated Michelle's case to suit his own design.

Could she prove it, though? That was the question spinning in her head.

Journey's palm slammed onto the table. "He must have fed that same line of BS to my sister's coworkers in forensics. That's why I didn't come to you all sooner. But there's no way." Journey crossed her arms. "Michelle wouldn't do that. She wouldn't take a vacation and neglect to tell *any*one. Unless she conveniently told Joseph Larson and no one else." The venom in Journey's voice could have wiped out an army battalion.

Spencer rubbed his chin, appearing thoughtful. "The main issue we've had with declaring foul play in Michelle's case is that we haven't had a friend or family member to give us information. Now that we do, and with that message Michelle sent to you, I think we can say there was foul play in Michelle's disappearance."

The announcement was like music to Amelia's ears. For the past six months, she'd been trying to solve a puzzle with at least fifteen missing pieces. "What about jurisdiction?"

Spencer nodded. "That's something we can take care of now. We'll see what Michelle was working on around the time she disappeared. Since she was in the employ of the FBI, if there's a possibility she was kidnapped due to her work, then the crime lands in our jurisdiction."

Amelia could read between the lines. They couldn't definitively prove Michelle had been kidnapped or killed because of the forensic analyses she'd been conducting at the time, but they also couldn't completely rule out the possibility. As long as there was a chance her work had led to the disappearance, then the Bureau could make an argument to take the case from the CPD.

The Chicago Police Department worked hard, but their manpower and resources often were stretched too thin. Plus, with Joseph's meddling in the Michelle Timmer missing persons case, who knew what other evidence was still out there waiting to be found?

Spencer smacked the table with his palm as he rose to his feet. "All right. I'll take this to SAC Keaton, and we'll pull this case into our jurisdiction. I'm not sure how long this'll take, considering we're nearing the end of the workday, and the SAC is in meetings until five. Familiarize yourselves with the information that's been collected by the CPD in the meantime."

Amelia was confident she could recite the CPD's case file verbatim, but she didn't protest as Spencer took his leave.

Finally, she had the resources and time necessary to devote to Michelle.

Anything involving Joseph Larson turned into a rabbit hole, but Amelia didn't care.

One way or another, she'd find the truth behind Michelle Timmer's disappearance. And if that truth was Joseph, then she'd finish the job she'd started by caging him like the animal he was.

3

Bright and early the next morning, Amelia and Zane arrived at the field office, lattes in hand. The hour hadn't quite reached seven as Amelia followed Zane off the elevator and onto the sixth floor. As expected, the Organized Crime Division was sparse this early in the morning.

Late the night before, the FBI had officially taken jurisdiction of Michelle Timmer's missing persons case. More importantly, they'd slapped the label of "foul play suspected" onto the investigation. Justifying the use of federal resources in the search for Michelle would now be markedly easier for the powers that be.

Amelia and Zane claimed the same small incident room they'd utilized during their most recent investigation. On the whiteboard, Amelia could still make out a couple names that had been written on one side. Sammie Howard and Desiree Bauer—two of their latest serial killer's victims.

A psychopath had been fixated on a specific eye color, light brown ringed with green. During the investigation itself, none of them had a single clue why the sight of hazel eyes so enraged the young man. Only an explanation provided by the suspect during his plea agreement had yielded them an answer to the bizarre question.

Journey Russo joined Amelia and Zane before seven-thirty, and the three of them had set about creating their investigation board.

With Michelle's sister in the room, Amelia was hesitant to use the term *murder* board. Michelle's death was a distinct possibility, and Journey was an intelligent woman. No doubt, she'd already considered the possibility.

Tapping a dry-erase marker against the heel of her hand, Amelia took a step back to observe the scant information. She'd reserved a section for Joseph Larson on the lefthand side of the board but hadn't been able to add much to it. There was slightly more information by Michelle's photo, but still not enough.

The door creaked open at Amelia's back, and she turned as Zane stepped over the threshold with a mug of breakroom sludge in one hand. Amelia was fairly certain the FBI office used toxic waste in its coffee brewers, but she still couldn't prove her theory.

Journey had arrived on Zane's heels, but she'd had the good sense to buy a soda from the vending machine.

A woman of taste, I see.

Amelia waved her marker at the whiteboard. "All right, well, we've got a rough timeline. The CPD's case file came with Larson's statement, which claimed he last saw Michelle on July eleventh when he was walking her home from a date. His statement says Michelle was acting jumpy and that she kept looking over her shoulder. Allegedly, he didn't go inside with her, and that's the last time they interacted."

Journey's expression was what Amelia would expect from someone who'd just bitten into a lemon. "He didn't ask her why she was worried? Didn't do any *investigative* work even though he was a federal agent at the time?"

"Sounds like Larson." Zane frowned as he took his seat and woke up his laptop. "In that statement, he also claimed that he didn't follow up on Michelle's paranoia because their relationship 'wasn't that serious.' But everything we've gathered tells us they were more or less together for more than a month, at least. Journey, do you recall the first time Michelle mentioned Joseph Larson?"

Gaze fixed on the whiteboard, Journey pressed her lips together. "I want to say she first mentioned him to me in early May. There was something about how they were keeping things on the down-low because they both worked at the FBI office, but she thought he was fun and liked spending time with him."

Amelia couldn't fault Michelle for falling for Joseph's bullshit. After all, Amelia'd first met Larson during her brief tenure at the Boston FBI Field Office, and the two of them had become friends. Back then, the only aspect of Joseph she'd truly disliked had been his music preference.

Hell, he'd even been the one to put in a good word to get her a transfer to Chicago. He'd known Chicago was her hometown, and he'd been supportive of her decision to return to Illinois.

Acted. He acted *supportive. That man's entire personality is an act.*

Amelia's mouth went dry when she considered how close she'd come to trading places with Michelle. She'd never been romantically interested in Joseph, but she *had* considered him a friend. Now, knowing what she did, Amelia wouldn't put it past Joseph to make a friend disappear if he thought the decision would benefit him.

"We need to take Larson's statement with a grain of salt."

Amelia figured that much was apparent, but it never hurt to vocalize the obvious.

Zane twirled a ballpoint pen in his fingers. "Agreed. But unfortunately, Larson's statement is just about all we've got. Other than the neighbor who supposedly saw Michelle leaving with a suitcase and a carry-on."

"Then we need to go to the source." Journey took a long swig of her soda. "We need to go back through Michelle's neighbors and refresh their memories. If Joseph Larson's the only one who did any field work on Michelle's case, then we need to go back and do it ourselves."

Amelia liked Journey a little more every time she spoke. "You took the words right out of my brain. Or mouth, however that saying goes."

A slight smile passed over Journey's face. "All we've really got to go through are Michelle's neighbors and her coworkers. She moved to Chicago last March, and she hadn't made any friends aside from her coworkers."

Amelia had discerned as much from her review of the case file, but she was grateful for the confirmation.

"I can talk to her coworkers." Zane took a sip of his coffee, and Amelia almost laughed at his expression of distaste. "I'll talk to some of the janitorial staff too. That's where I found out she and Larson were dating in the first place, so it makes sense to follow-up with them."

"Perfect." Amelia hesitated and turned to Journey. "Do you think Michelle's apartment was rented to someone else after all this time? Or that any of her possessions are even there?"

Concern clouded Journey's features. "I don't know. I guess we can check the complex, and if her place has been rented out, maybe the manager can give us an idea of where her belongings are. And of course, we can still recanvass her neighbors."

"Sounds like a plan." Amelia offered Journey a quick smile. "If her place hasn't been rented out, it'll be good to have someone there who knew Michelle. Maybe you can tell if anything looks out of place for her."

Zane rubbed his hands together and pushed away from the table. "All right. Meet back here in a couple hours?"

"Right." Amelia reached for her coat.

They were beginning Michelle's case from far behind the starting line. Before they could make any real headway, they had to undo the damage Joseph had already done.

If any, she reminded herself. Just because she detested the man and just because her gut was screaming he'd done something to the forensic tech didn't mean it would ever be anything she could prove.

Though Amelia was committed to keeping an open mind, she didn't want her mind to be so open that her brain fell out of her skull. For months, her instincts had been nagging at her, hinting that Joseph was involved in Michelle's disappearance.

Why else would he have personally involved himself? Amelia had pieced together enough of Joseph's personality to confidently label him a chauvinist pig. There was no way in hell he'd jump up to help in a missing persons investigation of a woman he'd screwed for a couple months.

Not unless he had something to gain, or he was covering his own ass. Or both.

Amelia and Journey didn't converse much on the drive to Michelle's apartment. As much as Amelia hated driving in Chicago traffic, she wasn't about to make Journey traverse a city with which she was unfamiliar. Fortunately for Amelia and her traffic-related sanity, Michelle had opted for a residence close to the field office.

Back when Amelia was a kid, Wicker Park was known as one of the more artsy communities in the city. Now, after popularity of the area had surged, property prices and taxes had risen steeply—too steeply for the former residents to afford.

These days, she associated Wicker Park with wealthy hipsters. However, she couldn't fault Michelle for wanting to live somewhere nice. And Wicker Park sure as hell was *nice*, especially compared to the Englewood neighborhood where Amelia had grown up.

Englewood was the antithesis of West Town. Where West Town and its communities such as Wicker Park had been bought up and gentrified by wealthy real estate moguls, those same tycoons wouldn't touch Englewood with someone else's money. Year after year, Amelia's former home raked in some of the highest rates of violent crime in the city.

She pushed aside the thoughts as she parallel parked in front of a brick apartment building. Double-checking the address was correct, she stepped out into the frigid February morning.

"Michelle lived in apartment 307. The notes from her case say the neighbors in the three apartments next to hers on the third floor were interviewed, and it says the unit above hers was empty at the time she went missing."

Journey eyed the brick building as if it had stolen her lunch money. "So, they didn't talk to the person who lived *below* Michelle?"

"The case notes say they weren't home when the detectives spoke to the other neighbors." The city of Chicago had a bad reputation when it came to crime and policing, and Amelia was struck by a compulsion to defend the CPD. "The CPD is spread thin all over the city, except maybe in the richie-rich neighborhoods. They didn't have any indication of foul play in Michelle's case, so they had no choice but to shelve the file and move on to the next."

The agent sighed. "Yeah, I know. It doesn't mean they did anything wrong."

"Plus," a spark of anger warmed in Amelia's chest as she pulled open the front door of the apartment building, "the detectives who worked this case had Joseph whispering in their ear the entire time, telling them his version of events, offering to help, or whatever else he did to make it look like he'd tried to find Michelle."

They'd have to talk to the detectives in person, but if Joseph could fool the federal agents with whom he'd *worked* for so long, she was certain he'd have no problem pulling the wool over the CPD's eyes.

Journey seemed to follow Amelia's unspoken logic. "We'll have to see if Larson came by to talk to any of Michelle's neighbors."

"Let's start with the one neighbor the CPD missed. Her name is Trudy Cordova. Or was. Hopefully, she's still living here." Having lived in an apartment for almost all her adult life, Amelia was well-aware that many complexes—especially those catering to the working class—had a revolving door of tenants. If Trudy's lease had expired any time in the last seven months, then Amelia and Journey would have to track down her new address, and...

She shut down the series of what-ifs and mentally crossed her fingers. They'd traverse that bridge if they came to it. Hell, Amelia wouldn't be surprised if Joseph had already spoken to Trudy, conveniently losing the notes from the discussion before they could be added to the case file.

Orange and white carnations were woven into a spring wreath that hung on the door to apartment 207. The flowers were fake, but they added a sense of liveliness to the beige and gray hall.

Amelia rapped her knuckles against the dark wood,

receiving a muffled, "One second," in response. Though she was curious to observe Journey's demeanor, Amelia kept her gaze straight ahead. Only a few seconds after the knock, the door creaked inward to reveal a short woman in her late-thirties or early-forties.

Her eyebrows creased as she glanced from Amelia to Journey and back. "Hello. Can I help you ladies?"

With a polite smile, Amelia flipped open her badge. "I'm Special Agent Amelia Storm, and this is my partner, Special Agent Journey Russo. We're looking for Trudy Cordova."

The woman swallowed, managing a faint nod as her gaze darted from one badge to the other. "Yeah...that's me."

The variety of responses Amelia received when announcing her title never ceased to amaze her. A sizable chunk of civilians went on edge the instant they learned they were in the presence of an FBI agent, even when they were completely innocent. Perhaps they were worried they'd been accused of a crime they hadn't committed, or perhaps they'd merely been raised to be wary of law enforcement.

Amelia could relate. She'd grown up in Englewood, which wasn't a community known for its affinity for cops.

Journey chuckled quietly, surprising Amelia with her good humor and warm tone. "It's all right, Ms. Cordova. I know seeing two FBI badges before lunchtime can be a little...jarring. I can assure you you're not in any trouble."

Trudy's tense stance relaxed at the reassurance. "It doesn't help that I haven't quite finished my first cup of coffee yet. I am curious, though. Does this have anything to do with that agent who came to talk to me back at the end of August?"

Amelia blinked a few times as she worked to conceal a look of surprise. "You were visited by an FBI agent at the end of August? Do you recall their name?"

Trudy pursed her lips. "Oh, jeez. What was it? It was a

really common name. Hold on." The woman's attention jerked downward, and Amelia followed her eyes to where she was using her leg to corral an orange and white cat. "Stop it, Mister. You don't want to go outside. I *know* you don't want to go outside."

"My cat does the same thing. She thinks she's this grand adventurer, but when she gets into the hall of my apartment building, she completely loses her cool." Amelia hoped the personal story would help set Trudy more at ease. If she'd been visited by Joseph, only god knew what he'd told her.

"That sounds about right." Trudy knelt to gather the tabby in her arms. "Sorry about that. Come on in, Agents. I can't remember that man's name right now, but I do remember that he left me a card. He left it under my door while I was on vacation. He wrote a note on it asking me to call him when I got back."

I knew Joseph had been here.

Amelia flashed Trudy an appreciative smile. She and Journey stepped over the threshold, pausing to remove their shoes at Trudy's request. The scent of sandalwood and vanilla grew stronger as they followed Trudy to the living room, where the yellow-orange flames of a candle flickered cheerily atop a bookshelf. Though Trudy apologized repeatedly for the cat hair on the cushions of the couch and loveseat, Amelia hardly noticed.

After offering Amelia and Journey each a cup of freshly brewed coffee, which they both accepted, Trudy took her spot on the loveseat perpendicular to the couch.

As Amelia took the first sip of the steaming coffee—which was at least seven million times better than the FBI's breakroom brew—Trudy leaned forward and placed a business card on the wooden coffee table. "Oh, I found that agent's business card when I was getting our coffees. You can keep it if you need to."

Glancing at Journey, Amelia plucked up the card. Sure enough, the text beneath the FBI logo read *Special Agent Joseph Larson, Organized Crime Division, Chicago Field Office.*

Amelia's stomach did a maneuver like it was trying out for the Olympic gymnastics team. Larson had never denied his relationship with Michelle but witnessing physical evidence of his involvement reinforced her gut feeling that something about this case was very twisted.

She used the sentiment to renew her focus and dedication. The days of Joseph Larson's intimidation were gone, and she was going to rip this case apart piece by piece to get to the truth.

Clearing her throat, Amelia replaced the coffee mug on the table. "Thank you for hanging onto that business card, Ms. Cordova. It's really very helpful. Now, I apologize if this seems repetitive, but could you walk us back through everything you and Agent Larson discussed at the end of August?"

Amelia wanted to know every little thing Joseph had said or done during his interaction with Trudy Cordova, but at the same time, she didn't want to make the Bureau seem incompetent or corrupt.

To her relief, Trudy's expression belied no signs of judgment. Based on her hospitality so far, Trudy was the helpful type, if a bit uneasy at first. "Sure. Um, let's see. He came by on a Tuesday. I remember because I used to have yoga on Tuesdays, and I was trying to get him to hurry up so I wouldn't be late. I feel a little bad for it now that I think back."

Oh, honey. Joseph is the last person on the planet you need to feel bad about being short with.

Trudy's gaze shifted to the corner of the room, her expression thoughtful. "He wanted to know about what Michelle had been doing on July eleventh. Apparently, that was the last time anyone saw her. It was the last time *I* saw her. I know that for certain."

"Could you run us through the last time you saw her?" Journey's calm, kind tone surprised Amelia. If it was *Amelia's* sister who was missing, she wasn't sure she'd be able to maintain the same level of professionalism.

Perhaps that was Amelia's military background talking. When the military or the CIA wanted information, they weren't usually nice about it. After ten years in the Army, at least part of the sentiment had worn off on Amelia.

"Yeah, I remember it pretty well, actually." Trudy reached down to scratch behind her cat's ears. "I always noticed when Michelle was coming and going. One time, shortly after she moved in, I believe, Mister got his wish and actually got *outside*-outside. I couldn't find him, but Michelle helped me. We used some treats to lure him back home, and I just remember thinking how, in a city like Chicago, it was such a nice thing to do for a neighbor who barely knew me. After that, I'd always made a point to wave or say hello to Michelle when I saw her coming or going. Which wasn't often, since I'm a nurse and I work a lot of overnights."

A hint of sadness touched Journey's smile, eliciting Amelia's sympathy.

Amelia sensed it was a good time for her to take over the interview. "And on July eleventh, did you see anyone with Michelle?"

Without hesitating, Trudy shook her head. "No, no one. I was at work until four in the afternoon that day, covering a shift for a friend of mine. I had a vacation coming up, so I came home, packed up my stuff, and then hung out on the balcony to enjoy the warm weather. I want to say it was sometime around six when I saw Michelle leaving. She was wearing a cocktail dress and heels, so I waved goodbye and told her she looked great. She waved back, but she seemed...*nervous.* I figured since she looked like she was headed to a party, maybe it was just social anxiety."

To Amelia's side, Journey scrawled out some notes on a little pad. Inanely, Amelia hoped Journey's handwriting was better than Zane's. "Did you see what kind of car Michelle got into?" The question was a longshot, but Amelia would be remiss if she didn't try.

Trudy sipped her coffee. "I...I'm sorry, Agents. I can't remember much about it. Just that it was an SUV." Concern clouded her eyes as she met Amelia's gaze. "I'd asked Michelle to cat sit for me while I was on vacation, but when I knocked on her door the next day, there was no answer. I tried again later in the day but wound up having to call a friend of mine to come hang out with Mister every other day while I was in Hawaii. Honestly, I've lived in this city for the last two decades. I didn't think anything of it, just figured she'd gotten preoccupied with work or something."

Amelia softened her expression. "Other than Agent Larson, did anyone come to talk to you about Michelle? Anyone at all?"

"No. Agent Larson was the only one."

Of course he was.

Joseph Larson, the man who was arguably their primary suspect in whatever had led to Michelle's disappearance, was the only person who'd interviewed Trudy Cordova. And conveniently, he'd neglected to add his interview notes to the case file.

Had Joseph neglected to notate the case because he wanted to cover his own ass? Was the explanation so simple?

Trudy Cordova came across as perfectly accommodating, kind, and glad to be of help. Still, an itch persisted in the back of Amelia's head.

Joseph Larson had been here at least once before.

Had he returned since then? Had he bribed Trudy or one

of the other neighbors to alert him if anyone else came searching for Michelle?

What if Michelle was still alive? If Joseph caught wind of Amelia and Journey investigating her disappearance…

No, not if. *When.*

The clock was ticking.

4

As Alex Passarelli slid into the cushioned booth across from his mother, Sofia, a pang of anxiety played against his ribs like a xylophone. Nervousness was a rare feeling for Alex. He'd been a capo in the D'Amato crime family since he was twenty-four, and he'd lived in the mafia lifestyle since he was born. He'd never been under any illusion of leaving this world behind, except for maybe a year or two toward the end of high school when he'd dated a girl outside "the life" who ultimately wound up breaking his heart.

Even then, his thoughts had been just that—a teenage fantasy, a way to mentally rebel against his parents. Something to hold over their head, to remind them he was his own person.

He glanced up from the menu to observe his mother, and the trepidation fizzled out, a nauseating anger rushing to take its place.

Sofia Passarelli's ebony hair fell over her shoulder in soft waves, and her olive skin always glowed, even when Alex knew for a fact she hadn't left the house in weeks. At first blush, Sofia was the perfect mafia wife. Beautiful, articulate, and classy.

Beneath the veneer, the woman was a trainwreck.

For the vast majority of his childhood, Alex had been raised by his family's help. Their housekeeper slash former nanny was still one of his favorite people on the planet, and she was more a maternal figure than Sofia had ever been.

Alex's mother had given birth to him at the tender age of nineteen, though young mothers weren't particularly uncommon in Italian crime families. One of Alex's aunts had her first two kids at nineteen and twenty-one, and she'd been a doting, loving mother since day one.

Sofia was different. She was...detached. From Alex, from the D'Amato family, from everything. Sometimes, Alex envied her. But more often than not, he wished he could take hold of her shoulders and shake her until she acted like a real human being.

Seeming to sense his stare, Sofia turned her attention to him. "How's Liliana doing? She hasn't come by the house in a few weeks."

The casual question about Alex's fiancée—not by his own choice, the marriage had been arranged by Alex's father and Salvatore D'Amato himself—created an unpleasant twist in his chest. Liliana D'Amato was nearly ten years Alex's junior, but like him, she'd been raised in the mafia lifestyle. In fact, she carried herself like most women Alex's age.

Still, Alex couldn't help but feel as if the arranged marriage was stealing something from Liliana. Alex was thirty-two, and he'd had the opportunity to live his youth as he pleased, for the most part. Liliana's entire life had been planned out for her by men more than twice her age.

Guilt. That's what he was feeling.

Alex liked Liliana, admired her, even. *That's probably why I feel guilty. If she was a stuck-up bitch, I doubt I'd care.*

He shoved aside the solipsism like it was an overcooked piece of meat. Thinking about how Liliana had been all but forced to marry him was a surefire way to irritate him, not to mention the unsavory reason he'd asked his mother to lunch.

"She's good." He placed his menu on his place serving. "She's been busy working on an honors thesis."

One of his mother's manicured eyebrows quirked up. "Really? What about?"

Alex resisted the urge to roll his eyes. He doubted Sofia gave half a shit about what Liliana was studying in college. "Cybercrime."

Sofia was a lot of things, but she wasn't stupid. She caught onto the significance right away and then did something Alex hardly ever witnessed.

She smiled. A genuine, pleasant expression, not one of the fake smiles she reserved for family gatherings. "Good for her. Having a woman at your side with a degree in software engineering will be great for both of you, I'm sure."

She wasn't wrong. One of Alex's major goals in the D'Amato family was to lead them away from high-risk industries like running guns and drugs, replacing them with low-risk, high-profit gigs like counterfeiting and identity theft. While penalties for selling illegal firearms or cocaine could land a person in prison for the rest of their life, cyber-crimes often resulted in a slap on the wrist, comparatively.

Before Alex could reply, a waiter stopped by to collect their drink orders. The hour couldn't have been later than twelve-thirty, but Alex ordered an old-fashioned anyway. His mother was the last person on the planet to judge him for drinking too early in the day.

Once they'd received their beverages, the same server took their food order and departed. With each passing second, the subject of this impromptu luncheon weighed more heavily on Alex. Like he was caught in a tomb from

Indiana Jones, and the ceiling was closing in on him, threatening to flatten him into a pile of blood and viscera if he didn't find a way out.

His mother continued to ask questions about Alex and Liliana's wedding, which was planned for September.

Has she picked out her dress?

She and her mother and closest female cousins were heading to the bridal store in a week.

Will you have a honeymoon?

He and Liliana hadn't discussed a honeymoon yet, but if she wanted one, Alex would give it to her.

Good, I'm glad to hear I raised you right, Alex.

She hadn't raised him much at all, but he didn't protest. He was only halfway involved in the conversation. Once the food arrived, Alex would bring up the real reason for the lunch.

A couple weeks ago, Amelia Storm, the girl who'd run off with his heart more than eleven years ago, the girl who'd grown up into a *Fed*, had brought him a disturbing piece of information from her so-called *confidential informant*.

Alex had done his damnedest to figure out who had given Amelia the intel, but he'd hit a brick wall each time. His contacts at the Chicago P.D. didn't have a clue, and his sources of information inside the Bureau were limited these days.

Hopefully not for much longer, but that was a topic for him to agonize over another time.

More than ten years ago, not long after Amelia left for the military and whatever war zone had become her home back then, Alex's little sister, Gianna, had been kidnapped without a trace. For years, Alex and his father had scoured the criminal underworld, searching for clues as to who might have taken her. Time and time again, they'd come up empty-handed.

Finally, when they were certain they'd tapped the well of information dry, they'd enlisted the help of a Chicago P.D. homicide detective.

Trevor Storm had gotten close to finding the truth of Gianna's kidnapping. Too close, and he'd paid the ultimate price.

Amelia would undoubtedly resent Alex and his family for Trevor's death for the rest of her life. Alex sure as hell would if their roles were reversed.

Now, more than two years after Trevor's death, his younger sister was searching for answers. At first, Alex hadn't wanted Amelia to involve herself because the endeavor would be fraught with risk. In typical Amelia fashion, however, she'd shut down his concerns, reminding him of her gun and badge, not to mention her decade of military experience.

If he was honest with himself, he was glad he hadn't managed to dissuade her. A week ago, they'd met up for the first time in months.

According to Amelia's newest confidential informant, before Sofia married Luca Passarelli, she'd had a relationship with Stan Young. Amelia's theory was that Stan Young had kidnapped Gianna as revenge for an old grudge with Sofia Passarelli. After giving the situation more consideration, Alex was inclined to agree with her.

Dammit.

Even thinking about the prospect set Alex on edge. He was unsurprised to learn the seemingly upstanding Senator Stan Young was as dirty as a urinal at an interstate truck stop, but the fact that the man had been personally involved with *his* family?

That wouldn't stand.

The waiter's pleasant smile, along with the scent of baked chicken and herbs, returned Alex's full focus to the table.

Once the food was deposited and drinks refilled, the young man took his leave.

Alex glanced to his chicken parmesan, but his stomach lurched in protest. His nerves had more of a hold on him than he'd realized, and he was too wound up to eat.

His mother didn't have the same problem. Her fork and knife scraped the plate as she cut into her steak.

Clearing his throat, Alex set aside his own silverware. "I need to ask you about something."

Sofia's gaze jerked up from her food. "What do you need to ask me?" The pale blue hue of her eyes was rare for someone of Italian lineage, and there was no end to the compliments she received.

Gianna had those same eyes.

Remembering his sister and her bright grin strengthened Alex's resolve. "Before you married Luca, did you have any other relationships?"

Alex had stopped calling his father by anything other than his first name years ago.

Sofia's mouth drooped open for a beat before indignation flared in her features. "Did I have a *relationship*? Why the hell is my *son* asking me about who I slept with before I married his father? Have you lost your mind?"

No, but I think you lost yours a long time ago.

He kept the sarcasm to himself. "It's relevant, Mama."

Her nostrils flared. "Relevant to what, exactly?"

"Gianna."

A tense silence settled between them. Where Alex had expected a display of her Italian roots and the passion for which his ancestors were known, she remained quiet, her jaw clenched so hard Alex could have likely heard her teeth grind together if it weren't for the ambient noise of the restaurant.

Knuckles white where she gripped her cloth napkin,

Sofia's stare bored into Alex. If he didn't look away soon, the heat from her glare would burn his retinas.

I'll take my chances.

He'd set up this lunch date to get answers, and he wouldn't leave without them. There was no way in hell Amelia Storm would have passed along bad information about something she knew was this important to him. He and Amelia would never be able to be openly friendly with one another, but he still trusted her. If she was sure her confidential informant's intel was good, then it was good enough for Alex.

Finally, she broke away from the intense stare, pretending to be interested in her food. "How is it relevant to Gianna, Alex? What exactly are you hinting at?" His mother's words crossed over to him through clenched teeth.

Keeping his expression carefully blank, Alex set down his fork. "It is relevant. We've turned over every stone looking for my and Luca's enemies, trying to figure out which of them might have held a grudge deep enough to kidnap Gianna. The Leónes wouldn't have been that stupid, unless…"

Though Alex rarely talked work with his mother, Sofia remained in tune with the D'Amato family. She was aware of their many enemies, as well as the long history of bad blood with the Leóne family. "Unless what?"

"Unless someone ordered them to kidnap her. And I'm not talking about a job they were paid to do. They would've been smart enough to turn that down. The Leónes are a lot of things, but they haven't survived this long by abducting teenage girls from their rivals during a period of peace. Not without a damn good reason."

His mother's eyes narrowed ever so slightly. "And who exactly do you think orders around the *Leóne* family?"

Though Alex had become adept at reading the people

with whom he worked, his mother might as well have lived on a different plane of existence. Her tells were never the same, her tics were subtler, and her demeanor far more volatile.

The men who worked for Alex were levelheaded. Sofia Passarelli was not.

Rather than feed her a little bit of information at a time to observe how she reacted, Alex elected for a change of plans. "Stan Young orders around the Leónes. When he says 'jump,' the Leónes ask how high." Alex leaned his elbows on the table and leaned forward, his gaze fixed unerringly on his mother. "Which begs the question of *why*. He was settling an old score, but not with me or Luca."

Panic flooded Sofia's eyes, her stance tensing like a child caught misbehaving. Anger consumed the nervousness in the blink of an eye, but the crack in her armor had answered Alex's question before she spoke again. "You think Stan Young has a vendetta with me? That he kidnapped my only daughter because of something *I* did to slight him?" Alex could tell she'd intended the statement to come across as ridiculous, but to him, it was factual.

"That's exactly what I'm saying. You had an affair with Stan Young, and he's held onto a grudge for all these years. That grudge manifested in him kidnapping Gianna, and more than likely killing her." The words sounded cold to Alex's own ears, but he didn't care. He wanted answers, and his mother was hiding something.

Clang.

Sofia dramatically pitched her silverware onto the plate as she rattled off a series of Italian curse words. "Is this why my son brought me to lunch? To accuse of screwing another man before I married his father? To insinuate that same man kidnapped my baby girl ten years ago?" Through the wicked blue flames in her eyes, there was a distinct sadness, of regret. "Who was supposed to keep Gianna safe, huh? Was it me? Was I the capo, the one with the gun?"

Guilt sawed at Alex, but he ignored it. "Don't try to change the subject. Blaming me and Luca doesn't get us any closer to finding out who *actually* took Gianna, and you know it. You also know the one place we haven't searched, the one grudge we haven't inspected yet, don't you?"

"I don't have to put up with this from my own son!" In a blur, she leapt to her feet and scooped her handbag off the booth. "This conversation is over, Alex. My past is none of your business. It's all said and done and digging it up now won't be productive for anyone."

Alex opened his mouth to respond, but Sofia spun around on her heel and stalked toward the front doors.

He could have followed her into the cold streets of Chicago to continue to badger her with questions, but he suspected he wouldn't get much further. Her defensiveness was an answer in and of itself, but it wasn't enough to go after Stan Young. Not yet.

Heaving a sigh, Alex glanced down at his food. This place made some of the best chicken parmesan he'd ever eaten, and even though he'd lost his appetite, he wasn't about to let such a high-quality meal go to waste.

As he ate, Alex began to form the rough workings of a plan. If he couldn't get his answers from his mother, he'd find them elsewhere.

He didn't have the first clue who Amelia's confidential informant was, and he knew she'd be beyond livid if she learned he was sneaking behind her back.

But by this point, he didn't care. He'd failed for so long to find the bastard responsible for kidnapping Gianna, and he had no intention of quitting when he was the closest he'd ever been.

Alex didn't care how. He'd find who was responsible for taking the one bright shining star he'd had left in this life.

One way or another, he'd learn the identity of Amelia's CI. If his and Amelia's tentative friendship went down in flames afterward, then so be it.

He'd pry the answers out of the informant, piece by agonizing piece.

5

Sweeping my gaze along the view of Chicago's early afternoon skyline, I reached for one of the foil-wrapped candies in a dish at the edge of my son's mahogany desk. From the fortieth floor of a downtown skyscraper, the vessels moving through Lake Michigan were like toys in a kid's bathtub. I'd always liked the view from up here. Though I still held an office down the hall from my son's, my duties with the U.S. Senate commanded my attention much of the year.

The cushions of my squat armchair rustled as I stood, popping the chocolate candy in my mouth.

My movement seemed to snap Josh out of his trance. Rubbing one temple, he swiveled his seat around to face my direction. "Sorry, Dad. I just had to reply to an email from the director of human resources."

Chuckling, I waved a dismissive hand. "Don't worry about it. I worked that same job for years before I campaigned for the Senate. I know how busy it keeps you."

Tentative relief edged its way onto Josh's face. His high cheekbones and defined jawline were almost a perfect likeness to my own. Truthfully, the only real differences in our appearance were his green eyes, where mine were gray, and dark hair where mine was a lighter shade of brown. Otherwise, the kid could've been my clone.

Josh rested his elbows on his knees, his gaze similarly fixed on the view of the city. "Ever since those mafia goons tried to use our Kankakee County farm for their human trafficking bullshit, we've tightened background checks across the board. We had to get some more manpower in HR, but I think it's paying off. I've got a better feel for what's going on at all our major sites now."

I flashed him an approving smile. "Good. With the primary election coming up in June, that's exactly what voters will want to hear. We can translate that to politics too. If we're able to maintain a multibillion-dollar agricultural business without corruption, then we can do the same in Washington. Something like that."

My son's response was a weak nod, his eyes still glued to the city.

Over the summer, the FBI had busted a labor trafficking ring being run by the Leónes at one of my company's vast properties. This business, Happy Harvest Farms, had been founded more than a century ago by the Young family, and we'd held onto it as the business evolved.

I had intentionally distanced myself from what was happening in Kankakee County, wanting to maintain plausible deniability throughout the entire debacle. Though I'd known the gist of what had occurred, I obviously hadn't been privy to all the dirty details.

Namely the fact that the Leóne men who'd snuck into management positions had been running a kiddie porn ring out of the warehouse basement.

I'd dumped a hell of a lot of money into cleaning up my and my business's image after that mess. In the immediate aftermath, I'd been tempted to burn down the entire Leóne family.

Literally. I'd wanted nothing less than to set those mafia bastards on fire like I was Emperor Nero and they were rebellious Christians in the Roman Empire.

Their kiddie porn business should have been a permanent black mark on my political reputation, my business, and every other aspect of my life. But, as luck would have it, my son was a marketing genius, or genuinely felt terrible about what the Leónes had done and how our infrastructure had made it possible, or both.

No, luck didn't have anything to do with it. Josh was capable because he'd learned from the best...me.

All the effort had kept Josh busy. Maybe a little too busy. Aside from our business updates, such as today, the kid hardly came around for family functions anymore. Any time he was at the house, stress seemed to emanate from him.

For the life of me, I couldn't figure out if he was working himself half to death or if he was hiding something. My wife, Cynthia, was insistent on the latter, but I wasn't as convinced. Cynthia had always disliked Josh, and I assumed the sentiment had to do with the fact that Josh would inherit Happy Harvest Farms when I died, not her.

Greedy bitch.

She was desperate to sink her talons into it, as if that half-wit could run a multibillion-dollar business. At least with Josh, I knew Happy Harvest Farms would survive long after I was dead.

I'd needed her to portray the perfect wife toward the start of my political career, but now, I was an incumbent. I had support across the aisle in D.C., and I'd won the last two elections by a landslide. Her usefulness had run its course. Of course, there was the little matter of how much dirt she had on me.

And where that dirt was hidden…

Sometimes, I wondered why I hung onto Cynthia, why I didn't just take my chances and have someone like Joseph Larson arrange a little "accident."

At the thought of former Special Agent Larson, my chest tightened with rare emotion. Anxiety.

Neither Brian Kolthoff nor I had heard from Larson in a full two days, which was odd. As the minutes turned into hours, my unease regarding the entire situation grew.

Was Joseph going rogue? Did he know something Brian and I didn't?

I shook off the notion like an annoying insect.

Later. I'd deal with the Larson issue later.

Though I'd brushed off Cynthia's concerns during our conversation, her suspicion regarding Josh had gotten under my skin. I hated when that woman was right about anything, least of all my own kid. She certainly didn't possess any maternal instincts. The woman wasn't capable of maternal.

I cleared my throat to get Josh's attention.

For the second time in five minutes, Josh blinked a few times, appearing as if I'd woken him from a trance.

"Something on your mind, son?"

Josh leaned back in his chair, dragging a thumb along his jaw—a common tell when he was deep in thought. "Just… busy, I guess. Still cleaning up this shit from Kankakee County, making sure it doesn't happen again somewhere else."

Oh, believe me, it won't. If it does, if those sons of bitches draw any more negative attention to me before this primary election, I swear to god…

I tossed the wrapper from my candy into a wastebasket as I returned to my seat across from Josh. "That's understand-able. But you need to take time for yourself, too, son. We haven't seen you much at the house lately. Mae misses her big brother."

Now, it was Josh's turn to rise to his feet. Crossing his arms, he peered down at the city. His stance was tense, tenser than it should have been.

Suspicion crackled along my back like lightning.

Cynthia wasn't right. She couldn't be right.

"Son, if there's anything you want to tell me…anything that's been bugging you, you know I'm here to listen, right?" Josh had never made a habit of sharing his secrets with me, and to be perfectly honest, that's how I preferred our relationship.

A muscle in his jaw ticked, and he dragged in a long breath. As he released the air from his lungs, he rubbed his eyes.

There *was* something on his mind. I swallowed a sudden urge to jump out of my chair and shake my son's shoulders until he spat out whatever secret he was keeping, large or small. I hated being kept in the dark when I asked a question, and Josh knew it.

I snatched another candy, eager to keep myself busy in the tense silence.

Josh turned to me and sighed. "Have you ever met someone you wish you hadn't? Or wasted weeks, months of your time on something that didn't pay off in the end?"

I snorted to mask a frown. "Who hasn't?"

His expression turned pained, almost regretful. "Carolina and I broke up. With everything going on here, and with the election coming up so soon," he shrugged, "I didn't have time. Or maybe I subconsciously didn't want to make time. Jesus, I don't know."

Realization and relief flooded my bloodstream. Shit, the kid was torn up over a woman? No wonder he'd been acting so weird.

Women had that effect on a man, especially those closest to him.

An image of a particular redhead populated the screen of my mind, and my mood sank even lower.

I offered my son a few platitudes, hoping he'd take it as fatherly advice, and not just me trying to excuse myself because the conversation had become boring. That kid was my legacy, but despite his business savvy, he was missing...*some*thing.

Ruthlessness, maybe. But perhaps his conscience was for the best. If he had no qualms with deceit and violence, he'd make it a priority to push me out of the way so he could have the keys to our empire.

It's what I did.

I traveled down forty stories, escorted by one of my security detail, all the way to the back of a waiting SUV. After shutting my door, he climbed into the passenger's seat, and we were off.

Sinking into the comfort of the leather seats, I let my mind drift to other luxuries I afforded myself. Astronomically priced scotch. Vacation homes in all the most exclusive locales. And activities like visiting Kolthoff's yacht.

And that fucking redhead. I couldn't keep her from haunting my mind...

As I closed a heavy metal door and descended the stairs to the second-lowest level of the Equilibrium, *I stopped abruptly. Voices filtered up to me, one belonging to Kolthoff, and the other a woman's pleading tone.*

Had that asshole called me to meet with him and lost track of time again? It'd be just like him to let me wander through an open doorway to see him railing someone. Neither Brian nor Joseph had any semblance of boundaries when they were down here.

Approaching the only open door in the hall, I steeled myself for the sight of Brian screwing his latest purchased piece of ass.

A wet thud *reverberated out into the corridor, and I hesitated. I knew that sound—some bitch's head had just been bounced off the floor. That was a show I'd like to see.*

Smoothing a hand down my pastel blue tie, I eagerly shoved open the door.

Brian was a mess. His brown hair was disheveled while his white dress shirt was unbuttoned and spattered with blood. His belt was undone, but at least his pants were on.

Not that it mattered. This wouldn't be the first time I'd watched him fucking a girl.

The fluorescent lights caught the sheen of sweat on his forehead, as well as what was visible of his upper body. Though he looked like he'd just run a marathon, the crumpled form of a woman at his feet told me the real story.

Someone had been caught disobeying him.

He wiped the back of one hand over his mouth, his gaze finding mine. His shoulders heaved with each ragged breath he took. "Nice of you to finally make it, Stan."

I rolled my eyes. "Seems like you were able to pass the time just fine. Who the hell is she, and what did she do?"

Brian raked a hand through his hair and knelt next to the woman. "Can you hear me, you stupid bitch?" He took a fistful of her auburn hair, and when he lifted her face, I nearly pissed myself. I was rooted to the spot like I'd stared directly into Medusa's eyes.

The woman Brian had beaten to within an inch of her life was my mother.

I jerked back to reality with a start. Had I just fallen asleep, or had I succumbed to a twisted sort of flashback?

Glancing to the two men in the front of the SUV, neither of whom seemed to have noticed my little lapse, I massaged my temples and held back a sigh.

The woman on Brian's yacht was the spitting image of my dead mother, right down to the shade of auburn she dyed her hair. Maybe she and my mother had used the same brand of dye.

Flames of anger licked at my nerves as I recalled the woman who'd brought me into the world. The woman who was supposed to nurture and care for me, but who'd done the exact opposite.

Coming face-to-face with Michelle Timmer for the first time, I'd been certain this was my second chance, my opportunity to change the unfortunate story of my youth. Though I wasn't particularly religious these days, the Catholic superstition from my younger years was never far behind.

I'd wanted to do things different this time, I swear. She and I didn't have to be enemies. We could have conversations, could start anew.

With my mother, nothing was ever that simple. That bitch had betrayed me, just like I should have known she would. Only now, I was an adult. I could overpower her. Could force her to bend to *my* will.

Which was exactly what I'd done. As I'd landed the first blow across my mother's...no, Michelle's face, nothing had ever been so satisfying in my entire life. Or so scary. I'd almost expected the woman to rise from the floor and sink her fangs into my neck.

The thought made me shiver, which angered me even more.

I'd pay her back for everything she'd done to me, and I'd laugh as I did it.

Despite the witch being adrift off the East Coast, my anticipation was anchored to one goal.

I couldn't wait until Brian sent her back to Illinois.

I couldn't wait to have her all to myself.

6

Amelia didn't realize she'd fallen asleep on the couch until the pillow slid out from underneath her head. No, that wasn't her pillow. She'd been snoozing on Zane's lap, and he'd gotten up to do...something. His voice had permeated her dream, but now that she was awake, she couldn't remember a word he'd said.

Squinting at the clock on the television stand, she rubbed her eyes with the back of her hand. Not even seven-thirty in the evening? God, she was getting old. Older than a thirty-year-old woman should be. Next thing she knew, she'd be heading to the early bird dinner special before crawling into bed at six.

The sudden rush of water through pipes brought her the rest of the way to the land of the living. "A shower. That's what he said he was doing."

At the sound, Hup perked up from where she'd been napping on the arm of the sectional couch. She let out a squeak as she leapt to the floor and darted toward the sliver of light from the half-open bathroom door.

Amelia straightened and swung her legs off the couch.

She could use a shower while the water was warm, not that she was under the illusion she and Zane would get much actual showering done if she joined him. They never did, and Amelia always wound up having to wait for the hot water heater to refill so she could actually get clean.

Her lustful thoughts brought a smile to her face as she stretched and rose to stand. She'd taken a full two steps before her phone buzzed against the coffee table. The smile morphed into a frown as she paused mid-step.

They *were* in the beginning stages of an important case, and the caller might have time-sensitive information.

Dammit.

Amelia cast a longing glance at the shaft of light before clenching her hands into fists. Turning on her heel, she marched to her cell. "This better be good."

As she scooped up the device, she noted the number wasn't one she'd saved in her contacts. The area code was from Chicago, so she doubted the caller was Journey. No, she'd saved Journey's information.

Maybe it's just a spam call.

She swiped the screen and raised the phone to her ear. "Storm."

"It's me." Alex Passarelli's voice sent a jolt through her.

"Alex, you okay?" She shook off the surprise. "What can I...help you with?" The words sounded awkward, even to her own ears.

"I need to talk to you about your informant."

What the hell?

"You're my informant."

"Ha ha. That's not what I mean. This is about our meeting the other day. About the information you gave me regarding my mother and her *fling* with a certain U.S. Senator."

Don't worry, Alex. I haven't forgotten.

She swallowed the remark. "Okay. What about it?"

"I talked to my mother." His clipped tone was about as irritated as she'd ever heard him. If Alex Passarelli was pissed off, then that didn't bode well for anyone. "She denied everything. How do you know your informant isn't just feeding you a line? What is it about them you're trusting so much?"

The fact that he'd be tortured and killed if anyone found out he was talking to me. Or the fact that he's turning on his own damn father because he wants to do the right thing. Take your pick.

Amelia would never give up Josh Young's identity to Alex or anyone. She could only imagine how a mafia capo would extract information from him. "Look, I asked you to trust me, remember? I told you I'd vetted my source and that I was confident they were telling me the truth. Has that slipped your mind already?"

In the silence that followed, Amelia could practically sense the tension through the phone.

When Alex spoke again, his voice was less irascible, but she could tell he was holding back. "I didn't say I don't trust your judgment, but *I* have some questions I'd like to ask this person."

"Then give them to me, and I'll ask." She'd only ever referred to Josh as *they*. She didn't even want Alex to know his gender.

"I want to know where they got their information. Obviously, this is someone close to the Young family. Close enough to pick up on a skeleton they buried in the closet more than thirty years ago. I can't use hearsay to accuse my mother of cheating on my father while they were engaged, all right? If I want a straight answer from her, I need a leg to stand on."

He had a point. The Italians were traditional, and an accusation of adultery—toward a woman, at least—was serious. Amelia wasn't shocked to learn that Sofia had denied everything.

She also knew Alex well enough that she was confident he wouldn't throw his own mother to the wolves. Odds were, he wanted answers for his own peace of mind. Possibly to make sure he wasn't the illegitimate child of Sofia Passarelli and Stan Young.

"All right." Amelia swallowed a sigh. "Here's the deal. I'm not going to give you my informant's name, period. End of story. But I can see where you're coming from, and I do want to help you with this. That much should be obvious, right? I wouldn't have told you any of this if I didn't want to help you."

"I know. This is complicated in my world, you know?"

She snorted. "Oh, believe me, I'm aware."

"It's just…have you thought that this person might be trying to screw with you? This person is probably close to the Young family, so what if they're someone trying to point you in the wrong direction? We've got fewer than four months before the Senate primary election. Stan Young could be up to anything right now."

Amelia's chest tightened. The exact same thoughts had run through her mind on plenty of occasions. Stan Young was a dangerous man, and there was no doubt in Amelia's mind that he'd do anything humanly possible to maintain his political power.

That was the whole point of the handful of meetings she and Josh had before he'd dropped the bombshell about Sofia Passarelli's relationship with Stan. They'd built a mutual trust, had established an understanding that they were on the same team. They both wanted Stan to burn, and they wanted to get to the truth about Gianna Passarelli's kidnapping.

She was sure of it.

Wasn't she?

The last thing she needed was Alex casting doubt on Josh

Young's credibility. All because Sofia had denied screwing around with Stan Young.

Of course she'd denied the fling. What sane human being wouldn't have?

Realizing she'd been quiet too long, Amelia forced herself to speak. "What do you want me to do about this? Be specific. I'm not a mind reader."

"I need evidence. Something physical, something that solidly ties Stan Young to either my mother or...my sister. Corroboration, that's what you guys call it. Maybe with that, I can get the truth from her."

Amelia had been relying on Alex to pry more information out of his mother, but Sofia Passarelli was apparently even more stubborn than either of them had anticipated. "Evidence," Amelia repeated. "New evidence for a ten-year-old case. You realize what you're asking, right?" Even as she posed the question, an idea had begun to form in her mind.

"I know, but this is the only way." Finality rang in his words, and Amelia found it hard to disagree.

"Fine. Let me see what I can do. I'll reach out to you when, *if*, I find something."

"All right. That's all I ask."

As they said their farewells, Amelia's stomach tightened with a combination of unease and annoyance. Unease because Alex had given voice to some of her own concerns, and annoyance because she was tired of rehashing the same topic.

Worry niggled in the recesses of her imagination. *What if he's somehow playing me now? Is he so hell-bent on protecting his mother's honor that he'd do something rash?*

Why couldn't Alex accept that his mother had messed around a little before she'd married? Was it really that hard to believe a mafia woman might be curious about what was outside her gilded cage?

After contacting Josh Young via a one-time-use email the two of them used to stay in touch, she went to tell Zane about her and Alex's phone call. There was a time when she'd kept her ties to the mafia a secret even to him, but these days, they shared almost everything.

Amelia couldn't have asked for a better confidante. Even without his wealth of knowledge about the inner workings of organized crime syndicates—gleaned from his tenure in the CIA, no doubt—Zane was levelheaded and smart. There was something in his perpetually calm demeanor that cut through Amelia's anxiety, even before they'd become lovers.

After Zane finished with his shower, Amelia relayed the news to him. Josh replied a little more than an hour later, setting up a time and place for him and Amelia to meet the next day. By now, Amelia recognized the address of the abandoned warehouse where they'd first met. At least she'd be in familiar territory.

The remainder of the evening was uneventful, with Amelia and Zane finally settling into sleep a little before eleven. Amelia's rest was fitful for the first half of the night. Naturally, when her alarm roused her, she felt as if she'd been yanked off another planet.

Rather than head to the FBI office with Zane, Amelia took off for an entirely different part of the city. As she pulled to a stop in front of the sprawling, decrepit building, she noted Josh's car was already parked. This was the fourth time they'd met in person, and each time, Josh was at the location first.

The crunch of gravel beneath her feet and the rush of the city followed her to the bench where Josh sat sipping a latte. Though he was only a couple years older than Amelia, the shadows beneath his green eyes added another five or ten.

All part of the soul-sucking journey to free himself from the shadow of his psychotic father.

Amelia's father had made his share of mistakes—Jim Storm had been a raging alcoholic for most of Amelia's life, having only sobered up three years ago—but her dad wasn't a bad person. He definitely hadn't been a saint as he dealt with his grief over the passing of Amelia's mother. Fundamentally, however, Jim was a good man.

"I'm sorry for the last-minute notice." Amelia's apology wasn't just a platitude. She was genuinely remorseful she'd had to put Josh in this precarious position. It couldn't be easy for him to risk so much by meeting with her.

"It's fine." He rose from the bench as she neared. "This needs to be fast, though. And it needs to be the last meeting we have for a long time."

Until after my father is in prison, was the unspoken stipulation in his statement.

Though Josh had never been exactly at ease during their meetings, Amelia hadn't witnessed him quite this paranoid. Alarm bells clanged in her head, and she reflexively glanced around the barren, pockmarked parking lot at their backs.

"Why? If you think someone knows, you can tell me. We can get you to a safe house. We can protect you if something's going wrong."

Josh's expression softened. "No, you can't. You know as well as I do that it'd only be a matter of time before one of my father's people got to me."

Amelia had no rebuttal. He was right. Aside from Zane, SAC Keaton, and only a handful of other agents, Amelia couldn't completely trust anyone at the FBI office when it came to Stan Young. Not after she'd been kidnapped and almost killed by a fellow agent and nearly raped by another.

Corruption was a fact of life in a city as large as Chicago. She didn't doubt the offices of other major cities had similar problems. Small cities too, most likely.

Stuffing her hands in the pockets of her knee-length

trench, Amelia sighed. The white cloud of her breath floated away on a mild breeze. "If you were in trouble, we'd at least try. I could always just hide you in my spare bedroom, provided you're not allergic to cats."

The hint of levity seemed to take the tension out of the air as Josh chuckled. "I'm not. I'll keep that on my short list, Agent Storm. Thanks."

She didn't permit the silence's tendrils to take hold before she spoke. "I'll just cut right to it so I don't have to keep you any longer than necessary. I need some help with the Gianna Passarelli case. Right now, it's sort of hanging in limbo because we don't have anything to tie Stan Young to the Passarelli family."

Josh's jaw tightened. "Yeah, I get that. It took me a while to piece it together, and I used to live with the guy. Here." He reached into his peacoat and produced two plastic baggies.

As Amelia recognized the contents, anticipation flooded her. "Toothbrushes?"

"DNA."

Even as hope's embers ignited, she gestured to the sparkly pink brush. "I assume that one is yours?"

Josh snorted out a laugh. "Yeah, right. It's Mae's. I labeled both bags just in case you needed it. The plain green one is mine. I'm assuming you can run an analysis to prove that I'm Mae's biological half-brother and that Stan is our dad. I don't know how you'll tie it to Sofia Passarelli, but…I trust you, Agent Storm. I know you'll figure it out."

Amelia handled the baggies with the delicacy she'd use to pick up a newborn kitten. "When I run this analysis, if I use it to get to Stan, they're going to figure out you gave it to me."

He lifted a shoulder as if it didn't matter. "Maybe. But if you get to Stan, you cut the head off the snake. Life will get a lot easier for me after that, I think."

She didn't share Josh's confidence. If the time came when

Stan figured out Josh had been the one to facilitate his down-fall, Amelia would personally stuff Josh in her trunk and take him to a safe house.

Amelia hoped it wouldn't come to such an extreme, but hope held little weight in matters of life and death.

As Zane shouldered open the door of their little incident room, he hoped Amelia would be sitting at the oval table. Any time she went to a face-to-face meeting with Josh Young, his anxiety spiked. He trusted Amelia's judgment regarding Josh, but the worry that someone might have caught onto the senator's son—and therefore Amelia as well—was constant.

To his chagrin, the only occupant of the room was Spencer Corsaw. The SSA's dark eyes were glued to the screen of his laptop, but his attention shifted quickly as Zane eased the door closed behind himself.

"Good morning again, Palmer. Did you get anything from the folks in forensics?"

Zane pulled out a chair and sat, reaching for his paper coffee cup as he did. He'd arrived at the field office bright and early that morning so he could catch a couple of Michelle's former coworkers as they were finishing up their overnight shift.

"Not much." Zane was disappointed to find his coffee had cooled to room temperature. "Just another woman confirming that Joseph Larson was a womanizing ass."

One of Spencer's eyebrows quirked up. "Do elaborate."

"Sandra Chen, one of the analysts on Michelle's team, said Larson had hit on her a few times. Which wouldn't seem like much, but Sandra happened to be aware that Larson was 'dating' Michelle at the time. Plus, Sandra is married, so…"

He left the thought unfinished and gulped down half of his tepid coffee.

Spencer twirled a pen in his fingers as he appeared thoughtful. "Did Sandra tell Michelle about Larson hitting on her? Or why not?"

"She didn't. She said she didn't feel like it was her business, and she wanted to stay out of it." Zane could already imagine what Amelia would say to Sandra Chen's decision to remain silent.

Amelia would frown and point out that women needed to look out for one another because creeps like Joseph were far more common than they ought to be. Most of them just didn't have an FBI badge.

Maybe if Sandra had said something...

Zane shut down the thought as he slugged back the rest of his coffee. Plenty of folks preferred to stay out of the personal lives of their coworkers, and there was nothing wrong with their decision. Setting boundaries was healthy and normal, and Sandra couldn't have known what an animal Larson actually was.

Is.

Zane held back a sigh. "There wasn't much else Michelle's coworkers could tell me about her disappearance. Her boss, Angus Gomez, was worried about her, but guess who was one of his work friends?"

Leaning back in his chair, Spencer groaned. "Joseph Larson."

"The one and only. Larson assured Gomez he was helping the CPD with Michelle's case, and he gave him periodic updates. Specifically, he told Gomez there were no signs of foul play. Gradually, Larson started addressing the forensic team's concerns about the plausibility of Michelle leaving town so abruptly by suggesting Michelle might have undiagnosed bipolar disorder and that she'd left the city in the midst of a manic phase."

Spencer narrowed his eyes. "Wasn't there a note about that in her case file? Something added within the last couple months?"

"A note left by Joseph Larson. And until Journey, we didn't have any way to really refute it."

"Shit." Spencer added six syllables to the word. "Larson's hands were all over this case."

"Which is why it didn't become a bigger deal." Joseph Larson was a master manipulator, and he'd handled Michelle's case like a game of chess. "There's part of Journey and Storm's interview with Trudy Cordova that didn't make it into Michelle's case file either. Michelle had volunteered to cat sit while Trudy went on vacation. What kind of person would volunteer to watch someone's pet and then suddenly go away?"

"According to Larson, someone with bipolar."

Zane waved a dismissive hand. "Still. It's a convenient tidbit Larson left out. According to the notes, Trudy even told Larson about it. He just neglected to include it in the case file."

Tapping his pen against the table twice, Spencer moved to stand. "Well, Palmer, I think it's about time we paid Larson a visit. By my estimate, we've got enough to get him in here for an interview. How he handled Michelle's case might not quite be criminal, but it was sloppy as hell. Say what you want about Larson, but he is most definitely *not* sloppy."

"No, and that's the problem." Zane reached for his coat as anticipation mixed with a slight hit of adrenaline flooded his veins.

How would Larson react to being questioned by his former coworker and supervisor?

Ten bucks says he lawyers up and slams the door in our faces.

Spencer snatched his coat off the back of a chair. "What are you thinking?"

"I'm thinking Larson isn't going to be happy to see us." *If he's even there.*

"Probably not."

Zane set aside the rest of his trepidation as he and Spencer took off for Larson's apartment. Joseph was dangerous, sure, but the man was also smart. There was no way in hell he'd react violently to their visit. Joseph only committed crimes when he was confident he could get away with them.

If they could get to him, a lengthy interrogation might cause him to slip up, even with a lawyer.

But they needed a reason to hold him first.

To Zane, it was like they were stuck on level one of a video game, and they couldn't progress to the second stage until they found a key that was located on level three.

He didn't often wish he was back in the CIA, but right now, he could use the extrajudicial freedom he'd had at the Agency. Dragging Larson out to a CIA black site and throwing him in a dark cell would surely do wonders in jogging the smarmy bastard's memory.

Alas, Zane was part of the FBI now, not the CIA. There were rules, regulations, and protocols in place to ensure a guilty person didn't go free and an innocent person didn't wind up behind bars. The system was far from perfect, but it was what they had.

On the short trip up to Joseph's apartment, anticipation tightened his muscles. Today would be the first time he'd interact with Larson since he'd been fired, and he doubted the prick would take kindly to it.

As Zane and Spencer came to a stop in front of Larson's door, they exchanged a quick glance. Spencer's jaw was tight, his posture tense.

Good to know we're on the same page.

Wary of any gunshots Larson might send as a greeting, Spencer and Zane stepped to either side of the doorframe before Zane rapped his knuckles against the door. He waited for a response.

Silence.

Blood pounded in his ears in time with his second, heavier knock. "Joseph Larson, open up. This is the Federal Bureau of Investigation." Zane figured Larson would recognize his voice, but he decided on the same greeting he used for any other person of interest.

All he received in response was more silence. Leaning closer to the door, Zane strained his hearing for the faint shuffle of footsteps, sound from a television, anything that would let him know Larson was dodging them.

There was nothing. Larson's apartment was as silent as a tomb.

Zane swore. "He's not here. We can check the parking garage for his vehicle, but I guarantee it's gone."

"Shit." Spencer glanced up and down the hall. "All right. Let's see if his neighbors know anything."

Deep in Zane's gut, he was already certain they wouldn't. Someone as clever as Joseph Larson wouldn't have given anyone notice if he'd skipped town. If that's what he'd done.

Their key wasn't on level three anymore. Now, it was on level ten.

7

Michelle's dreams were almost as unpleasant as the waking hours of her life. Every now and again, her mind would take her to better times, like when she and Journey had attended Yale together for their undergraduate degrees. She was almost always aware she was in a dream, but she was powerless to stop her brain from replaying the events. Usually, her thoughts were much darker...

The metal door of her cell swung inward, and blood drummed in Michelle's ears as her anxiety spiked. Any time that godforsaken door opened, she wondered if it would be the last. Had the sick bastard finally grown tired of her like he assured her he had and decided today was the day he'd put her out of her miserable existence?

In truth, the prospect of death wouldn't seem frightening if she knew her end would come swiftly.

Kolthoff wouldn't let her die quickly. He'd rape her first, probably more than once. Then, he'd beat the hell out of her. Lather. Rinse. Repeat, for god only knew how long.

Stop it!

She needed to stop thinking about it. Stop giving him that power.

Don't let him live in your head rent-free, dammit.

Michelle gritted her teeth, shoving the mental imagery away, though it would undoubtedly return.

Like now…

As a man stepped over the threshold of her room, Michelle bit the inside of her cheek to suppress a sigh of relief.

Instead of Kolthoff's eerie, pale green gaze, the visitor looked down on her with gray orbs as cold as the walls of the cell. The black and blue striped tie around his neck was loosened, the sleeves of his dress shirt rolled up to the elbow.

Michelle's breathing calmed, though only slightly. The night she'd come to Brian Kolthoff's yacht for the so-called fundraiser, she'd placated herself with the sight of Senator Stan Young and his wife, Cynthia. She'd been certain any corruption wouldn't run all the way to the United States Senate.

How utterly naïve she'd been.

As the door closed behind the senator with a clack, Michelle swallowed to return some semblance of moisture to her mouth. After pulling up the thin blankets of the bed over her crossed legs, Michelle sat as still as a statue.

Though she'd only seen him a handful of times after the first day he'd struck her, Michelle had sort of come to look forward to his visits. Not forward as in excited, but simply because it gave her something to do. It broke up the monotony of the four walls surrounding her. Plus, Michelle enjoyed trying to figure the man out.

Stan never looked her in the eye to start—he'd only make eye contact after he'd been in the room for a while, like he was a diver adjusting to a change in depth.

His stance was tense, hands clenching and unclenching almost in time with his ragged breathing. He was reliving a sliver of his past each time he entered her cell, but she was still attempting to piece together what that sliver was. She'd gathered by now that she resembled his mother, and there were a whole host of issues with that relationship.

During her time at Yale, Michelle had taken one whole psychology course, and only because it had been required. Introduction to Psychology had taught her some useful information, but sitting in this cell with a man who was clearly laden with mommy issues, she wished she'd taken more classes. Anything to give her an edge.

"How has Brian been treating you?" Stan's words were pinched, like he was squeezing out the last little bit of toothpaste in the tube.

Like most of their previous encounters, he seemed to be trying to be...accommodating. He'd start out looking angry, but the moment he came closer to her, the anger faded, and he appeared to transition into someone different.

"I...I don't see him very often. Usually, one of his guys brings me food, and that's about it."

With an approving nod, Stan rubbed his jaw. His fingers trembled, she noticed. "Good. I told him and Joseph not to touch you anymore."

As much as Michelle wanted to know why in the hell Larson and Kolthoff would listen to him, she bit her tongue. Clearly, the senator was the ringleader. Why? She didn't have a clue. "Um... thanks. Can...can I ask why?"

His flat gray eyes latched onto hers for a brief moment before moving away. "Because you remind me of someone. Someone I never got to make amends with."

The remorse in his tone would have ignited Michelle's sympathy a while ago. But after being beaten and raped and treated worse than an animal, she'd lost any illusions that these men could be redeemed.

Now, all she wanted to know was how to play this man's weakness to her benefit. She had to choose her next words carefully. "Can I help with that?"

"I don't know. I'm not sure if she'd want to make amends with me."

"But you want to make amends?"

He glanced away and nodded.

"She was your mother?"

"Yes." He shifted his weight from one foot to the other. "She was a terrible person, and she did horrible things to me. Her only child. I don't think she ever wanted children, and she resented me because of it. She should've never been a parent."

Michelle grieved for the little boy he once was, but she silently cajoled herself for the moment of empathy. She'd heard plenty of stories about Stockholm syndrome—she'd even written a paper about how the film Beauty and the Beast clearly manifested the condition. Never in a million years had she imagined she'd be fighting off twinges of sympathy for a man who was partially responsible for her being held captive.

No matter how tragic Stan Young's past might have been, he was the enemy. Period. End of statement.

Stan didn't say much more before leaving, but he returned the following day. At least, Michelle assumed it was the following day. He revealed a little more about his abusive mother, and Michelle pretended to empathize and nurture, all while steadfastly reminding herself he was the enemy.

She wasn't Belle. Stan Young sure as hell wasn't the prince.

The dream world warped her sense of space and time, and the next thing she knew, she'd arrived at the fateful day of their most recent interaction.

Rather than sit on the bed, Michelle stood face-to-face with the corrupt senator. Every sense in her body was on high alert, searching for the slightest change in his demeanor.

He hadn't exaggerated when he'd told her his mother was a terrible person. If even half his stories were true—and Michelle suspected they were all true—Renee Young was a grade-A piece of shit.

"She was married and divorced twice, but she always kept the Young surname." Stan smoothed his shiny purple tie. "That was a rarity back then, but no one really questioned the heiress of a multibillion-dollar business."

"Kind of like how famous actors never change their surnames." Michelle made her best effort to sound helpful.

Stan nodded. "Yeah, like that."

The conversations didn't bore her, so to speak, but anxiety was slowly eating away at her patience. This man needed a therapist and about a century of hardcore cognitive behavioral therapy, not a woman taken captive by his BFF, Brian Kolthoff.

But she was under Stan's protection. Because of him, Kolthoff and Larson hadn't laid a finger on her, and Stan himself had displayed no sexual interest in her whatsoever. She'd rather be Stan Young's therapist than Brian Kolthoff's sex slave.

Michelle licked her lips, carefully considering her next move. She didn't want to relinquish Stan's protection, but the idea of not knowing what lay in store for her was becoming more unbearable with each passing day.

Following pure instinct, Michelle opened her arms to Stan, beckoning him into an embrace. He hesitated before cautiously moving toward this ghost from his past. Once Stan was close enough, Michelle wrapped her arms around him gently. She soothed him before offering what she hoped he wanted to hear.

"I'm so sorry for how horrible I was to you growing up. I wasn't fit to be a mother." Stan tensed in her embrace, but Michelle didn't let him go. "I made so many mistakes, and I hurt you so badly. I can't undo the past. But I want you to know how very sorry I am for hurting you, dear."

Stan's tension released, and he buried his head into Michelle's shoulder and began to sob.

Michelle's mind raced as she desperately sorted through the options of how to proceed. But Stan gave her that opening.

"All I ever wanted was for you to love me." His tears soaked

Michelle's t-shirt. She patted his back and gently stroked the back of his head.

"Stan, honey. We can start fresh. We can have the relationship we never had."

He lifted his head and searched her eyes. "What do you mean?"

"I want another chance to be the mother I should have been. The mother you deserved."

A faint smile began to form, and Michelle could almost feel a lifetime of pain and sorrow lift from the senator's soul.

But the brief trace of lightness was replaced with concern. His eyebrows pinched together. "And how would we do that?"

Worry crawled into her bloodstream like a parasite. Was she about to say the right thing?

"Let's run away together, just you and me. We can make a fresh start!" The words spilled from her lips before she could stop them.

Stan's face contorted into a mask of rage so quickly, and Michelle knew she'd made a fatal mistake. "You deceptive bitch!"

Michelle took a swift step back, but he closed the distance immediately. Icy terror flitted up her back, clamping down around her rapidly beating heart.

He sneered. "You're just like her. Any time you act civilized, you're up to something, aren't you? Well, you're not the one in control here."

As he arced his hand over his shoulder, Michelle had no time to react. The back of his knuckles collided with her cheekbone, the force of the blow snapping her head to the side. Pain radiated from the site of the blow like an earthquake, and the tang of iron flooded her tongue.

Michelle's eyes flew open, pulling her from the memory, her breathing ragged as if she'd run a marathon. A light sheen of sweat coated her forehead. She clenched and unclenched her fists before touching the healing mark on her cheek.

As warm as her body was now, the perspiration provided

a fast track for the cold to seep into her skin, permeating through muscle all the way to her bones. She suspected Kolthoff provided her with these flimsy blankets on purpose, as some form of subtle torture.

Stan Young hadn't come by her cell since the incident. If the man was a normal human being, she might have been struck with a pang of guilt for pressing on such a volatile old wound.

He wasn't normal, though. Just because he hadn't raped her didn't mean he was a closeted saint—he was friends with Brian Kolthoff after all. There were no noble intentions behind his request that Kolthoff and Larson keep their hands off her. He simply wanted her to himself.

Letting her eyelids droop, Michelle ran through the reminders like a prayer. She refused to succumb to Stockholm syndrome and become attached to one of these pricks. Reiterating their true nature to herself was the best method she had to keep herself from a warped perception of the senator.

He wasn't here to save her.

No one would save her. Not even Journey.

Journey. Her best friend and sister. After Michelle's parents had died, she had been put into the system and was a permanent ward of the state of Pennsylvania. After bouncing from place to place through no fault of her own, good fortune had placed Michelle into the foster home of Journey's legal guardians, her grandparents.

While the Russos had fostered many other children, Journey had truly been a sister to Michelle. The pair were inseparable, even attending Yale together.

Michelle had found a loving and caring family in the Russos. She could almost smell the homemade oatmeal cookies fresh from the oven…

Just as Michelle's taut muscles relaxed with the beginning

stages of sleep, the metal lock of her cell disengaged with a *click*.

Even as every pore of her body was on high alert, she didn't move, silently willing the visitor to drop off her meal and leave.

"I know you're awake." Kolthoff's matter-of-fact tone dripped with self-satisfaction.

Shards of ice formed in her veins.

Don't let him into your head!

She gritted her teeth and rolled over to face him. The fluorescent fixture overhead sputtered to life, forcing Michelle to blink back tears as light stung her eyes.

The sight only seemed to amuse him. "I'm happy to announce that, in twelve hours, you'll no longer be my problem. I've been keeping you alive for months, and in the last several, I haven't even been able to fuck you."

She'd no longer be his problem? What the hell did that mean?

He flashed her an exaggerated frown. "I'll miss all our good times, but at least I filmed a few of them so I can take a stroll down memory lane if I'm feeling in the mood."

Her stomach lurched, but she kept her expression as neutral as possible. The recordings weren't news to her, but *months*?

That's all?

Surely, she'd been trapped in this hell for most of her adult life.

At the same time, she could scarcely believe she'd been missing for a huge block of time, and no one had come looking for her. Was Journey still on her secret assignment? Had Larson found a way to delete the message she'd sent her sister before accompanying him to the so-called fundraiser?

Maybe.

Michelle shoved aside the what-ifs, returning her focus to

the monster wearing a suit and tie. "What do you mean I won't be your problem anymore?"

A lazy smirk crept to his face. "Wouldn't you like to know?" He set a plastic container of food on the same table he always used.

I would, actually.

She bit her tongue to keep the remark at bay. Kolthoff was cold, detached, and highly unpredictable. Larson had always enjoyed making threats he never carried out, but Kolthoff's threats were promises. Stan and Larson both had human emotions buried deep down in their twisted brains, but not the man in front of her.

Brian Kolthoff was a stone-cold sociopath.

Tilting his head, he stuffed both hands in the pockets of his slacks. "I guess I can share the good news. You belong to Stan now, and you're being relocated to a location under his control."

The thinnest sliver of hope pierced through Michelle's glum thoughts, and she wasn't sure if she ought to revel in the emotion or run from it. Last time she'd been moved, she'd made a desperate attempt to escape while they were on the road.

The memories were scrambled from the beating she'd sustained at Kolthoff's hand afterward, but she could distinctly recall the look on a stranger's face as she approached and pleaded with him to help her. First, he'd been shocked. Then the surprise had morphed into skepticism, and then...something resembling contempt.

When Michelle returned her gaze to Kolthoff, his smirk had turned into a wolfish grin. "You're remembering the last time you tried to escape, aren't you?" He took a couple steps closer. "And you remember how far that got you, right?"

Though he was still several feet away, she shrank away until her back met the cold carbon fiber wall.

"You'll be on your best behavior this time, understand? I won't be there personally but trust me..." he crouched, his stare like a pair of laser beams, "if you pull some shit again, Stan won't be the one to deal with you. I think that's an important distinction to make. Until you're relinquished to him in person, you're still mine. I'll deal with you, and I'll make your last failed escape seem like a walk in the park. Then, when I'm done with you, maybe I'll kill you, or maybe I won't."

It was as if roiling black clouds moved in, almost completely obscuring Michelle's pitiable moment of hope.

"I've got some Russian friends who I think could come up with some...*creative* uses for a woman like you." He reached out for a condescending pat to her cheek. "Go ahead, Michelle. Try to pull the same shit you did last time. It'd make my day."

With the ominous warning lingering in the air, he rose to his full height and left.

Kolthoff had almost killed her the last time she'd tried to escape, and this time...

I don't have a choice. This is it.

In her gut, Michelle had never been more certain of anything. If she didn't try to make a break for freedom during the upcoming relocation, she'd never have another opportunity. Though she would suffer greatly if she failed, she had to try. If she didn't try, then there was no sliver of sanity to which she could cling.

She'd learned from her mistakes last time. No bystanders would help her—not because they didn't want to, but because Kolthoff's goons would convince them Michelle was lying.

The only person she could rely on was herself.

8

Rubbing my tired eyes, I scrolled absentmindedly through the text of a piece of legislation I was supposed to sponsor when I returned to D.C. I had a little over a week left until I was expected back in the capitol, and fortunately, my to-do list was dwindling. Josh was guiding Happy Harvest along as smoothly as ever, as if nothing had ever happened out in Kankakee County.

Though I'd initially put my son in charge of the company to make it appear as if there was no conflict of interest with my senate seat, the kid had performed remarkably well. I was still unofficially in charge of the business, but with Josh, I didn't have to worry as much about the daily operations when I was busy in D.C.

A light *ping-ping* from the computer monitor snapped me back to reality. The notification noise for incoming video calls was different from any others on the PC, and I realized with a start that I'd been distracted for a solid fifteen minutes.

As I took a sip of coffee that had become lukewarm, I glanced to the closed door of my home office. Everyone in the household knew better than to meander up here when I was working, except perhaps my nosy wife. Since my caller was Brian Kolthoff, I'd prefer no one overhear the conversation.

Better use the earbuds just in case she's standing outside the door.

I placed the coffee back on the dark wooden desk, retrieved my earbuds, and hit a key to answer the video call. "You're on time."

Brian let out a quiet snort as his video feed populated a new window. "Sorry. I was busy taking care of your little pet. Someone has to feed her, and you're never here to do it." The contempt in his voice prickled the hairs on the back of my neck.

My knee-jerk reaction was to throw the petulance right back in his face, but this wasn't just any business associate. This was Brian Kolthoff, a billionaire venture capitalist turned D.C. lobbyist.

I massaged my temple and swallowed my irritability. "I was just looking over that bill I'm sponsoring. The one we were discussing when I was in D.C. most recently."

Brian's distaste fell away in an instant. "How's it shaping up?"

I offered a slight smile. Every now and then, I had to remind Brian who held the political power in our relationship. "A definite improvement from the last version. I think there are still a few tweaks that can be made, but we'll work those out when I'm in the capitol soon. I'll send you the current draft after our call."

"I appreciate it." The suave, charming Brian Kolthoff had returned. The man possessed so many masks, I couldn't keep them all straight even though I'd known him for more than twenty years. Kolthoff was the textbook definition of a sociopath.

"What about the girl?" As confident as I was in the security of the application we'd used for the video call, I still hesitated to say her name. Part of me knew my reluctance had little to do with my concerns regarding encrypted networks.

Brian shrugged noncommittally. "She's fine. Alive, for now, anyway. My guys will be heading out with her in about eleven hours."

"Starting the trip in the middle of the night?"

"It's the best time to pull her off the yacht. Fewer onlookers."

"Fair enough. I'll trust you know what you're doing. That means she should be here sometime tomorrow night, then." I'd already made the necessary preparations at the location where I'd be keeping Michelle. Not that there had been many to make.

She wouldn't be alive for long.

Some part of my bitch of a mother was alive in that woman. I didn't know how I was so certain, but there was no doubt in my mind. Just the thought of her fair complexion, that auburn dye she used for her hair...

"Get in the cellar, Stan. Don't make me tell you twice."

Tears streaked down my cheeks as I peered up at her, silently pleading for mercy I'd never receive. The cellar outside our lake house wasn't like the clean, finished basement at home. "But I don't like it down there. There are bugs and spiders. When I try to lay down and sleep, they crawl all over me. They even bite me sometimes."

An orange glow illuminated her irritable expression as she took a long drag of her cigarette. "I didn't ask if you wanted to, you little shit. I'm your mother, *and when I tell you to do something, you'd damn well better do it!"*

I flinched at the raised volume of her voice. Usually, when she shouted at me, the words were followed with a swift backhand. A mark on the side of my face was still healing from the last time she'd hit me with her left hand, and the diamond on her ring finger had gouged my cheek.

This was a losing battle, but it was the only one I had. "Please, Mom. I'll do anything else. I just...I don't want to go down there again."

Her gaze bored into me as she pulled in another drag. Dropping down until we were eye-level, she pinched the half-finished smoke between her thumb and forefinger, smiled sweetly, and held the cigarette out to me. "Fine. If you don't want to go down to the cellar, then put this out for me?"

My mouth went dry, blood pounding in my ears. I was only seven, but I still had the good sense to realize this was a trap.

Licking my lips, I reached a trembling hand out to take the cigarette. Since we were outside, I figured I'd just stub it out on the ground like I'd watched my mother do plenty of times. It was an easy way to avoid a night alone in the cellar, right?

Wrong.

Just as I was about to take hold of the cigarette, she jerked it out of my reach. "Not on the ground, Stupid Stan." Her eyes landed on my khaki shorts. "On your leg. Right here." With one cherry painted nail, she prodded the inside of my thigh.

Tears welled up in my eyes, blurring my vision. "But...but Mom, that'll hurt."

In one swift motion, she reached out and smacked me in the back of the head. "It's supposed to hurt, you idiot! Do you think I'd let you get out of staying in the cellar just for putting out my cigarette? How stupid are you? You know what, just for that, you're going to do both. You're going to put out my cigarette, and then you're going to stay in the cellar until I come unlock it to get you out! I'm supposed to be on vacation, but it's never really a vacation when I have to deal with you."

I'd pleaded two more times, but each had merely earned me another backhand.

Contempt rose in the back of my throat like bile, drawing

me back to the present. There were seventeen different scars on the inside of my legs, all of which were visible to this day. Any time I'd been asked about them, I'd lied and said they were from the chickenpox.

And that wasn't even close to the worst thing she'd done to me.

To think I'd entertained the idea that I could use Michelle to make peace with my dead mother. To think I'd find closure, some novelty peddled by Hollywood to sell more movie tickets.

Closure was no longer on my agenda. When my knuckles had collided with her face, and the force of that blow had zipped up my arm...I'd felt more satisfied than I ever had screwing one of Brian's whores. Even Gianna Passarelli's tender body hadn't brought me this much relief. The ultimate satisfaction would be watching the life drain from my mother's likeness.

After my interactions with Michelle, perhaps I needed to revisit the idea of taking Sofia for myself.

A contemplation for a different day, but a tantalizing possibility nonetheless. My reach had grown longer in the years since I'd had Gianna kidnapped, and these days, I was quite sure I could get to the pretty mafia queen herself.

"Have you heard from Joseph Larson?"

Brian's voice shook the pleasant fantasies from my head. "No. Have you?"

"No." Brian leaned forward in his office chair, his eyes flitting to something off-screen and then back to the camera. "Not for about five days, same as you. One of my guys told me there were FBI agents at his apartment recently."

As unease settled in my gut, I clenched one hand into a fist. "FBI agents? Is he under some kind of criminal investigation? Or is it an internal thing after he resigned?"

"I don't know. We don't exactly have any sources in the

Bureau to let us know. After Kantowski caught a bullet to the head, Joseph was our only source. I can't tell if he's hiding from the Feds or if he knows something we don't, and that's why we can't find him. I sent guys to a couple of his safe houses, one in Indiana and one in Michigan. They were both empty."

"Maybe he's trying to rat us out." I'd mulled over the possibility already, and as much as I hated to admit it, I had no real recourse if Joseph decided to spill his guts to the FBI. Brian and I would have to cross our fingers that our expensive lawyers and plausible deniability would keep us out of a courtroom.

And I really, *really* didn't need this shit so close to the primary. Ben Storey was gone, but a new contender had risen in his place. My campaign strategist assured me I was in no real danger, unless…

A repeat of Kankakee County. Another scandal, another blow to the appearance of my integrity.

Brian crossed his arms. "We need to find him and deal with him. I know you and him were never best buds or anything, but don't underestimate him. Just because he's sixteen years younger than me and doesn't have a graduate degree doesn't mean he's stupid."

"I know he's not stupid. But you should also know how catastrophic it would be if he decided to rat us out to the Feds."

Joseph had been in my and Brian's inner circle since before he even joined the Bureau. Though I hadn't been all that impressed with Joseph to start with, I'd learned over the years just how calculating he could be. I hated to admit it, but without Joseph, Brian and I would have been in deep shit a long time ago.

But then Joseph had to go and resign…if that was even the truth. I still didn't know why or how he'd lost his position at the FBI. Maybe if the son of a bitch had come to me instead of holing up wherever in the hell he was, I could've put political pressure on the Special Agent in Charge of the Chicago Field Office. As part of the Senate's Intelligence Committee, I had an in with the FBI.

Judging by his clenched jaw, Brian's musings were in the same realm as my own. "We need to find him, and if it comes to it, put him down. Joseph's not like us. He came from nothing, grew up in some shithole in southern Missouri. If the choice comes down to him going back to that type of life or selling us out, there's no doubt in my mind which he'll pick."

I rubbed my jaw as I worked to conceal my surprise. Joseph and Brian had always been more tightly knit than I was with either man. To witness Brian so casually suggest we kill Joseph was a stark reminder of who this man truly was.

Would Joseph roll over on us that quickly, or is Brian projecting?

If I didn't have a form of leverage over Brian, like the current legislation I was sponsoring—legislation that would make Brian even wealthier and would reaffirm his influence in U.S. politics—then dealing with him would be like handling a stick of lit dynamite.

As we said our farewells and concluded the video call, the significance of my realization weighed down my stomach like a ball of lead.

Once I had my mother...*Michelle*, I either needed to distance myself from Kolthoff or find a new political incentive to hang over his head. I wasn't particularly confident in the latter, but perhaps Brian and I parting ways would be for the best. With Joseph in the wind, we needed to lay low for a while. Brian could continue to run his exclusive sex trafficking business from the lower deck of the *Equilibrium*, catering to the twisted desires of the world's wealthy elite.

I'd keep my distance. All I wanted was Michelle.

9

Alex squinted as a pair of headlights lit up the screen of his laptop. As the car passed, signaling its turn into a gently sloping driveway, he turned the computer toward the man in the passenger's seat. Gabriel Badoni's gaze snapped away from the white glow of his cell, and he offered Alex an approving nod.

For the past day and a half, Alex and Gabriel—his most trusted lieutenant—had been scoping out Josh Young's residence.

Josh Young. Senator Stan Young's son.

Parked safely three blocks north of Josh Young's house, the risk of being spotted or raising an alarm was virtually eliminated.

In the twenty-first century, their means of surveillance had less to do with staking out the gray stone house in a cable van and more to do with a couple strategically placed wireless cameras. The batteries could last up to seventy-two hours, but Alex wouldn't need that much time.

He and Gabriel would make their move tonight.

Two full days after Amelia and Josh's meeting, Alex still had a hard time believing what he'd witnessed in front of that abandoned warehouse.

Any time he was hit with a stab of guilt for betraying Amelia's trust, he reminded himself who she'd met yesterday. How long had they been exchanging information? What had Amelia given him so far?

Amelia was a big girl, and Alex was confident she could take care of herself, especially in a firefight or a physical brawl. He wasn't so sure she understood the nuances and complexities of the criminal underworld, though. Being a Fed was a lot different than being part of a mob family.

How could Amelia possibly think Josh was on her side? He was Stan's *son*, for god's sake. Josh Young ran Happy Harvest Farms. Would the man really risk a multi*billion*-dollar agricultural empire because he'd discovered his father was morally unscrupulous?

In Alex's world, a man's son was his legacy. By extension, he was confident Stan viewed Josh in the same light. Once Stan was gone, Josh would take his place, both in the legitimate business and Stan's ties to organized crime.

Whatever in the hell those were.

The bottom line was simple. A son wouldn't betray his father. Not the son of a capo, and sure as hell not the son of a billionaire senator.

What part of their relationship—the photos of Stan and Josh side by side at various campaign functions, wide grins on both their faces—made Amelia believe Josh would turn on his *father*?

Young was pulling the wool over her eyes. At the absolute least, he was working as a double agent, relaying information from his and Amelia's meetings back to Stan.

Well, Josh's charade ended tonight. Alex had recruited

Gabriel, his lieutenant with the most experience handling sophisticated security systems, to help him pluck Josh from the comfort of his home. Alex had entertained the idea of simply putting a bullet in the back of Josh's head, but the senator's son could still prove useful.

Though Alex used his role as a capo in the D'Amato family to steer him and his people away from high-risk industries like running drugs and guns, the role of violence would never diminish in his world. A beatdown, or in extreme cases, an execution-style murder was the only language some men understood. Even if the D'Amatos switched over their entire business to a legal industry, Alex suspected they'd have to kill or maim the rival Leóne family to send a message through their thick skulls.

In any case, Alex had never laid a hand on a person who wasn't part of this life—and that included cops, unless they were dirty. He held his men to the same standard, and it had been years since someone in the D'Amato family had stepped out of line.

The suspicions ran through Alex's head on a loop as he and Gabriel kept watch on the cameras to monitor Josh's nighttime activity. Fortunately, the guy didn't seem to have much of a social life.

Alex glanced at the clock in the corner of the screen. "Almost ten. He's been home since…eight-thirty, right?"

"Eight-thirty, yeah." Gabriel offered him an expectant look. "Suppose it's time?"

Alex turned the key over to bring the engine to life. "Yeah. Let's get closer, then we'll put the cameras on a loop. Just like we planned."

During their surveillance, Alex hadn't spotted any security personnel, but he'd noted plenty of cameras. Fortunately, neither of Josh's neighbors were as paranoid as he was. The neighbors' surveillance was limited to the fronts of their residences. Technology was the D'Amato family's specialty, however, and Alex had tampered with so many security cameras he'd lost count.

Once he and Gabriel were satisfied the home surveillance had been neutralized—at least until Josh took a gander at the footage and realized his cameras were on a loop—they parked, crept through a neighbor's backyard, and scaled a wrought-iron fence. Dried leaves and vines scraped at the black fabric of Alex's hooded sweatshirt as he eased himself down onto a patch of brown grass.

Careful to stick to the shadows, he followed Gabriel up onto a wooden deck. As his lieutenant produced a credit card-sized device from his pocket to disarm the security system, Alex glanced around the backyard.

Compared to Stan Young's residence, Josh's home was modest. A black tarp covered a grill in the corner of the deck, and a handful of chairs were stacked beside it. Otherwise, the yard itself was approximately the size of a postage stamp.

Curious. Josh had more than enough money to live like a king for a thousand lifetimes, but here he was, in a one-hundred-year-old gray stone house with a tiny yard and little space between him and his neighbors.

Unease crept down Alex's back like an insect. Was he making a mistake? Was *he* wrong about Josh Young?

Doubt it. Daddy probably just doesn't let him have free reign over the family fortune.

A quiet beep drew Alex from his diligent surveillance. With the alarm system down, Gabriel retrieved a lock pick and went to work on the sliding glass door. The lock disengaged with a *click*.

Alex readjusted his hood, pulling up a face scarf to conceal his identity. As Gabriel slid open the door with a barely audible hiss, Alex closed one gloved hand around the nine-mil tucked beneath his arm.

The kitchen was cloaked in just as much shadow as the backyard, and Alex was grateful his vision had already adjusted. The soft glow of two different digital clocks, one on the microwave and the other on the oven, were the only sources of illumination.

Closing the door behind himself, Alex gestured for Gabriel to take the nearby hall. They'd snagged the layout for the place from an old real estate listing and had divided up the house earlier in the afternoon. Knowing the kitchen was blocked from view of the living area by a dining room and a large pocket door, Alex and Gabriel had agreed the deck was their best point of entry.

One hand grasping the nine-mil, the other clutching a syringe, Alex crept past the kitchen island. Aside from the tick-tock of a wall clock, the dining room was as dark and silent as a tomb.

Satisfied the room was unoccupied, Alex wove back into the hall and headed toward the living room. Finally, he spotted a flicker of light and the quiet drone of a woman's voice.

"The forecast tomorrow is looking just about as cold today, but don't worry. A warm front is coming through the city later this week, just in time for the first days of March."

I guess March won't be coming in like a lion... Alex wondered where he'd learned that idiom.

He slowed his pace to a veritable crawl, resting his back flush against the wall as he leaned forward to catch a glimpse of the living room.

As his gaze settled on the man lying on the sectional couch, he steadied his breathing. A fleece blanket covered Josh Young up to his neck, his cheek resting on a plush throw pillow. The glow of the television reflected off Josh's tired eyes, but so far, he hadn't noticed Alex.

Ducking back behind the wall, Alex placed the syringe between his teeth and started to plot his approach. Josh would see him no matter what he did, so he'd be best served by letting his silenced handgun lead the way. Maybe if he—

Creeeeak.

Fueled by a sudden rush of adrenaline, his gaze shot up toward the source of the sound—the ceiling.

Gabriel.

Stupid old house.

He tightened his grasp on the nine-mil and dared another glance around the wall, hoping like hell Josh hadn't noticed the groaning floorboard upstairs.

No such luck.

The fleece blanket was on a pile next to the throw pillow, and Josh's gaze was glued to the doorway. Alex pressed his back into the wall until he thought he might bruise his shoulder blades. A scrape of wood told him Josh had opened a drawer, and that could mean only one thing...

Young was armed. Alex's endeavor had just become ten times riskier.

His only shot now was to take the man by surprise as he exited the living room.

Alex had little time to prepare himself before Young crept into the doorway. His stocking feet made little more than a whisper of sound against the hardwood.

Despite Alex's best efforts to meld into the drywall, Young swiveled to his right to check the hall. Alex had only a fraction of a second to react as Young's eyes met his.

He still had the element of surprise. He could shoot Josh and leave him dead in a pool of his own blood for his father to find.

But then, who would answer his questions? Who would tell him why in the hell Josh had been meeting with Amelia?

At the last second, just before Josh had brought his handgun to bear, Alex took a swift step forward to close the distance. Wrenching Young's arm behind his back, Alex released his bite on the syringe and jammed it into the man's neck.

Holding him tight, Alex waited until Josh's body went limp. Alex guided his unconscious form to the floor with one hand under his armpit.

After collecting Gabriel, who muttered a handful of apologies for his mishap, he and Alex loaded Josh into the trunk of his own car. One forty-five-minute drive later, they dragged the still-unconscious Josh Young down to the basement of a seldom-used house outside of the city.

Alex handcuffed Josh's wrists to a sturdy iron ring bolted to the cinderblock wall. He wasn't sure if the ring had been installed specifically to bind captives or if it had been used for something less sinister at some point in the past. Either way, it worked for Alex's purposes tonight.

Young had been out like a light for almost an hour and a half when Gabriel snapped a smelling salt capsule under his nose.

The man's eyes flew open like they'd been set on a timer. With a sharp inhale, Josh tugged on his binds as he scrambled to sit upright. His gaze darted from Gabriel to Alex, then to the shelf of supplies at Alex's back. There was no rhyme or reason to the items on the shelf—garden shears, a wrench, a long-dead cordless drill, a coaxial cable—but Alex had already come up with a few creative applications for each.

Readjusting his black face scarf, Alex stepped forward into the halo of light illuminating his captive.

Young's mouth gaped open, but he quickly smothered the awed expression. "What…" Young's voice was a hoarse croak, and he paused to swallow, "what the hell is going on? Did my father send you? Where is he?"

Alex fought to keep the confusion out of his tone. "Your father?"

Josh gave a vicious yank to his binds. "This isn't necessary. Just let me talk to him! I'll sort this out. I guarantee it's not what you think."

As Alex dropped to his haunches to bring himself down to Young's level, he tugged down the scarf. "Tell me what I think happened?"

Josh stopped mid yank, his eyes wide as a pair of saucers. "No...y-you. Alex Passarelli. I know who you are. Oh, shit." Rather than continue the feeble attempt to free himself, Josh's shoulders slumped.

Alex's curiosity only deepened, but he didn't want Young to know. He needed to appear in control of the entire situation. "Well, I guess I can skip the introductions. I'd say it's nice to meet you, Josh, but it's not. You're heavier than you look."

"Thanks. I've been working out. I like to think I've built up some muscle mass."

If the comment hadn't come from Stan Young's kid, Alex might have laughed. "We can cut the shit, then. Do you know why you're here?"

Josh pressed his lips together, his gaze fixed on a point over Alex's shoulder. "I *thought* my father had sent you, but I seriously doubt it now that I know who you are. Dear ole Dad isn't on great terms with the D'Amatos."

"Who did you think I was before you knew I was part of the D'Amato family?"

"Figured you were some Leóne goon."

Curiosity dug into Alex's brain like an ice pick. "Leóne? Why would Stan Young have a Leóne soldier kidnap his own son?"

Young's eyes narrowed. "Why else? Because he wants me dead. Maybe he just woke up in a bad mood and decided to have me killed, or maybe his bitch of a wife finally convinced him that I'm secretly plotting his demise. Pick one. I don't know why that man does half the shit he does. He's a twisted son of a bitch."

Alex hadn't wanted to be wrong. He'd been so certain Josh was playing Amelia for a fool, but now...

Keep a level head. Don't let down your guard.

"Why have you been meeting with Amelia Storm?"

The color drained from Josh's cheeks. "I don't know what you're talking about."

"Why are you lying about it?"

He glanced to Gabriel, then back to Alex. "What do you want with Agent Storm?"

Alex snapped his fingers in front of Josh's face, satisfied when the man flinched. "No, you're not answering my questions with another question. I asked you why you've been meeting with Amelia Storm. Answer me."

Irritation flashed in Josh's eyes, as if Alex had made him late for an appointment. "If you were anyone else, I'd tell you to just kill me now. I want to make that part perfectly clear, okay? If you weren't Gianna's brother, I'd tell you to go fuck yourself."

The mention of Alex's little sister stole his cantankerous remark before he could make it. All he could manage was, "Why?"

"I'm helping Agent Storm, just like I tried to help her brother. She wants to find out who kidnapped your little sister because whoever that is, they were behind her brother's death too."

Though Young appeared to be sincere, Alex hadn't survived the mafia lifestyle this long by being naïve. "So, you're turning on your father? Why the change of heart? Do you want to take him down so you can have the Young family fortune all to yourself?"

"Are you familiar with the concept of *enough*, Mr. Passarelli?" Young tried to adjust where he sat on the concrete floor, but the position of his cuffed wrists didn't allow for comfort.

"What did I tell you about answering my questions with a question?" Alex put as much annoyance in his tone as he could manage, but admittedly, he was losing steam. Maybe he shouldn't have questioned Amelia's judgment. She hadn't gotten to her position as a special agent by blindly trusting and ignoring red flags.

Josh gave another perfunctory tug at the handcuffs. "People like my father, like his pal Brian Kolthoff, they always want more. No matter how many zeroes are in their bank accounts, they'll never be satisfied. They'll step on whoever gets in their way. They'll *kill* whoever gets in their way if they can't smother them legally. All because they never have *enough*."

Alex could relate to Josh more than he cared to admit. The mafia was loaded with men who'd never stop hustling, who'd never be satisfied. "And you're saying you're not like them?"

Josh raised his chin. "I'm not. My family has more money than god. I have *enough*. I won't bore you with details, but I'd like to leave a better legacy than my asshole of a father."

You and me both.

The picture was becoming clearer to Alex. He and Josh were on the same side. Hell, they even seemed like kindred spirits. "What have you told Agent Storm so far?"

Josh glanced to where Gabriel leaned against a cinderblock wall, both arms folded over his chest.

"Oh, sorry. I guess I forgot to introduce the two of you." Alex's tone bled sarcasm as he gestured to his lieutenant.

"Gabriel, this is Josh Young. Mr. Young, this is Gabriel. Whatever you say to me can be trusted with him."

"If any of this gets back to my father, I'll wish I was dead."

Gabriel tilted his head. "Believe me, we're two of the last people who'd ever give Stan Young or his Leóne goons the time of day."

Young sighed, making another feeble attempt to move his arms to a more comfortable position. "I was Trevor Storm's informant when he was investigating Gianna's case. I gave him much of the same information I've given Agent Storm so far, and he wound up dead."

Alex exchanged a quick glance with Gabriel, confirming they were on the same page. "We can handle ourselves."

"Clearly." Josh's tone was flat. "I've been piecing this together for a long time. *Something* happened between my father and Sofia Passarelli. An affair, a fling, whatever you want to call it. Obviously, it ended, but Stan doesn't let things go that easily. He's obsessed over Sofia for years, *decades* at this point. I caught it on his web browser history back before he knew how to clear it. Whatever they had or did, he didn't let it go."

Did Alex's mother know about Stan Young's prolonged infatuation with her? Had she already suspected that Stan was involved in kidnapping Gianna?

Embers of rage burned in Alex's chest, but he kept the sentiment out of his face. He didn't want Josh to misconstrue his ire. "Then Stan took my sister as retribution?"

"Exactly."

"Do you have any proof of this?"

Josh licked his lips and nodded slowly. "Yeah. The proof is my sister, Mae. I already gave Agent Storm samples of Mae's DNA and mine so she can run an analysis."

The embers threatened to burn Alex alive as the implication of Josh's statement settled in. Anger wasn't an emotion

Alex liked to entertain. Weaker men made rash decisions out of ire. They lashed out violently and allowed the rage to dictate their actions.

Alex wasn't like them. He was always in control of his emotions, but right now, hearing from another person's mouth that Stan Young had kidnapped Gianna, raped her, and then stolen her child—Alex's niece—to raise as his own?

Any human being's limit would be tested.

Save it. Save that anger for the person who deserves it, and no one else.

Running a shaky hand over his mouth, Alex swallowed hard. Guilt nibbled at the back of his mind, slowly eating away the moment of white-hot rage. He shouldn't have second-guessed Amelia. He should have trusted her judgment.

"All right." Alex rose to his feet and reached an expectant hand out to Gabriel.

Wordlessly, Gabriel placed a small silver key in Alex's palm. Josh's wide eyes followed each movement as Alex unlocked the cuffs.

The instant his hands were free, Young began to massage his wrists. Still, he didn't speak. Wariness was plainly visible in his face as he moved to stand. "Is that...it?"

"That's it." The rush of anger had sapped Alex's energy. "Sorry for the, uh, whole kidnapping thing."

Young shrugged without a hint of anger. "Classic misunderstanding. It happens sometimes."

Alex had never imagined the day would come, but he thought he actually liked Josh Young. It took guts to defy one's own father, especially in Alex and Josh's worlds. Men viewed their sons as their legacies, and for the son to break away from those expectations to forge his own path was dangerous.

But to do so when the stakes were so incredibly high, as they were for Josh, was impressive.

Unfortunately, Josh was in the midst of navigating a minefield. One wrong move and the consequences would blow up not just on Josh but anyone with whom he'd been involved.

They all had to be careful where they stepped next because a single misstep could be their last.

10

B arren fields whipped by, vanishing behind the SUV as they hurtled down the highway. Michelle viewed the scenery through a fishbowl, her head dizzy and vision unfocused. A couple hours ago, at their last stop, the man in the passenger's seat had dosed her with some type of synthetic opiate. Whatever in the hell it was, the effects were almost identical to what she'd been given during her recovery after Brian had beaten her to within an inch of her life.

This time, there was no medicinal intent. The drugs were used to keep her disoriented and docile for the long trip to…

Where were they going? Michelle could have sworn one of the men had mentioned a destination, but she couldn't recall it. Time was a blur in her fugue-like state.

She'd never been a fan of any substance that dulled her senses, not that she'd tried many. Michelle had always preferred her mind to be sharp, even when she wished she was anywhere else.

Fighting through the opiates was like treading water in a riptide. If she hadn't had practice a couple times already, she'd have likely succumbed to exhaustion by now.

In order to keep her brain grounded in reality—like holding the string to keep a balloon from floating off into the sky—she forced herself to focus on road signs, passing vehicles, the pattern of the surrounding landscape. Anything to give her more of a feel for where they were and where they were headed.

Blinking repeatedly, Michelle squinted at an upcoming road sign.

Chillicothe 8 Miles.

The name of the city was vaguely familiar, but in her current state of mind, Michelle couldn't quite place it. Based on the license plates she'd spotted on passing vehicles, they were currently in Ohio. The golden glow of the sun cresting the horizon behind them meant they were traveling west.

Wisconsin. We're headed to Wisconsin. That's what one of them said.

Not long after the Chillicothe sign, Michelle made note of a billboard advertising a truck stop, gas station, and a fast-food joint at an upcoming exit. She'd spotted a half-billion similar signs already, three of which her captors had used.

At each stop, Michelle had asked to use the bathroom, and each time, her request had been granted. She could only assume the men didn't want to clean human waste off the sleek leather seats. One of the men—a young, broad-shouldered guy with a remarkably flat crew cut—would fuel up the SUV while the other accompanied Michelle inside.

Both men repulsed Michelle, but she particularly disliked the guy who'd escorted her to the ladies' room at their three stops. With his beady eyes and pug nose, he reminded her of the kid in movies who'd beat up the geeks and steal their lunch money.

Only now, he'd become an adult and had grown into his bulk. Rather than learning the error of his bullying ways, he'd doubled down and now worked for Brian Kolthoff.

The motion of the vehicle veering onto an exit on the right pulled Michelle from her contemplation. Dammit. She'd spaced off again. Maintaining vigilance with an opiate flowing through her system was becoming more difficult as the hours dragged on. All she wanted to do was sleep, but she knew if she gave into the temptation, she'd wake in a brand-new hell.

Licking her dry lips, she carefully studied the surrounding area as they approached the stop. A strand of trees lined the creek running behind the gas station, essentially separating the cluster of buildings from the farmland beyond. On the other side of the road was the promised fast-food joint, along with a ramshackle motel.

Though the fueling area of the gas station was large enough for multiple eighteen-wheelers and other large vehicles to fit at the same time, the building itself was no larger than an average convenience store. A strip of grass separated the gas station from the truck stop and restaurant next door. Michelle assumed, based on her travel experiences, that the truck stop provided showers, an assortment of foodstuffs, and a warm meal to those passing through.

The hour was early, but the stop was already bustling. Michelle couldn't decide if the extra people were a blessing or a curse. Her prior escape attempt taught her that she couldn't rely on any of them to help her.

As the SUV slowed to a stop beside a fuel pump, Michelle cleared her throat. "I need to use the bathroom."

Pug Nose snorted as he turned to face her. "Of course you do. You women always have to piss every twenty minutes on a road trip, don't you?"

Michelle let her head loll to the side but didn't reply.

Crew Cut chuckled. "She's high as a kite."

That's what you think, dipshit.

Truthfully, she *was* high. But she wasn't as messed up as she'd led the pair to believe.

Leaning to the side, Pug Nose held open his canvas jacket to showcase the matte black handgun holstered beneath one arm. "All right, toots. You know the drill. You pull anything, and," he squinted at the rear windshield and pointed, "see that happy little family getting fuel behind us? They're all dead. Not today, but I'll make it my personal mission to find them and put them down. Understand?"

Michelle dipped her chin in a lazy nod. "Uh-huh." She believed Pug Nose's threat. From the snippets of dialogue she'd caught between him and Crew Cut, neither man was fit to walk free in a civilized society.

Pug Nose zipped up his jacket and stepped out into the cold morning. After pretending to fumble with the door, Michelle stumbled out of the back seat. The scent of gasoline and car exhaust wafted up to greet her, along with the chatter of the nearby family Pug Nose had threatened.

The cool breeze, the sound of laughter, and the sensation of real, solid land beneath her feet were becoming more familiar with each trip to the truck stop bathrooms she made. Before this excursion, those sense-awakening experiences were so foreign to Michelle, she might as well have been deposited on a different planet. Ironically, if her senses weren't dulled by the opiate, she was certain she'd have stood on the precipice of a panic attack brought on by sensory overload.

Pug Nose prodded her in the direction of the gas station, and she offered no resistance. She tried to ignore the silvery bell that tinkled as she pushed open the advertising-laden glass double doors, the scent of roasting hot dogs and fried food, and the hiss of the soda machine in the back corner.

At her side, Pug Nose pointed toward a hallway next to the fountain drink dispenser. Michelle shuffled past a few aisles, noting the four different doors in the short hall. On the right was the men's room and a second door labeled *Employees Only*, and on the left was the ladies' room, a water fountain, and another *Employees Only* door.

"Make it fast." Pug Nose gave her another slight shove before he turned toward the fountain drinks.

Michelle's plan was half-cocked at best, but it was all she had. All she needed was a window. Half-walking, half-staggering into the women's bathroom, she thought she might be hallucinating.

On the wall opposite the stalls was a glorious pane of glass.

She blinked a few times to focus her vision, to reassure herself she wasn't so high she was hallucinating.

The window was still there.

Though she told her feet to hurry, Michelle was certain she was slogging through mud or sand as she scrambled over to the wall. The sill was at chest height, granting her an easy view of the two brass locks. She prodded and pulled at the first, her fingers as precise as a pair of bratwursts.

In her current mental state, the menial task was akin to solving a Rubik's Cube.

By the time she finally disengaged the second lock, she was certain at least an hour had elapsed. Any moment now, Pug Nose would come charging into the bathroom, spouting curses and reiterating how badly she'd screwed up. Maybe Brian Kolthoff would crawl out of the drain like Pennywise.

Gritting her teeth, Michelle wrenched open the window. The creak of the sill was as loud as an air raid siren, and she hesitated, half-expecting Pug Nose to barge in demanding to know what all the racket was. She glanced over her shoulder, blood pounding in her ears, but the door didn't move. God, she wished she knew how long she'd been in here. Her sense of time was too warped to make an accurate estimate.

Michelle turned her focus back to the window. There was a way to pop out the screen without damaging it, but the sudden surge of panic had rendered her movements even clumsier.

Rather than waste even more precious time trying to solve another stupid puzzle, she leaned her weight into the screen and pushed.

To her relief, the screen popped out of place and clattered to the ground. Poking her head out the window, she gasped and pulled it back in. Though his back was turned to her, she spotted Crew Cut easily enough, and she knew he could turn her way at any moment.

Shit.

Did she risk being seen? No.

Glancing around the restroom, Michelle came up with Plan B.

With a quick glimpse toward the door to ensure Pug Nose hadn't crept up on her, Michelle lifted the bottom of her hoodie to reveal the hem of her t-shirt, hooked it on one of the lock levers, and pulled back until it ripped. Satisfied that a scrap of fabric had been left behind, she looked around for a place to hide.

Please, God, let this work.

If she was being transported by Brian Kolthoff himself, the trick might not have worked. Brian was as smart as he was sadistic, but Pug Nose and Crew Cut were a different story. Michelle'd had nine hours to study the pair, and though the men had enough brawn to stand in as linebackers for a professional football team, they weren't especially clever.

In a rare stroke of good fortune, the bathroom appeared to have been recently remodeled. Though it wasn't part of any chain she knew, the place did enough business to warrant a restroom with a number of stalls. The stalls were set back in the wall, and between each, a faux stone divider ran from the floor all the way to the ceiling. Though the space was unoccupied aside from Michelle, each of the doors was almost closed, leaving only a sliver of the toilet visible. On one of them was a handwritten "broken" sign.

Noting there was no vanity beneath the granite counter and the three sinks, Michelle's decision was made for her.

Grabbing the sign and securing it to the door in front of her, she slipped into the stall nearest the window and, using a metal safety grip to steady herself, climbed to sit atop the tank of the toilet.

Then, she waited, straining her hearing to make out what was happening in the gas station. Her mouth was dry, her breathing was shallow, and her stomach was in knots—none of which were the result of the opiates. If anything, the drugs calmed her to the point where she was able to successfully sit still.

As the door of the ladies' room swung inward with a *whoosh*, Michelle tensed. She fully expected to hear Pug Nose or Crew Cut rattle off a series of obscenities, but to her surprise, a woman muttered, "Wow."

Michelle's sluggish brain took a few seconds to realize the woman was likely impressed with the quality of the bathroom. Gas stations were notorious for disgusting facilities.

The woman took the stall closest to the exit, but as soon as the lock of her stall had clicked into place, the swinging door opened again.

Adrenaline spiked in Michelle's veins, and for a beat, her mind was clear and sharp. The newcomer didn't speak, and Michelle knew right away it was Pug Nose or Crew Cut. His fist pounded against the woman's stall, nearly causing Michelle to jump and lose her balance.

"What the hell's taking you so long?" Annoyance dripped from Pug Nose's tone.

"Excuse me?" The woman's shout rang around the room.

In spite of the dire situation, Michelle wished she could have caught the look on Pug Nose's ugly face.

"Oh, I'm sorry, ma'am. I thought you were someone else." Pug Nose shuffled forward a couple steps, and then his movement stopped.

He saw the window.

"Dude, I don't give a shit who you're looking for! Get the hell out of here!" Indignation practically radiated from the woman's bathroom stall.

Pug Nose swore.

Time plodded by at the speed of cold molasses, and Michelle was certain that if Pug Nose didn't find and kill her, she'd die from a heart attack if he didn't leave soon.

"Dude, get out! Now! Before I pull out my phone, film your creepy ass, and make you the worst kind of TikTok famous!"

Michelle wished she could hug the woman. If she made it through today alive, she promised she'd make her best effort to find the woman and send her flowers, chocolates, or just cold hard cash.

Muttering a half-assed apology, Pug Nose trudged back to the door, hesitated, and left.

Relief crept into Michelle's tense muscles, but she shooed away the sentiment before it could take hold. She wasn't out of the woods yet—not even close.

The woman finished up her business and washed her hands. For a split second, Michelle was tempted to creep out of her stall and plead for help.

All she had to do was picture the disgusted expression on the face of the last person she'd asked for assistance, and her fantasy died.

Trust no one.

Once the woman was gone, Michelle came down from

her perch. She couldn't hide in the bathroom for long. Crew Cut and Pug Nose weren't the brightest bulbs in the box, but chances were good they'd come back to the ladies' room.

She paused in front of the swinging door.

If either of the men were standing in the hall, her escape was over before it ever began. They'd wrangle her back to the SUV, and no matter how big a scene she caused, she'd have no hope of getting away from them.

Chillicothe had sounded familiar to Michelle when she'd first spotted the sign, and now she remembered why. The city was notorious for human trafficking and a heroin and opiate crisis. There was no way in hell Brian Kolthoff couldn't buy off cops from Chillicothe.

The first portion of Michelle's plan had worked, thanks in part to her outspoken savior who'd shooed Pug Nose out of the bathroom, but there were plenty more steps until she was in the clear.

Pulling in a long, uneven breath, Michelle counted to three and tugged open the door. Like a soldier checking for an enemy ambush, she poked her head out into the hall. The little family from the fuel pump beside Pug Nose and Crew Cut's SUV were browsing the aisles, searching for snacks for their road trip.

They're all dead. Not today, but I'll make it my personal mission to find them and put them down.

Michelle couldn't turn back now. If she made it away from Chillicothe with her life, she had to trust that Pug Nose and Crew Cut would be in too much hot water to take the time to track down and murder an entire family. Brian Kolthoff didn't strike her as the type of boss to forgive such an egregious mistake.

When she didn't spot either of her captors, Michelle side-stepped to the *Employee Only* door next to the ladies' room.

Without pausing to second-guess herself, she shoved open the door and hobbled over the threshold.

As she turned around, a television screen caught her eye. A worn, leather couch rested against the wall beside the door, and a rectangular table stood beside a kitchenette.

The employee breakroom.

To her relief, the space was unoccupied, but she wasn't sure for how long. For the second time, she needed a place to hide.

A sliding closet door stood directly opposite the entrance —coat storage. With a quick glance out the window beside the wall-mounted television, Michelle pushed open the closet door and stepped inside. It was deeper than she'd expected, with shelves built into both ends. The shelves were stacked with brand-new polo shirts still in their plastic packaging, as well as a few pairs of khaki pants. Michelle quickly recognized the clothing as the uniform worn by the employees she'd spotted behind the counter.

Unless they were hiring someone new in the next couple hours, Michelle doubted they'd pay close attention to the space between the lowest shelf and the floor. Dropping down to her hands and knees, Michelle wedged herself into the tight space. Lying on her side, she crossed her legs to fit into the opening and pressed her back against the wall, satisfied she was mostly concealed beneath the shelves.

Then, she waited.

And waited.

And waited.

Though she made a valiant effort to maintain her vigilance, she nodded off at a couple different points as her adrenaline receded, only to be jarred awake each time a noise penetrated her safe haven.

When the breakroom door creaked open, she was ripped back to the world of the waking once more.

Was this it?

Had Crew Cut and Pug Nose searched the perimeter, only to determine Michelle must still be somewhere in the building?

God, she wished she had a watch. She couldn't tell for the life of her how long she'd been here. It felt like an eternity.

"Hey, babe." A man's quiet voice was followed by the *click* of the door latching in place.

When Michelle didn't hear a response, she assumed he was on the phone.

"It's been all right. Steady flow of customers but not slammed. Yeah, I'm off at two. Do you want me to pick up something to eat on my way home?"

Another pause.

"Really? That sounds much better than takeout. I can't wait."

Fabric rustled as he sank into the couch.

"Speaking of strange, there were a couple weirdos wandering around the store earlier. Not the dope fiends we sometimes get. Neither of these guys was from around here. Their plates were from Virginia, and one of them had a little bit of a Southern accent. They were just…creepy. They came up and asked me and Maryann if we'd seen a woman sneaking around. Said she was high or schizophrenic or something, I don't know. Their vibes were all sorts of messed up, you know?"

Michelle pressed her back into the wall until she worried her skin might bruise. Crew Cut and Pug Nose had been asking the clerks about her, filling them with lies about her mental state. She'd made the right call by not interacting with the woman from the bathroom.

She might have been hidden for the immediate future, but she needed to get the hell out of here. Out of this trafficking hub, away from Pug Nose and Crew Cut.

The employee's conversation shifted to a television show he and his partner had started bingeing, and then they said their goodbyes. Michelle's legs were falling asleep, and her knees were killing her, but she waited for the man to leave before she dared shift in her uncomfortable position.

Once the feeling was restored to her calves and feet, she steadied herself with the lowest shelf and moved to stand.

How in the hell was she supposed to get out of here without drawing attention to herself? She couldn't live in the employee breakroom forever.

No, that would be too easy. This place was a paradise compared to where she'd spent the last several months.

Focus, Michelle. You need to get out of here.

Pug Nose and Crew Cut would search the surrounding area for her before they dared to call in reinforcements. Knowing how Brian Kolthoff would react to the news, Michelle doubted they'd alert him until they were absolutely certain they'd lost her.

By that point, she wanted to be long gone. Considering she was still high on synthetic opiates, had no identification, and had no money, there was only one way she could leave Chillicothe behind her. She had to sneak onto a vehicle headed out of town—preferably a vehicle with out-of-state plates, lest she wind up right back in Crew Cut and Pug Nose's hunting grounds.

To do that, she had to leave the relative safety of the gas station.

She took stock of her clothes. The black parka, navy blue hoodie, and jeans weren't conspicuous by any stretch of the imagination, but Pug Nose and Crew Cut would recognize the attire.

Good thing you're in a closet full of employee uniforms.

Glancing to the shelves and then the handful of coats on hangers, she shrugged out of her coat. Michelle had never been a thief, but her current circumstances warranted a break from the usual. Changing clothes in the narrow closet was awkward, and she took almost twice as long as she'd have if she had free range of motion. She abandoned the worn parka, figuring Pug Nose and Crew Cut wouldn't be able to immediately identify her hoodie. Her jeans went next, and though the khakis closest to her size were too large, they'd work.

Was there valuable evidence on her old clothes?

Probably, but she had to ignore her forensic mind. The evidence would be worthless if she was caught.

Pushing open the closet door a crack, she confirmed no one else was in the room before stepping out into the light. After her vision adjusted to the new brightness, she crept over to the window, careful not to show her face.

The black SUV in which she'd ridden not long ago was no longer at the fuel pump, but the vehicle was partially visible where it had been moved to a parking stall in front of the building.

As she scanned the pumps, she gasped.

Crew Cut stood at the rear of a large dump truck, the back of which was covered by a tightly pulled tarp. A shorter, gray-haired man Michelle didn't recognize was at his side. Crew Cut gestured to the truck, and the older man shook his head. Based on his plaid jacket and worn jeans, the guy was the driver, and Crew Cut was asking him if he'd seen Michelle.

Michelle tensed as Pug Nose trotted over to the two of them. The older man's tense posture told Michelle he wasn't keen on the conversation, providing her a slim measure of satisfaction. She couldn't imagine a world where either Pug Nose or Crew Cut were what any normal person would consider tactful.

As the truck driver started toward the gas station, Pug

Nose and Crew Cut exchanged a few words Michelle wished she could hear. Pug Nose waved a hand at the nearby truck stop, and Crew Cut nodded. Spinning around, Crew Cut marched toward the SUV with Pug Nose on his heel.

With a sharp breath, Michelle ducked away from the window. Her paranoid gaze shot straight ahead as she flattened her back against the wall. Seconds ticked away in relative silence, maybe even minutes, before she dared to peek out the window again.

The SUV was gone. Judging by Pug Nose's gesture to the truck stop, they'd decided to check for Michelle there.

A dump truck wasn't ideal for catching a ride out of town, but beggars couldn't be choosers. Once she was away from Chillicothe, she could get her bearings and figure out the next step. Her window of opportunity was open, but only a crack. She had to act quickly before it slammed shut like a guillotine.

Tucking her hair beneath the hood of her sweatshirt, Michelle turned her gaze down as she slipped out into the hall.

Her anxiety-ridden brain insisted every pair of eyes in the store turned to her as she exited the hall, but she kept her head down and focused on putting one foot in front of the other. With each step, she became more and more certain someone was about to recognize her, that they'd drag her back to Pug Nose and Crew Cut, and then...

Back to Brian Kolthoff.

Michelle's throat tightened.

Out. Get out. Get to that lifeline of a truck.

She shouldered open the glass door with the ad for a seventy-two-ounce fountain drink for only ninety-nine cents. The chill, early-morning wind smacked her in the face as the tile beneath her feet turned to concrete.

Starting in the direction of the truck, she quickly took

stock of her surroundings. The family Pug Nose had threatened was long gone, leaving only the dump truck, a red pickup, and a beat-up Honda Civic hatchback.

Across the road, the truck stop was marginally busier. Michelle searched for the black SUV and immediately broke off her gaze when she spotted it. Eyes back on the ground, she hurried the rest of the way to the dump truck.

Another scan of the area assured her no one was paying attention to her movements. The truck driver was still in the gas station, and the young man fueling up his Honda was focused on his phone.

Adrenaline surged through Michelle's veins as she hoisted herself up the side of the truck. Her confinement workouts had paid off. Even through the lingering haze of the opiates, the tremor in her body from the adrenaline, and her near exhaustion, she easily picked her way up to the edge of the tarp.

She only gave herself a second to consider the contents of the truck before squeezing under the canvas. As her foot sank into sand, relief washed over her in a wave. Though she'd have toughed it out no matter what the contents were, she was grateful she didn't have to hide in a pile of animal carcasses or busted concrete.

She quickly worked to resecure the tarp, blocking out the light of the rising sun, as well as much of the sound. Lying on her back atop a heap of sand, only the sound of Michelle's labored breaths kept her company. She'd bury herself for warmth when they got on the road.

She didn't mind. The isolation was a significant improvement from the lousy company of Pug Nose and Crew Cut.

A voice in the back of her head reminded her the men might have spotted her. On cue, every muscle in her body tensed as a pair of booted footsteps neared the truck.

"I'm just outside Chillicothe." An unfamiliar voice drifted

up to Michelle, and she finally permitted herself a quiet sigh of relief. "Grabbed myself a little something to eat. 'Bout to head up north now. Got a little delayed when some guy approached me about his missing crazy sister or some shit."

Metal creaked as the man climbed into the driver's seat, and his conversation was abruptly cut off as he slammed the door closed.

Against all odds, Michelle was on her way out of this godforsaken town.

Whether or not she'd be able to get far enough away from the men who sought her, she still couldn't be sure.

But she knew she'd rather die than let Brian or Stan catch her alive.

11

Though the forecast promised warmer weather in the coming days, Amelia found the prediction hard to believe as she stepped out of her car on Monday morning. The trees of Adams Park shielded her from a portion of the blustery day, but not all of it. Teeth chattering, she tugged up the collar of her coat as she closed the car door.

Alex Passarelli had called her late the night before to set up a last-minute meeting, which he claimed was an emergency. He'd upended what had been an otherwise uneventful but pleasant weekend spent with Zane and Hup cloistered in Amelia's apartment. Needless to say, her sleep had been restless, and she was on edge as she approached a familiar gazebo.

Like always, Alex had gotten to the park first, not unlike Josh always beating her to their clandestine meetings. Amelia suspected Alex's early arrivals had less to do with punctuality and more to do with him savoring a moment of peace and quiet away from his busy life as a mafia capo.

How he managed to seemingly breeze through the gridlock known as Monday "rush" hour was a mystery.

Hunching her shoulders against the wind, Amelia hurried up the wooden steps into the relative shelter of the gazebo.

Alex's gaze flitted to her, and he pocketed his cell. "Good morning. How was the drive?"

"Annoying." Amelia hadn't intended for her tone to come out so clipped, but she *had* just spent forty-five minutes driving through some of the worst traffic in the United States.

"Sorry about that." He took a sip from the paper coffee cup in his hand. "But this couldn't wait. It's important, and it's time sensitive."

She took a quick glance around the small parking lot. Satisfied they were indeed alone—not that any sane person would come to a damn park on a day like this—she dropped down to sit on the edge of the bench across from Alex. "I've gathered that. What's up?" She tried to make her tone amiable, but the result was only awkward.

As Alex sighed, the white cloud of his breath disappeared, whisked away by the cold breeze. "I figured out who your informant was. I know you've been meeting with Josh Young."

"You...*what?*" Anger flared in Amelia's chest. "You figured out...*how?* What the hell did you do?"

Alex held up his free hand. "Look, just hear me out, all right? First of all, I'm sorry. I screwed up. I should have trusted your judgment to begin with."

Worry sneaked in beside her anger, but she didn't let the sentiment show. "Did you do something to Josh? What the hell happened?"

Blowing out another sigh, Alex took a drink of coffee. "I followed you to the meeting you had with him a couple days ago. I'm sorry. I shouldn't have done that. It's just...this is the closest anyone's ever been to figuring out what happened to

Gianna, and I had to know who it was. To make sure they weren't feeding you a line of BS."

The puzzle pieces clicked together in Amelia's head, further stoking the ire threatening to bubble over like magma seeping through a crack in the earth's crust. "You called me the other night so I'd set up a meeting with Josh. So you could *follow me?*"

He held up both hands, as if he might need to protect himself. "I'm sorry, Amelia. I was so sure I was doing the right thing, that I'd be helping both of us by butting in. But I screwed up."

If Alex had been anyone else, if he was anyone other than a D'Amato capo, and anyone other than Gianna Passarelli's big brother, she'd have spat a long string of four-letter words at him and stalked away from the meeting.

Knowing Alex was just as desperate to find out who'd kidnapped his sister as Amelia was to learn who'd killed her brother held her anger at bay.

She opened her mouth to admonish him but stopped. A rare expression flitted over Alex's face, though only briefly.

Shame.

Amelia paused. What would she have done if their roles were reversed? Could she have taken him at his word and resisted digging to learn the identity of his informant?

Doubtful.

She and Alex were birds of a feather. There was a reason they'd been drawn to one another in their younger years.

Her surge of anger began to subside. "Josh is okay, isn't he?" She suspected she already knew the answer but was compelled to ask anyway.

"Yeah, he's fine. We just…talked." He shifted in his seat as he took a long drink of coffee.

Amelia knew Alex was glossing over his and Josh's inter-action. "You didn't just talk, did you?"

Alex waved a hand. "No, we did. We just…didn't tell him we were coming over beforehand. You were right about him, though. He's a good person. I've got Gabriel helping to keep tabs on him now, another layer of security. Just in case Stan starts to think something's going on."

As much as Amelia hated to admit it at first, the knowledge that Alex and his lieutenant were looking out for Josh was a welcome reassurance. There was only so much Amelia could do without landing Josh on the FBI's—and by proxy, Stan Young's—radar. Alex and the D'Amatos could stealthier and could offer Josh a blanket of security without raising any alarms or leaving a paper trail.

The more she mulled over the situation, the more relieved she became. Alex's methods had been unorthodox, as they often were, but she was more confident in Josh's safety now.

With her anger slipping away, she stuffed her freezing hands in her pockets. "So, was that all you wanted to discuss today? Or was there something more?"

Alex slugged back the rest of his coffee. "Josh told me about how he thinks that his sister is…" he paused and licked his lips, "how he thinks Mae is my niece. I know he already gave you samples of his and Mae's DNA, but with just those, you still need to be able to prove that Mae was related to Gianna."

"True." Amelia had been waiting for the results of the analysis before she came to Alex with the news. "Even if it proves Stan is Mae's biological father, I don't think we'd have enough to arrest him. We might not even have enough for a warrant at that point. Because technically, anyone could be Mae's mother."

He held out his empty cup. "Here. You can run my DNA, and it should tell you if I'm Mae's uncle."

There was little doubt in Amelia's mind that the results

would indeed confirm the genetic relation, but stranger things had happened. Stan could have still kidnapped Gianna and then knocked up some other woman around the same timeframe.

She accepted the cup, holding it gently until she could stuff it into an evidence bag. She always kept a few in her car for unexpected moments such as this. "Thank you, Alex. This will be a huge help. And since it's a paper coffee cup, I won't have to tell anyone you gave it to me. I can just say I was a creep who followed you around and stole your garbage."

A slight smile crept to his face. "Do whatever you need to do. My only requests are that you don't tag that DNA with my name, and that you let me know the results."

It was a fair offer, but Amelia didn't miss the ominous undertone in his voice.

What would Alex do if or when he learned for certain that Stan Young had raped Gianna and stolen her child?

Honestly, she couldn't say. Alex had surprised her at so many points over the last year, she wasn't confident she could predict what was going through his head.

She'd cross that bridge when she came to it. For now, her plate was full.

If the DNA analysis implicated Stan Young in Gianna Passarelli's kidnapping, then the senator and his cohorts—including Brian Kolthoff—would immediately fall into damage control mode.

Amelia didn't have to be a fortune teller to realize what that would mean for Michelle if she was still alive.

From the instant Alex had handed Amelia his cup, Michelle's life hung by a thread.

If the poor woman was even still alive.

12

Michelle had no earthly idea where she was. As the cobwebs of sleep fell away from her tired brain, she was convinced for a beat that she was still in the back of the dump truck.

No, that wasn't right. The surface beneath her was cushioned and comfortable, and a pillow was tucked beneath her head. After searching her foggy memory, she recalled crawling out into the daylight like a bear emerging from its cave after a lengthy hibernation as soon as the dump truck had made its first stop. From there, she'd located a new ride —a camper attached to a shiny silver pickup.

When Michelle had discovered the camper was unlocked, she'd been struck by a pang of guilt. Once upon a time, she'd lived in a small town where no one locked their doors. Where everyone had trusted their neighbors not to invade their space.

She'd hidden in a closet until the family of three returned from inside the gas station. Though Michelle had briefly worried one of them would climb into the camper, all three loaded into the cab of the pickup—as the law required.

Helping herself to the family's bottled water and a can of baked beans had come with another wave of guilt, but she didn't have much choice. Her throat had been dry and scratchy, and a dehydration headache had loomed just behind her eyes.

The food, water, and sleep had helped, and as she cracked open her eyes, she was relieved to discover the world was no longer quite so hazy. Finally, the effects of the synthetic opiates were wearing off.

Her moment of reprieve was short-lived.

As the door of a vehicle *thudded* closed, Michelle became hyperaware of her surroundings. Her mind had been so foggy, she'd failed to notice what had roused her from the fitful slumber in the first place.

The muffled howl of the road beneath tires had lulled Michelle to sleep like a bizarre, post-modern lullaby, but the white noise was gone. The camper was as still as a tomb.

Michelle's skin prickled with goose bumps. She needed to hide.

Footsteps crunched against gravel as a person neared the bedroom window. Pastel blue curtains covered the glass, allowing Michelle to make out only the petite shape of the person outside the camper.

Michelle glanced frantically around the room. Beneath the bed was storage, so she immediately ruled it out as a hiding spot. Tiptoeing over to the sliding closet door, she held her breath.

The person outside halted in their tracks. Michelle's senses were in overdrive as adrenaline helped to clear the fog from the opiates still in her system.

A more distant voice spoke, but they were too far away for Michelle to understand.

When the girl near the camper replied, however, Michelle almost jumped out of her skin at the sudden volume. "Okay.

I'm going to get my bags out of the camper. Do you want me to get yours and Dad's too?"

The other person's response was shorter this time. "Sure."

"Okay. I'll be inside in a second."

A second.

The word echoed through Michelle's head like a gunshot. She had a *second* to conceal herself from the young woman who was headed inside to collect her family's bags.

Gritting her teeth until her jaw ached, Michelle eased open the sliding closet door. If she wasn't so panicked, she might have chuckled at the fact that she was spending the day slinking from one closet to another like the world's weirdest stalker.

Though faint, the scent of lilac laundry soap greeted Michelle as she crammed herself into the shallow space. She still had sand in her socks, but at least her hiding places had gradually been improving.

Just as she shut herself in the darkness, the door to the camper squeaked open.

Michelle concentrated on keeping her ragged breaths silent, though she was almost convinced her pounding heart would give her away. As far as she could remember, she'd cleaned up the can of baked beans and the two water bottles she'd drunk. Since there had still been a little trash in the kitchen wastebasket, she'd tucked the three items beneath what was already there.

Otherwise, she'd slept on top of the neatly made bed, using her hoodie as a blanket. Chances were good she'd left behind some sand, but she doubted the girl would look *that* closely.

Staying as still as a statue, Michelle remained perfectly silent. Floorboards creaked beneath the girl's light footsteps as she made her way down the narrow hall.

Directly toward the room where Michelle was hiding.

Michelle swallowed a bout of panic and squinted through the crack between the door and the wall. She didn't hold the position for long, fearing the teenage girl might spot the slightest movement through the narrow opening.

Adrenaline, ice-cold and burning all at once, rushed into Michelle's veins as the girl crossed the threshold into the bedroom. The girl was humming, a clear indication that she had no idea there was a strange woman hiding in the closet of her family's camper.

Closing her eyes, Michelle sent out a quick prayer to any deity that might have been listening. A prayer that the bags the girl had come to collect were stashed under the bed, back in the living area, the kitchen, or anywhere else.

Please, anywhere but the closet.

A pronounced *creak* ripped Michelle from her silent plea. Her eyes snapped open, and her breath caught in her throat as time slowed to a crawl.

The wooden door glided along its track with a quiet groan, all while Michelle made a futile, last-ditch effort to meld into the paneling at her back.

She failed, of course.

Blue eyes popping open wide, the teenager's mouth fell open. A shriek split the still air as she leapt backward.

"Help! Mom! Dad! There's someone in here!"

Michelle hardly heard her cries.

Now or never.

Michelle couldn't stay here. She hadn't been granted enough time to formulate a comprehensive plan, but she needed to get the hell out of this camper and away from this family.

Seizing the moment of confusion and fright, Michelle bolted past the terrified girl and sprinted down the hall. She skidded to a stop next to the breakfast nook, flung open the door, and leapt down to the concrete.

At least, she *tried* to jump onto the driveway, but her path was blocked. Instead of landing on the ground, she slammed into the hulking form of a man in a red and black plaid coat. The impact was so unexpected, much of the breath *whooshed* from Michelle's lungs in a violent gasp.

She caught herself on the side of the camper to regain her balance. Preparing to bolt, she scanned her surroundings. The shadows of tall, leafless trees crisscrossed the quaint neighborhood. Each house was at least two stories, and judging by the number of barren flower beds and brown lawns Michelle spotted, the area was family friendly. The air was crisp and clean, and there were no sirens or honking car horns in the background.

That rules out Chicago, or any other major city, for that matter.

To her chagrin, the exact *where* was still a mystery. She'd figure it out, but she needed to get the hell out of here first.

She'd not taken the first step when the broad-shouldered man in plaid stepped directly into her path. "Where do you think you're going? What the hell were you doing in my camper?"

Michelle's mouth was as dry as a desert. She licked her lips, digging deep in the recesses of her mind for a plausible excuse. "I, um, I was…hitchhiking. And I swear, I'm just trying to get home." Her hoarse voice sounded alien to her own ears.

A crease formed between the man's dark eyebrows. Clearly, he was unconvinced. "Uh-huh. So, you're a vagrant, and you broke into my camper so you could catch a ride to the grand city of Hagerstown, Indiana? Doesn't seem like a likely story, lady. Try again."

Hagerstown, Indiana.

Try as she might, Michelle couldn't drum up the faintest recognition of the town. Indiana was adjacent to Illinois and even shared a border with Chicago, but there was a hell of a lot of open space in the state.

Besides, did Michelle even *want* to go to Chicago? Brian had been in the process of moving her to Wisconsin so she'd be under Stan Young's control.

If not Chicago, then where?

She silenced the whirlwind of thoughts.

Focus. This guy wants an answer. You need to get out of this without involving the police.

Michelle pulled in a deep breath. "It's the truth. I know it's wrong, and I'm sorry. But I don't have two dimes to rub together, and I really needed to get out of…of the place where I was. I'm just trying to get back to my sister, or at least get somewhere I can get ahold of her. She's an FBI agent."

Mentally, Michelle slapped herself on the back of the hand for blurting out Journey's profession. It was true, but to this small-town dad who was built like an NFL linebacker, the proclamation only made her sound like she was losing her marbles.

The skeptical glint in his eyes told her that was exactly what was running through his head. "Your sister is an FBI agent? And you're trying to get back to her…why? Why didn't you just call her?"

"I don't have a phone. They took it."

Dammit, Michelle. Stop it. Stop giving him information. You don't know who he is or who he'll tell about this.

She doubted a random Indiana man was connected to Brian Kolthoff, but if he told the authorities what she'd regaled, the odds of the information making it back to Brian were significantly higher.

"Who took it? The little green men?" The mocking edge in his tone made the hairs on the back of Michelle's neck stand on end.

His obvious condescension also strengthened her resolve. He wouldn't help her. No one would.

"It doesn't matter who took it. Fact is, my phone's gone, and yes, I'm trying to get ahold of my sister. And yes, even if you don't want to believe me, she *is* an FBI agent. Look, I didn't mean to scare your daughter, okay? I'm just…in a bad spot right now, and I need to find my sister."

His stony expression didn't waver. "Right. Well," he pointed to a spot over Michelle's shoulder, "maybe he can help."

Hope sinking like a stone, Michelle whirled around just in time to spot a brown and gold cruiser turn onto the quiet street. The vehicle was already close enough that Michelle could make out Henry County Sheriff's Department printed on the side.

Seriously?

The acidic burn of bile crawled up her throat.

No.

Whatever she did, she couldn't let herself fall into the hands of law enforcement.

Law enforcement was the entire reason she was here— Joseph was an FBI agent, for Christ's sake. Stan Young was a *senator*.

Before she was consciously aware of the motion, Michelle turned to bolt down the driveway. Logically, she was well-aware of the hopelessness of running away from the police on foot. Especially since she had no idea where Henry County and Hagerstown, Indiana were.

Michelle was about to make her second step when a large hand closed around her upper arm.

"No!" The word ripped from her like a scream, and for a beat, she was back in that horrible cell.

Lumberjack Dad was replaced with Brian Kolthoff, and

the expression of concern and trepidation morphed into a malicious grin.

She already knew what happened when she pleaded with Brian to let her go, or when she tried in vain to wrest herself away from his grasp. He liked when women fought back, and he'd always made sure Michelle was aware how much he'd enjoyed her struggle.

As soon as it had appeared, the memory fell away like a curtain in a theater.

A crisp breeze whispered down the small-town street, rattling tree branches and cooling Michelle's flushed cheeks.

"Ma'am?"

Still paranoid and now slightly embarrassed at her outburst, Michelle jerked around to face the deputy.

He held one hand up in the air, palm facing her. The other rested near the holstered taser on his belt. "Ma'am, I'm going to need you to come with me. You're under arrest for breaking and entering."

No!

The voice in Michelle's head shrieked like a banshee, but she couldn't summon so much as a squeak to her lips.

His stance made their respective roles clear—she was a criminal, and he would zap her with tens of thousands of volts if she tried to make a break for it.

Tears sprang to her eyes. She'd come so far. From pretending to be high as a kite the first time she was dosed with opiates, to deceiving Pug Nose and Crew Cut at the gas station bathroom outside Chillicothe, to hiding in a dump truck filled with sand…

All to get *here*. To be arrested and thrown right back to a place where Brian Kolthoff's corrupt tentacles could easily grasp her.

What choice did she have?

Her fate, her life, her livelihood, were in the hands of the Henry County sheriff's deputy standing at the bottom of the driveway.

13

With Joseph Larson nowhere to be found, Zane had begun to worry their leads regarding Michelle Timmer would soon fizzle out. In the event Joseph had indeed been involved in Michelle's disappearance—and, personally, Zane was ninety-nine percent sure the former agent was—the man had gone to great lengths to conceal his role.

So far, though, Larson hadn't used his phone or any credit cards. A warrant to search his apartment hadn't revealed any hints of where he might have gone. Even his car had been found only a block away from his building. The man was truly in the wind.

They had twenty-four-seven surveillance at his apartment, though. If the bastard showed up, they'd know.

Leaning back in his office chair, Zane tapped a couple keys on his laptop and sighed. At least Amelia's morning meeting with Alex Passarelli had been productive. With Alex providing Amelia a DNA sample, they'd be closer to proving that Stan Young had played a part in Gianna Passarelli's kidnapping ten years ago.

Only if the DNA is a match. It's still possible Mae isn't related to Alex at all.

Zane doubted it, but he reminded himself of the possibilities to avoid tunnel vision.

He blew out a sigh and retrieved his cell from the interior pocket of his suit jacket. His research on Michelle Timmer had run into a brick wall, but he still had one avenue left to explore.

A large part of the reason SAC Keaton had been able to get rid of Joseph Larson so decidedly was Zane's connections to the Central Intelligence Agency. One of his former coworkers and good friends, Nate Tennick, worked as an intelligence analyst for the Agency. As a result, Nate had access to an immense trove of information.

The CIA's reach was long, to say the least. Surveillance footage from an old covert operation on the East Coast had backed up the photos Amelia had received of Brian Kolthoff and Joseph Larson together.

If they could figure out exactly where Michelle had gone the night she'd disappeared, perhaps Nate would be able to dig up more corroborating evidence. They'd still need a hell of a lot more than video surveillance to get to Joseph Larson and his pal Brian Kolthoff, but messaging Nate was a good start.

I wonder if I can just get the CIA to take him out.

Zane snorted to himself at the thought. It wasn't out of the realm of possibility, but Larson would have to commit an egregious offense against international security to become a blip on the Agency's radar.

Just as Zane finished typing his message to Nate, the door swung inward to reveal Amelia. She held a paper cup of coffee in each hand. A smile warmed her face as her forest green eyes settled on him.

"I got you a peppermint mocha, but the barista said

they're on their last stock of whatever it is they use to make these." She elbowed the door closed and handed him the drink.

"Thank you." He took a tentative sip of the latte, savoring the chocolate and mint combination as Amelia pulled out a chair.

"Of course. Have you found anything in your research this morning?"

"No, not really." He felt like a horse chasing a carrot on a stick, but he kept the thought to himself. "I sent a message to my contact, the same guy who helped us with Larson. If we can narrow down where this 'fundraiser' Michelle attended was located, then he might be able to get us something. Provided it was in a location that was being monitored at the time. For now, I think it's reasonable to have him check the main docks on Lake Michigan in the Chicago area. If it turns out the event was held elsewhere, I'll ask my contact to check there." If the vessel was near any remotely significant port, then Zane would bet money there was a video recording.

Amelia twisted the paper sleeve around her cup, appearing thoughtful. "The corroboration would definitely be helpful, but I still think we need more."

Zane could understand why the case had been shelved in the first place. Even without Larson omitting certain details from his interview with Trudy Cordova, there was little to point them in the right direction.

Before Zane had a chance to vocalize his concern, a decisive clatter nearly caused him to jump out of his chair.

In tandem, he and Amelia's attention jerked to the door of the little incident room.

Journey Russo's blue eyes were huge, her cheeks tinged with pink. Based on the heavy rise and fall of her chest, she might have run all the way to the field office from the equator.

Anticipation spiked in Zane's chest, and he sat a little straighter as Journey waved her phone in the air.

"I just got a call from a sheriff's deputy in Hagerstown, Indiana." She inhaled deeply and shoved the door closed. "He just arrested a woman for breaking into a camper that was being hauled by a family. That woman was Michelle."

Zane's coffee cup stopped halfway to his mouth, his palms suddenly clammy. "Is she okay?"

Journey nodded, relief and excitement radiating off her in waves. "She tried to run, but the deputy said he'd just wrapped up a refresher training for domestic violence a few weeks ago. He suspected there was more to her behavior, so he asked her some questions when they got back to the station. She wouldn't answer most of them, and she demanded that he call me. I talked to her on the phone."

Had he fallen asleep while he was waiting for Amelia to get back from her meeting with Alex?

He sipped the coffee. No, the taste of peppermint and chocolate was definitely real. None of the scene before him had been manufactured by his sleeping brain.

"Michelle?" Amelia's voice held the same level of awe. "What…what was she doing in the back of a camper in Indiana?"

"I don't know." Journey rubbed her eyes, and Zane suspected it was to stop herself from crying. "She didn't want to be on the phone for too long. She said she needed me…*us*…to come get her before someone else showed up. I don't really know who she was talking about, but we have to assume the worst."

Amelia leapt to her feet. "How far away is Hagerstown?"

"A little more than four hours. I told the deputy not to hand Michelle over to anyone else, no matter what." She paused, worrying at her bottom lip. "But I don't know how well that'll hold up. We need to get there ASAP."

"I'll go with you." Amelia snatched her coat off the back of the chair.

Zane's head was spinning. Michelle Timmer had escaped? How? And how had she found herself arrested?

Pushing the questions to the side, he shook the mouse to wake up his laptop. No matter how Michelle had managed to resurface so suddenly, Zane realized there had to be more to the story. The woman hadn't vanished for seven months only to randomly reappear in some family's camper in Indiana.

Were Amelia and Journey headed into a trap? Did Joseph Larson have something to do with Michelle's reappearance?

They had to be prepared for any possibility, which meant Amelia and Journey needed to have backup at the FBI office. "I'll stay here and hold down the fort."

Amelia shot him an anxious glance. "Are you sure?"

He offered her as reassuring a smile as he could muster. "Yeah. I think we want to keep this as quiet as we can, so it'll be best if I stay here and keep my ear to the ground."

Just in case there's another rat in this office.

Aside from the two women in the room, Zane only trusted a handful of other agents with information about Michelle Timmer.

He gestured to the laptop. "I'll take a look through the Henry County Sheriff's Department and let you guys know if I find anything that sticks out. Since it's going to take you more than four hours to get there, I can call periodically to check and make sure Michelle is still safe."

"Good idea." Amelia scooped a set of keys off the table. "I'll drive. We can take one of the Bureau's vehicles."

With a few parting words, Amelia and Journey disappeared out the door. Part of Zane wished he was going with them. In the unlikely event they were headed into a trap or were intercepted by Brian Kolthoff or Stan Young's people along the way, he'd rather be at Amelia and Journey's side than twisting in the wind at the field office.

But his first instinct to stay to monitor the situation was the right call. Amelia could handle herself, and he was confident Journey could as well.

Journey just got back from working undercover on a cult in Pennsylvania. Were brainwashed cult devotees really much different from Brian Kolthoff's goons? Zane was confident she could handle both.

The odds of an ambush or a trap were slim to none, but what were the chances Kolthoff's guys would beat Amelia and Journey to Hagerstown?

That was the real danger.

He hoped Amelia's lead foot would be enough to ensure Michelle's safety.

14

I was in the middle of scrolling through a takeout menu on my phone, trying to decide what to get for lunch, when an incoming call interrupted my mental debate between pad thai and yellow curry.

It was one of my burners. The one dedicated only to him.

I swallowed hard. Glancing over the sparkling granite counters and rich cherry cabinets, I ensured I was alone in the kitchen before answering. "Brian."

It was the only word I could manage through the anxiety tightening my throat. Kolthoff wouldn't call me in the middle of the day just to chitchat. I knew before he even spoke that something was wrong.

It didn't help that today was the day he was moving Michelle to my Wisconsin lake house.

"Afternoon, Stan." Brian's voice was tight, his tone clipped. Yes, something was definitely wrong.

If he killed her, I swear to god...

I didn't wait for him to elaborate. "What is it?"

He sighed. "Your...*package* is lost."

A red haze of rage teased the edges of my vision. I

clenched and unclenched one hand, not realizing I'd risen to stand until I was pacing. *"Lost?* Pray, elaborate. You didn't dispose of it, did you?" I wasn't sure why I was speaking in code. Even though I was certain neither of our home lines was monitored—yet another benefit of sitting on the Senate's Intelligence Committee—I used my burner as an extra safety net. But through the white-hot rage unfurling in my chest, logic was sorely out of reach.

"No. *It* is still very much unharmed, at least to the best of my knowledge." Brian's obvious irritability was like gasoline on the fire burning in my chest.

"Then what the fuck happened?"

"The two men I tasked with transporting the package lost it just outside of Chillicothe, Ohio. It'd been gone for nearly an hour by the time they finally called me. They assume it must have, um, found alternative transportation out of the city."

I needed to get my ire under control, or I was going to regret my next words.

Brian pissed me off sometimes, but he was a valuable ally. And whether I liked to admit it or not, he was dangerous. I held the upper hand because of a bill I'd be pushing as soon as I returned to D.C., but my political leverage would only get me so far if I started spouting off threats to my longest-standing ally.

Covering my eyes with one hand, I pulled in a deep breath and counted backward from four. As I exhaled, I rolled my shoulders to displace some of the tension. "When did this all happen?"

"Early this morning. They called me around eight. Now, before you lose your shit completely, I've just gotten an update about her, which is why I'm calling you."

A sliver of relief pushed past the storm clouds in my head as Brian switched from talking code, though I knew he'd be careful not to use Michelle's name. Brian was a lot of things, but incompetent wasn't one of them. "All right. Let's hear it."

"When I found out those idiots had lost her, I put out an alert. One of my contacts in the Indiana State Police says a woman matching her description was arrested by the Henry County Sheriff's Department in Indiana. She'd broken into some family's camper, and they called the cops on her. She tried to resist arrest, but they've got her in custody right now."

Though I wanted to succumb to a wave of relief, I stopped myself. Brian's irritable tone persisted, telling me his story wasn't finished. "But? What's the complication?"

"Did you know her sister was a Fed?"

I blinked as confusion marred my anger. "Did I...what? Larson never mentioned her family, other than to tell me her parents were dead."

Brian scoffed. "Well, that sure was convenient of him to leave out. Because, according to my sources, her sister is a field agent for the damn FBI. And apparently, the Henry County sheriff is holding her until the Feds show up to get her. My contact has a friend in the sheriff's office who told them a couple agents from Chicago are on their way to get her."

"Shit!" I spat out the word like it had been a bad taste on my tongue. "Your contact is in the state police. Can't they pull her out?"

"They have to get to her before the Feds, and they'll have to convince the sheriff's department to release her into their custody instead of the FBI's. Right now, my contact says the sheriff's department is under strict orders to only release her to the Bureau. They can probably get around that, but *only* if they get there first. If Joseph hadn't resigned or whatever in the hell happened with his job, then up and disappeared, we wouldn't have to worry about any of this."

Until now, I wasn't sure I'd ever truly understood what an asset Larson was. The man wasn't a billionaire lobbyist or a U.S. Senator, but his position at the FBI had yielded us a wealth of priceless information.

"All right." I dragged a hand over my face and held back a sigh. "What about a good, old-fashioned bribe?"

"That's the plan. I told my contact that if the sheriff's department won't let her go based on their authority alone, then they could tell them to pick a number. Any number."

Any number.

The words echoed through my head like I was standing in a cave.

If the Feds got ahold of Michelle, not only would the sweet release of killing her be taken from me, but my and Brian's livelihoods would be at stake. Brian had slipped out of sex trafficking charges last year when he'd been caught buying a sixteen-year-old girl, but Michelle?

Michelle was different. Michelle was a grown woman, a Yale graduate, and an FBI forensic analyst. Michelle had clout. Her words held weight.

Not only that, but Leila hadn't actually met Brian in person. Michelle had been the man's captive for over seven months.

Aside from smacking her upside the head that one time, I never touched her.

If worse came to worst, I could still get out of this mess a free man.

For now, however, I needed to focus. "Okay. Let me see if there's anything I can do to help on my end. If you don't mind my asking, what are you doing with the two dumbasses who lost her?"

"Oh, don't worry." Brian's voice was as welcoming as Death Valley. "They're being dealt with. At this point, they're loose ends."

And you know what we do to loose ends.

"Good. If you need anything from me, just call. I'll be in touch if I learn anything new."

I stood unmoving in the kitchen for a long while after my conversation with Brian. My head was a whirlwind of what-ifs and paranoia, but through it all, the voice I least wanted to hear persisted.

"See, Stan! You screwed it up, and now you want me to fix it! Jesus, you can't do anything right!"

My mother's voice.

Hatred thrummed in my veins, a form of venom in its own right.

I'd wanted to torment that woman like she'd tormented me. To make Michelle's time with Brian Kolthoff seem like a stroll through the park. To rip her apart piece by piece until the shrill of my mother's voice finally disappeared from my head.

Brian was resourceful, and I was certain his contact shared that trait. With his deep pockets to top it off, we had a shot at recovering Michelle.

As long as our emissary got there first.

THE SOFT *CLUMP-CLUMP* of footsteps and the jangle of a key ring ripped Michelle from her failed attempt at meditation. After scrabbling around the holding cell, searching desperately for a structural weakness, she'd given up hope of breaking out of the building. Not that she believed she'd had a chance in the first place.

Fists balled at her sides, Michelle stood rooted to the spot as a man's shadow grew nearer. If she was about to face down her doom, then she'd do it with her head up and not cowering in a corner.

She was done with that.

As Deputy Cornell emerged in front of the holding cell, a ray of hope threatened to crack Michelle's armored exterior.

With his slick, salt-and-pepper haircut, kind brown eyes, and reassuring smile bracketed by years' worth of laugh lines, Rory Cornell didn't *look* like the type of man to drag Michelle back to a psychopath like Brian Kolthoff.

They never did.

Monsters didn't sport horns or pointed tails, nor were their intentions immediately visible in their faces. In Michelle's world, the worst monsters wore custom-tailored suits, smiled easily, and offered charming responses to questions.

Some monsters even carried a gun and badge.

Michelle wouldn't let Deputy Cornell's soccer dad appearance chip away at her carefully crafted shell.

"There are a couple of FBI agents here to pick you up." Metal clattered as the deputy unlocked Michelle's cell. "They drove all the way here from Chicago."

Flexing her hands at her sides, Michelle maintained a neutral expression.

Chicago. The same office where Joseph Larson worked. The same city where Michelle had been stupid enough to follow Joseph to a so-called fundraiser hosted by Brian Kolthoff. Kolthoff was another Chicago native, and of course, so was Stan Young.

Journey had told her she was on the way, but she hadn't specified where she'd been. Or had she and Michelle's panicked brain had blocked it out?

Part of her wanted to turn around and cram herself into the corner of the holding cell. She'd rather spend the rest of her life in the Henry County Sheriff's Department than go back with Brian or one of his goons.

Perhaps if she stayed here long enough, she would simply

meld with the wall and become a permanent fixture of the holding cell.

"Come on. Your sister is waiting for you." Deputy Cornell's voice was calm, like the sort of reassurance Michelle's own father had given her when she was a little girl.

For the second time, Michelle almost lost her footing over the treacherous cliff that was hope.

Your sister is waiting for you.

Clenching her jaw, Michelle forced one foot in front of the other. The fabric of her too-large, stolen khakis swished quietly as she followed Deputy Cornell down a drab hall. As he shoved open a heavy, metal door to the check-in area, Michelle's legs nearly buckled.

The woman who stood at the end of the clerk's desk wasn't Journey.

Vaguely familiar, yes. But definitely not her sister.

Where had she seen this person?

The forest green of the woman's eyes was far different from Journey's indigo orbs. Michelle had been gone for quite a while, but not long enough for Journey's eye color to change.

She wouldn't have guessed Brian Kolthoff had women in his employ, but she also wasn't all that surprised. An article she'd once read had suggested that many women worked in human trafficking. Michelle couldn't understand how another woman could turn on her vulnerable counterparts in such a way, but power and money did strange things to people.

Michelle's thoughts teetered over a rabbit hole, a panicked vortex threatening to swallow her whole.

The impending dread was so strong, she doubted she'd have noticed the approach of another person if her senses weren't still on high alert.

As Michelle ripped herself from the onslaught of what-ifs, she turned to the newcomer.

All at once, the panicked voice in her brain silenced.

She let herself breathe.

Journey.

15

For the four-and-a-half-hour trip back to Chicago, Amelia was glad to be the driver. This way, she could keep her focus on the road and not on the litany of questions looming in the back of her head. There had been no signs of one of Brian Kolthoff or Stan Young's people lurking in the shadows waiting to abduct Michelle, but Amelia realized they could've been nearby.

The journey was made almost entirely in silence. A sedan zipping along at eighty miles per hour wasn't the ideal location to conduct an interview with a victim who'd just been rescued from more than half a year of captivity. Besides, they hadn't been driving for longer than thirty minutes when Michelle slumped over asleep, her cheek propped on the frame of the car door.

Keeping track of a tail on a trip over hundreds of miles wasn't an easy feat, but at least Amelia didn't have to shoulder the burden by herself. She and Journey spoke little, the other agent's astute gaze darting to the side view mirror at regular intervals.

Fortunately, by the time they pulled into a Chicago

hospital—conveniently located only minutes from the FBI Field Office—they were both confident no one had followed them from Henry County, Indiana.

Since Journey had called ahead to advise the hospital staff they were en route, no trip through a populated lobby was necessary. While Amelia planted her ass in a private waiting room, Journey accompanied her sister through a physical exam. Most of Amelia's focus was devoted to ensuring no suspicious characters, staff or otherwise, approached the short hall leading to Michelle's exam room.

Amelia had already reached out to Zane, Spencer, and SAC Keaton, but she was hesitant to call on any form of security. Kolthoff and his lackeys had operated for *years* with a source in the FBI. Their reach was long, their tentacles woven throughout the law enforcement of Chicago and beyond.

Unless Amelia personally vetted the officer or agent herself, she wouldn't trust anyone at the CPD or FBI with Michelle. She realized her paranoia would make setting up a safe house a monumental feat, but she already had a couple agents in mind who she trusted to do the job.

Sherry Cowen and Dean Steelman were part of the Bureau's Violent Crimes Division, but Amelia and Zane had worked a few cases with them over the past few months. They were competent, and just as importantly, Amelia trusted them. If Agent Layton Redker of the Behavioral Analysis Unit, formerly a special agent in Cyber Crimes, wasn't still recovering from a gunshot, Amelia would include him in her shortlist as well.

Amelia's contemplation was interrupted by the barely audible footsteps of a woman in pale blue scrubs and a white lab coat emerging from the hall. Her long, miniature braids were pulled back into a low ponytail, her chocolate brown eyes shrewd but kind. With the laugh lines bracketing her mouth and the faint traces of silver running through her braids, Amelia figured she was an experienced medical professional.

"Agent Storm, you can come with me. We've moved Michelle to a new room, one that should be more comfortable for you and Agent Russo to speak with her."

Amelia was on her feet before the doctor finished. The fact that Michelle was already willing to give a statement was more than impressive. It was courageous. Amelia wouldn't have blamed the woman a bit if she'd shrunk back and refused to speak for days, weeks, or even months. Or ever. Sure, she'd have encouraged Michelle to give a statement, but she wouldn't have thought less of her if she'd refused or been psychologically unable.

God only knew what she'd been through over the last seven and a half months.

Ignoring the embers of rage that had ignited in the pit of her stomach, Amelia followed the doctor down the hall, around a corner, and to a closed, windowless door. Amelia rapped her knuckles lightly, and the door silently swung inward.

"Dr. Burnett. Agent Storm." Journey glanced over her shoulder to where Michelle sat in the center of a hospital bed. "Come on in. Dr. Burnett, this might be a little bit of a weird question, but is it possible for us to order some take-out? My sis...Michelle hasn't eaten in more than a day. Other than a pilfered can of baked beans, anyway."

The doctor offered the three of them a smile, the type of look that could set just about any human being at ease. "Of course. Let me know where you want to order from, and I'll put in the orders for you."

So they can't be traced back to any of us. So no one will know Michelle is here.

This wasn't Dr. Burnett's first rodeo. Though she was an

obstetrician at the large hospital, her specialty was working with victims of human trafficking.

As Amelia stepped over the threshold, Dr. Burnett followed her and closed the door. "We're running some blood tests and should have the results back soon."

Michelle shifted in her seat. "What are you testing for?"

"Everything. It's standard procedure for a case like yours. Since you told us they dosed you with an injection, we'll know exactly what was in that syringe. Sometimes, traffickers will mix their own cocktail of drugs, and then the authorities can use it as evidence in a trial." Dr. Burnett's face softened. "But I'm sure with your occupation, you already knew that."

A ghost of Dr. Burnett's smile manifested on Michelle's face. "Right. Thank you, Doctor."

"Of course, dear. I'll leave the three of you alone for now. If you need anything at all, just let me or Nurse Aguilar know."

Michelle's stomach growled, a reminder of the promised food. The doctor smiled and took their order for ham and cheese sandwiches and tomato soup. Comfort food at its best.

After promising to deliver the order as quickly as she could, Amelia waited until Dr. Burnett had disappeared into the hall to sit. The chair appeared as if it had been around since the Cold War, but to Amelia's surprise, the cushioned seat was comfortable. Propping an elbow on the wooden armrest, she pulled a small digital recorder from the pocket of her cardigan.

Considering Journey's familial ties to Michelle, Amelia was in charge of the interview. Neither of them had said as much explicitly, but Amelia could tell Journey was a professional. Though Amelia would lead the questioning, Journey could still provide supplemental inquiries, and of course, reassurance to her sister.

Part of Amelia felt as if they were rushing to take Michelle's statement, but she pushed the bizarre sentiment to the side. Michelle's case was about as far outside the norm as they came.

Clearing her throat, Amelia held up the recorder for Michelle. "I'm going to use this to record our conversation. Is that all right?"

Michelle swallowed and nodded. "Yeah, of course." The dark circles beneath her eyes aged her by almost ten years, and her pale complexion straddled a line between alabaster and pallid. In the photos of Michelle Amelia had observed, the woman always had a healthy, sun-kissed glow.

Still, considering everything the young woman had been through, she looked beautiful.

Amelia pressed a button on the recorder and set the device on the table at Michelle's bedside. After stating the date, time, and verbally acknowledging Michelle's consent to be recorded, Amelia pulled up a list of questions on her phone. While she'd waited for Michelle's physical, she'd typed out a handful of queries so she would be sure to remember them. Normally, she didn't go to such lengths, but this might have been the most important interview of her entire career.

"All right, Michelle. Let's start back at the beginning. Back with your relationship with the former special agent, Joseph Larson. Could you walk us through the early stages of that?"

Michelle blinked. "Former?"

Amelia nodded. "Yes. I'll tell you more about that when we're finished."

A soft smile flickered on Michelle's lips, but she didn't ask for additional information. "I met Special Agent Joseph Larson back in early May. He was working a triple homicide.

He and his partner suspected the Armenian mob was involved."

"Do you recall who his partner was?"

Michelle's gaze drifted to the floor, her expression a mask of concentration. "Um, yeah. Fiona Donahue. I only interacted with the two of them once. Otherwise, it was just Joseph Larson coming to the lab for updates."

"And when did the two of you become romantically involved?" The words sounded stuffy and prudish to Amelia's ears, especially since she was confident Joseph's capacity for romance was nonexistent.

"He asked me on a date on May twenty-second." Her tired eyes met Journey's. "I remember because it was the day before my mom's birthday. We went to dinner, had a couple drinks, and wound up at his place. Maybe it was a little sudden, but it's not like we're living in the fifties, you know? I was still pretty new to the city at the time, so I was excited to have finally met someone I could...I don't know, hang out with, I guess."

Unease prickled the back of Amelia's neck. Joseph's relationship with Cassandra Halcott—an assistant United States attorney with whom Amelia had worked side by side on several cases—had started in almost the exact same way.

Joseph Larson was a calculated predator, and Cassandra was lucky she'd gotten away from him when she did.

As Michelle walked through the early and mid-stages of her and Joseph's relationship, Amelia continued to draw parallel after parallel between Michelle and Cassandra.

"For a little while, we were almost like a normal couple." Michelle pressed her lips together, her expression bitter. "I started staying overnight with him pretty early on, and sometimes, I'd just be there for a couple days at a time. That's when I noticed his weird phone calls. At first, I just assumed they were from his SSA or from his case partner, but then I noticed something."

Amelia kept her face carefully blank. She didn't want her loathing for Joseph Larson to bleed over into Michelle's recollection. Neutrality was the name of the game. "What did you notice?"

"The phone he was answering wasn't his personal cell. It was one of those old flip phones. A burner phone." She rubbed her eyes with shaky fingers. "At first, I thought something ridiculous, like he had a second family and I was his mistress, or that he was just screwing around with another woman, and he was going to these lengths to conceal it because of my background in forensics. But, like I said, those thoughts were ridiculous. It took longer than I'd like to admit, but eventually, I heard about the leak in the Organized Crime Division. I didn't hear about it until the Leila Jackson case went to trial, but it's like all the pieces clicked in my head."

Anticipation vibrated just beneath Amelia's skin.

That's why Joseph risked kidnapping a woman who worked for the Bureau. She was onto him.

Amelia kept the revelation to herself, silently nodding for Michelle to continue.

"Unfortunately, that's the same time I discovered that Joseph was banging some bartender down the street from where I lived." Michelle's mouth twitched in a scowl, though Amelia suspected her animosity ran much deeper than just an unfaithful boyfriend. "We got into a big fight, and he claimed he didn't realize we were monogamous. For the next week and a half, he groveled and pleaded with me to forgive him. Eventually, I decided to, but not for the relationship. It was stupid, but I pretended to give him another chance so I could snoop and see if I could figure out what he was up to."

Tension radiated off Journey in waves, and as Amelia

glanced at her, she noted the woman's knuckles were white where she gripped the armrest.

When Journey spoke, however, her voice was calm and even. "That's when you messaged me about going to a party with him, right?"

Biting her lower lip, Michelle nodded. "Yeah. I didn't know anyone else around here I could tell, so I just sent that message. Honestly, I thought I was getting all worked up about nothing. Thought my imagination was looking for intrigue where there was none, you know? But there was part of me that just wouldn't let it go. And another dumb, naïve part that thought maybe I was wrong about Joseph."

Though Amelia wished desperately that Michelle's story ended with her putting a bullet in Joseph Larson's ass, she knew they were only at the beginning. "Could you tell us where this party took place?"

"A yacht docked just a little north of the city on Lake Michigan." Michelle's response came with zero hesitation. The night must have been burned into her memory. "Joseph claimed it was a fundraiser for Chicago public schools. Obviously, that was a lie. I had no idea until it was too late, though. When I saw Senator Stan Young and his wife, I thought for sure the whole thing was legitimate."

A fresh wave of anticipation rushed through Amelia's body. "Stan Young was *there*? What about his son?"

"No, Josh Young wasn't there. I'd seen that guy's face on news talk shows plenty of times. I know I'd have recognized him if he'd been there."

Michelle ran through the party itself, including her first introduction to Brian Kolthoff. The Shark.

Amelia didn't miss the way Michelle's shoulders tensed any time the topic turned to Brian. Her gaze became distant, even a little hazy, as if just speaking about the man transported her somewhere she didn't want to be.

Then, as Michelle began to describe the beginning of her time as a prisoner on Kolthoff's yacht, Amelia understood the haunted look in her eyes. Though Joseph Larson was just as depraved as The Shark, and though he'd assaulted her at least as many times, Michelle seemed to regard him more with anger than anything.

Kolthoff was a different story.

Amelia wished she could go back in time to when she'd arrested Kolthoff for trying to buy Leila Jackson. If she'd known a fraction of what the man would eventually do to Michelle, she'd have…

What? What could she possibly have done differently? Kolthoff had more money than God. The guy had bought and paid for his own version of justice, which was exactly why he was still a free man.

When Michelle arrived at her first interaction with Stan Young while she was captive, she shifted in her seat on the hospital bed. "I don't remember it all that well, and I assume it's because of the head injury. I was lying there, sort of fading in and out of consciousness, when I noticed this man step into the doorway. They spoke to each other, but I honestly can't remember what they said. At some point, I must have lost consciousness. Next time I woke up, there was an IV in my arm and a doctor in the room."

"A doctor?" Amelia echoed. "Do you recall his name?"

Michelle's shoulders slumped. "Yeah. Dr. Jones. I never caught his first name, but…I *can* remember what he looked like. He was probably five or six inches shorter than Brian, white, with glasses and blue eyes."

Amelia offered her a reassuring smile. "We'll set you up with a sketch artist soon."

The statement seemed to inject life into Michelle's features, and she sat a little straighter as she went on to describe her interactions with Stan Young.

With each new tidbit Michelle revealed, the picture of the corrupt senator became more twisted. Stan's childhood had been just the right combination of traumatic and privileged to mold him into the lunatic he was today.

Michelle's recollection had peeled back many of Stan's layers—the polished businessman and politician, the successful, family friendly man he portrayed in news articles and campaign ads—revealing the start of his rotten core.

As damning as Michelle's statement was, they still needed more. Without corroborating evidence, they were working with Michelle's word against a prominent lobbyist and U.S. Senator.

Amelia was confident that with the vast resources of the FBI, they could pull together enough to confirm parts of Michelle's account, but it would take time.

Time was a commodity they were sorely lacking. Each minute Michelle remained in one place was another minute closer to Stan or Brian finding her.

No matter the precautions they took, they couldn't rely on a safe house to keep Michelle out of harm's way.

If Michelle was ever to have a shot at piecing her life back together, they had to cut the head off the snake.

Shifting in her seat behind the two-way mirror, Amelia took a swig of the bitter breakroom coffee Zane had brought her a half hour ago. Partially to let Brian Kolthoff stew and partially to give themselves an opportunity to caffeinate, Amelia and Spencer had left the man sitting in the interview room with his lawyer. Aside from a few hushed words, the pair had barely spoken in the past twenty minutes.

Acting on the information provided by Michelle, Brian Kolthoff had been paid a visit by the Coast Guard. Cornered on his yacht, Brian had no choice but to comply with the request to come in and answer questions. En route to the waiting transport on shore, he'd taken the opportunity to contact his lawyer.

Eight a.m. had come far too quickly for Amelia, Spencer, and Journey. Between Michelle's initial statement, follow-up questions, establishing a safe house, and arranging for Kolthoff to be brought in, they'd all been awake until the wee hours of the morning.

Michelle's stamina and resiliency were downright

admirable. Despite the horror she'd endured, Michelle had stayed awake to answer questions until her eyes had become bleary and each of her sentences was punctuated by a yawn.

Amelia hoped the woman was finally managing a restful sleep, but based on what had happened to her over the last seven months, Amelia doubted Michelle would find real rest until her tormentors were behind bars. Or maybe not even until they were six feet under.

But what of their ghosts?

On the other side of the room, Journey Russo sat in a chair identical to Amelia's, her blue gaze fixed on the pane of glass. Since Michelle was Journey's sister, and considering the sheer level of agony Michelle had suffered at Brian Kolthoff's hand, Journey had been benched for today's interviews.

The agent hadn't protested. She'd stated she wanted the entire process done by the book, letter by letter, each I dotted and each T crossed. If they covered their asses, they'd leave no weakness for Brian and Stan's lawyers to exploit.

Perhaps Amelia should be nervous for her and Spencer's interrogation of Brian Kolthoff, but she was as calm as she'd ever been. Kolthoff was wealthy, powerful, and depraved, but Amelia had looked him in the eye before, and she hadn't been impressed.

He was just a cruel man whose wealth and social status had allowed him to inflict pain on others for too long. There was a void inside him, one he filled by trying to control everything around him.

Amelia would gladly take that control away from him and watch him kick and flail until he drowned.

Stifling a sudden, unexpected yawn, Amelia chugged half her remaining coffee.

"You suppose it's time we grace them with our presence?" Between Spencer's flat tone and the clipped manner he'd spoken to Brian Kolthoff earlier, Amelia figured the SSA would rather wrestle a cactus than feign niceties with the men in the next room.

Amelia downed the rest of her coffee. "Probably. Let's get this over with."

Though Michelle's account of events might be one nail in their coffins, they still didn't quite have enough to arrest Brian or Stan, and Joseph was nowhere to be found.

Their goal for this morning was to collect Kolthoff's statement, all while striking the fear of god into him. It was a risk bringing him in, but one they needed to take. They knew he would be a tremendous flight risk, and by bringing him in, even without an arrest, they could at least request him to not leave the city.

Plus, they'd make sure the asshole's picture was plastered on every news channel in the country. Then, as soon as they had corroboration, Amelia would personally march into Brian's palatial estate or onto his luxury superyacht to slap a pair of cuffs on his wrists.

With a nod of acknowledgment to Journey, Amelia and Spencer let themselves out into the sterile hall.

Hand hovering above the lever handle of the interview room, Spencer shot Amelia a curious glance. "How do you want to do this? Good cop, bad cop?"

Amelia snorted. Kolthoff didn't deserve a good cop. "More like bad cop, bad cop. If it worked on Emilio Leóne, it'll work on Kolthoff." Amelia's reference was to her and Zane's not-so-legal interview of a Leóne family capo during the Leila Jackson case.

Chuckling quietly, Spencer nodded. "Sounds like a plan to me. All right, let's go."

The door swung soundlessly inward, revealing the impatient stares of Brian Kolthoff and his lawyer, Harvey Byrd. Harvey was a good six inches shorter than Brian Kolthoff, but with his stout frame, the men's weights were likely similar.

The harsh fluorescence of the interview room caught the light sheen of sweat on the lawyer's forehead before he swiped it away. Harvey *seemed* like a joke at first blush, but a cursory glance at his background told a different story. The man was competent, and in a courtroom, he was downright vicious.

He was the best that money could buy, but Amelia couldn't stop herself from mentally referring to him as *Harvey Birdman: Attorney at Law*—a ridiculous cartoon she used to watch late at night with her brother.

"Agents." Harvey's gravelly voice cut through the memory. "Nice of you to finally join us. We've been waiting for almost a half hour."

Spencer crossed his arms and leaned against the wall beside the two-way mirror. "Twenty-three minutes. I kept track. I realize mathematics isn't your strong suit, but twenty-three doesn't round up to thirty. We had paperwork to fill out before we could talk to your client."

Harvey's mouth twitched in a scowl. "Right. *Paperwork.* The joy of any FBI agent's career."

Spencer shot the lawyer a disarming smile. "I'm glad we understand one another. Now, why don't we address what's brought us all together today?"

The lawyer narrowed his eyes. "Yes, let's."

As Amelia pulled out a metal chair with a *screech*, she maintained an unreadable expression. She'd never seen Spencer's fangs come out, and she had to admit, the sight was impressive. Today, it was also motivational.

Bad cop, bad cop.

Rather than sit, she slapped a manila folder on the table and pinned Brian Kolthoff with a knowing stare. "It's been a while, hasn't it, Mr. Kolthoff?"

Without balking, his eerie, pale green eyes met hers. "It has. You look...older, Agent Storm."

She almost laughed at his attempt to insult her appearance. "I am older, Brian. That's how time works."

Annoyance passed over his face as he turned to Harvey.

Taking his cue, the lawyer gestured to Amelia's manila folder. "We're here because of Michelle Timmer's baseless accusations, are we not?"

Spencer flashed Harvey and Brian a smirk that oozed condescension. "If they were baseless, we wouldn't be here now, would we?"

"Well, my client isn't under arrest, so I wouldn't be so sure of that if I were you, Agents."

"Isn't under arrest *yet*." Amelia kept her tone amiable, but venom stirred beneath the words like a slow-acting toxin. With an exaggerated sigh, she took her seat. "Back in June, your client was arrested for the sex trafficking of a minor—"

"Those charges were dropped. There was no evidence to substantiate those claims. If I remember correctly, Emilio Leóne is the one who was tried for trafficking that poor girl."

That poor girl.

This prick honestly thought he was a real human being.

Ignoring the bitterness threatening to spill into her bloodstream, Amelia continued. "Those were the original charges that you whittled down to nothing, Counselor. But," she held up a hand before Harvey could interrupt her again, "the point isn't whether or not the charges stuck or made it to trial. The point here is what we at the Bureau like to call a 'pattern of behavior.' You say Ms. Timmer's accusations are baseless, but I beg to differ. I think Ms. Timmer's accusations are quite consistent with your client's past behavior."

Harvey scoffed. "That won't hold up in a courtroom, and you know it."

With a swift step forward, Spencer braced a hand on the

edge of the table and met the lawyer's glare. "Perhaps not, but you know what *will*?"

Keeping her focus on Brian's expression, Amelia flipped open the folder to reveal a glossy, eight-by-ten print of a gas station outside Chillicothe, Ohio.

The lawyer leaned back in his seat, unimpressed. "Mind telling us what we're looking at, Agents?"

A muscle in Brian's jaw ticked, and Amelia would have bet money his blood pressure had just shot up.

He recognized the location. He already knew that was where his goons had lost Michelle.

Confirmation they were headed in the right direction renewed Amelia's sense of determination. When she pushed aside the first photo and pointed to an image of a black SUV, Brian's ire was more tempered, but the sentiment was still there.

Seeming to sense Amelia's scrutiny, Brian's gaze shifted to her.

"This is where Michelle Timmer escaped from her captors." Amelia used her index and middle fingers to tap the two pictures. "They were transporting her to somewhere in Wisconsin. She smiled. "How quickly will they flip on you, I wonder?"

Kolthoff lifted a shoulder, but Amelia could tell his noncommittal attitude was feigned. "I've never been anywhere near that hole-in-the-wall gas station or those men. I still don't see what this has to do with me."

"Of course you don't." Amelia waved a dismissive hand. "All right, let's take it from the top, then. What's your relationship with Michelle Timmer?"

Harvey shot his client a vehement glance. "My client has never met Michelle Timmer."

"Is that true, Mr. Kolthoff?"

"It is. I've never met that woman before in my life."

"Uh-huh." Spencer returned to his full height, towering over the lawyer as he leaned against the table. "She was dating Joseph Larson. From what I understand, Brian, you and Larson go way back. How is it that you'd never even *met* her?"

Kolthoff folded his hands on the table and offered Spencer a polite smile. "I'd never *met* her, but I had heard of her. Joseph isn't exactly the type to bring his casual lays around, you know?"

The unsettling glimmer in his eyes told Amelia the exact opposite was true. "Tell us what you know about their relationship."

"Like I said, they were casual, at least as far as Joseph was concerned. Honestly, I don't see why you aren't talking to him about this. If something happened to Michelle, shouldn't you be looking into whoever was screwing her at the time? That's usually the prime suspect, right?"

Amelia almost laughed aloud, though the sound would have been mirthless. Was Brian Kolthoff really about to roll over on his so-called friend?

"I'd love to speak to Larson, actually." Amelia watched Kolthoff's expression closely. "Any idea where I can find him?"

Kolthoff's entire face grew tense, the muscles in his jaw rippling just under the surface of his skin. He recovered quickly, though, his features softening into a blank slate. "No idea."

Amelia would have put money on that being the truth. No one had seen hide or hair of Joseph Larson. Not even his crooked crony.

Well, that was an interesting development.

Why had Joseph up and vanished, even from his allies?

And why in the hell was Kolthoff so quick to shift the blame to Joseph?

Setting aside her curiosity about Brian's attitude toward Joseph, Amelia laced her fingers together. "What about the party Michelle attended on the eleventh of July? The fundraiser she stated was held on *your* yacht. You didn't even bump into her there?"

"I didn't." Kolthoff's response was quick. A little too quick. "Because there wasn't a fundraiser that night. I don't know where that woman pulled her story from, but she's delusional. Maybe she saw me in an article online and formed an infatuation, and that's where this is all coming from. It wouldn't be the first time a woman has tried to dig her claws into me since my divorce, but it sure is the most outlandish attempt."

To Amelia, his response came across as...practiced. Something he'd recited in the bathroom mirror earlier in the morning.

During the Leila Jackson case, Brian had been the exact same way. He'd had an answer for everything, even when Amelia was sure she'd caught him in a lie.

It was like he knew the questions before they were even asked.

Amelia leaned back in her seat. "So, Mr. Kolthoff. Are you stating, on record, to two FBI agents, that you never met Michelle Timmer on July eleventh or any other date?"

Kolthoff swallowed hard, his eyes flicking toward the video camera in the corner. "I've never met Michelle Timmer...ever."

Brian Kolthoff had just lied on camera. It would just be one of the long list of charges she'd toss at him once they were ready for an official arrest.

Amelia relaxed into her chair even more. "Do you think Joseph Larson and Senator Stan Young will agree with you about that?"

Kolthoff paled, and his attorney held up his hand. "We

have no control on what those two fine gentlemen think or believe."

This was getting fun. Just watching the bead of sweat appear on Kolthoff's upper lip was satisfying. Amelia smiled. "I think that just might be the first true thing you've said today. You have 'no control'" she air quoted the words, "over what they might be telling us right now."

Spencer leaned forward, his mouth practically carved into a grin. "No, no control at all. Mr. Kolthoff, you might have set a world record on how quickly you flipped on your good friend, Joseph Larson. I wonder if he'll be as quick to do the same to you."

Sweat rolled down Kolthoff's temple, but before he could speak, his attorney jumped in. "Is this all?" He made a show of yawning. "If you don't have anything more substantial to ask, we'll be going now."

It was Spencer's turn to hold up a hand. "Not quite yet."

She and Spencer went around in circles with Kolthoff and Harvey for another forty-five minutes before the lawyer finally called a halt to the interview. Though there wasn't enough evidence to arrest Kolthoff *yet*, Amelia and Spencer gave the man a stern warning to stay in Chicago.

Once Kolthoff was gone, Spencer organized a couple agents to keep an eye on the man. In addition, they sent out a notice for the Coast Guard to monitor Kolthoff's veritable fleet of seafaring vessels.

Amelia pondered how much evidence they might find in a search of his boats.

Though the interview had ostensibly not yielded any groundbreaking information, Kolthoff's demeanor alone was enough to tell Amelia and Spencer they were on the right track.

They just had to keep digging, and they had to do it fast.

Kolthoff had slipped through Amelia's fingers once

before, and she'd be damned if she'd allow the sick bastard to slither away again.

WITH A PLASTIC CUP of water in each hand, Zane shouldered open the heavy door and stepped into the harsh lighting of the interview room. Three sets of eyes—Stan Young's, his lawyer's, and SAC Keaton's—turned to him as the door fell shut with a quiet *click*.

The sudden scrutiny didn't bother Zane. Though the interview had barely started, Zane had excused himself after receiving a text message from Spencer Corsaw. He'd departed under the guise of offering water to Stan and his lawyer, but in reality, he'd slipped away for an update about Amelia and Spencer's discussion with Brian Kolthoff.

Like Kolthoff, Senator Stan Young had been surprised when two agents arrived at his home requesting he sit for an interview regarding the allegations against him. Also like Brian, Stan had come armed with the lawyer he kept on retainer.

Their idea to pull both Brian and Stan into the FBI office at the same time was purposeful. If they'd interviewed one man and waited to seek out the other, then the two of them could craft a make-believe story to absolve themselves of any wrongdoing.

Neither suspect knew the other was in the station at this exact time. SSA Corsaw had gone to great lengths to ensure the men's paths had not crossed. But he'd be sure they learned later that they'd both been questioned. Turning the men on each other was an important part of this game they were playing with them.

By bringing both men in at the same time, they hoped to minimize the level of collusion, at least for the first interviews. The goal was to catch them in a lie once the investigation had yielded some useful information.

Zane smiled at the thought. He'd already sent the date, time, and location of the supposed fundraiser to his CIA contact. Nate had been searching the Chicago waterfront and points nearby before Michelle provided the specifics he needed.

Not that Brian or Stan knew they'd been recorded that night. The Agency was covert about its surveillance.

Clearing his throat, Zane set a cup of water down in front of Stan, and then his lawyer, Curtis McKnight. Mentally, Zane crossed his fingers that Stan would take a sip and leave the disposable cup behind. Amelia had already sent a sample of Josh Young's DNA to the lab to compare with Alex Passarelli and Mae Young's, but evidence from the kidnapping rapist himself could potentially speed along the process by showing a direct link.

"Sorry to keep you waiting, Senator." Zane undid the buttons of his black suit jacket and took a seat across from Curtis. "It's been a busy morning at the office. I'm sure you can understand."

Stan's smile didn't reach his eyes. "Of course. Curtis tells me we're here to discuss an...*allegation* that I've mistreated a young woman. Is that correct?"

That's one way to put it.

"That's correct." SAC Keaton folded her arms on the table, her gaze alternating between Stan and his lawyer. "We'd like to know more about your relationship with Michelle Timmer. You may recall that Michelle was...*is* one of our own. We're leaving no stone unturned."

According to Michelle's statement, Stan had never looked at her suggestively, though he'd struck her at least twice. His infatuation with her stemmed from a different source. From childhood trauma.

As much as Zane wished he could delve straight into Stan's formative years, he reminded himself that today was to establish a baseline—Stan's version of events, untainted by his collusion with Brian Kolthoff. The two men had undoubtedly communicated since Michelle had gone missing, but Zane was banking on her escape coming as a surprise to them both.

With so little time to react, hopefully, they hadn't gotten their stories aligned just yet.

Stan smoothed a hand down his silver tie and heaved a practiced sigh. "I understand. But I'd also like to remind you both that the senatorial primary is only four months away. I realize Michelle is one of the Bureau's own, but you also realize the position I'm in. The political divide in this country is worse than it has been in a long while, and that means my opponents are willing to go to even greater lengths to gain an advantage over me."

If Zane still had a badge from the CIA instead of the FBI, he could've laughed in Stan's face at the suggestion that Michelle was simply trying to discredit him. Though Zane didn't miss his lengthy covert time spent in Russia, he occasionally wished he still had the free reign the Agency had afforded him.

Instead, he bit the inside of his cheek to maintain a neutral expression. "I understand, Senator. We're just doing our jobs."

"I'll do my best to be helpful."

I'm sure you will.

The SAC scooted closer to the table. "Senator, how well do you know Michelle Timmer?"

Stan readjusted his tie, and Zane realized right away the gesture was a tell. Based on the rigidity of his shoulders and his stiff posture, not all of which was due to the uncomfortable chair in which he sat, the tic was a sign of his nervousness.

"I didn't know her at all. I've never met her. I don't have the first clue where these allegations came from. Not unless one of my rivals recruited her to smear my name before the primary."

The irony wasn't lost on Zane. Only a few months earlier, Stan's only real political rival had caught a bullet to the head. A joint effort between former FBI Special Agent Glenn Kantowski and a Chicago Police officer had failed to frame Amelia for the crime. The pair had then failed to kill Amelia as their plan B.

Though Zane had always suspected there was more to Storey's murder than just the anger of his spurned mistress, Glenn, he'd found no proof to back up his theory.

Zane studied the senator closely, but his poker face was firmly back in place. "What about Joseph Larson? Were the two of you friends?"

Tilting his head, Stan pressed his lips together and appeared thoughtful. "Joseph Larson? He was a special agent here at this field office, wasn't he?"

Zane nearly laughed. The senator clearly knew that Joseph was no longer working for the Bureau. He said nothing about that, though. He'd let Stan back himself in a corner on his own.

"He was. Do you know him?"

Stan dipped his chin slightly. "I met him a few times, yes. I don't know if I'd quite call us friends, but we got along just fine."

"And Brian Kolthoff?"

"Brian has been a friend of mine for a long time. We work together in D.C., and he's been a generous donor to my campaign. We share many of the same political ideals." Stan glanced at his watch and then at his lawyer. "Look,

Agents. I've got a busy day ahead of me, and I need to get started on it. I don't know anything about this woman's claims. My face shows up on the news all the time, which is how I assume she pulled my name into her story. If you ask me, I think the poor woman probably needs some therapy and medication."

When the suggestion came from Stan Young's lips, it seemed perverse. Like it was a threat instead of a recommendation.

To Zane's dismay, there had been no breaking developments to warrant holding Stan for a longer interview. Since he'd denied any involvement in Michelle's abduction, and since he claimed he'd never even met her, their options were limited. With a man like Stan Young, Zane had to remind himself to tread carefully. They needed a surgeon right now, not a heavyweight boxing champion.

They didn't let him go quite yet, though. They asked for his alibi for the evening of July eleventh as well as yesterday. They let it "slip," that Brian Kolthoff was just down the hallway, singing like the proverbial bird.

Stan Young was used to scrutiny, though, and while his forehead did grow damp, and though he smoothed his tie more than once, he remained calm as they questioned him for another half hour.

It was hard to let him walk from the room. They simply didn't have a choice at this point.

For now.

The sooner Zane heard back from Nate Tennick, the sooner they could either prove or disprove Stan's claim that he'd never met Michelle.

In his gut, Zane realized this was the calm before the storm. Even with corroboration to prove Michelle's statement was true, Stan and Brian wouldn't go down easily. Not legally, anyway.

However, the court of public opinion was far more volatile than a real trial.

An idea took form in Zane's mind. He'd spent the majority of his career involved in information warfare. The CIA was hardly above smearing their targets in the press to discredit them or paint a target on their backs.

Stan and Brian both had access to the best lawyers money could buy, but those pricey attorneys couldn't save them from a flurry of headlines. If no one acted and the investigation progressed normally, Stan and Brian would squelch any mention of their wrongdoings before they could even be published.

Zane might not have been a CIA operative anymore, but old habits died hard.

17

B efore I even crawled out of bed, a tingle down my spine told me today was...*off*. I'd spent most of yesterday afternoon preoccupied with my impromptu meeting with the FBI, all while my contacts had scrambled to find a shred of information about Michelle Timmer's whereabouts. Brian's people were on the same mission, but considering the urgency of the situation, I figured we couldn't have too many spies on alert.

If Brian was still on my side.

I wasn't so sure about that any longer.

I'd initially been relieved that the Feds had no evidence against me, but that relief was short-lived. Almost as soon as I'd left the field office, Brian had called to let me know he'd also been questioned.

Sneaky bastards. Calling us both in simultaneously prevented us from aligning our stories. And how could I know what Brian had really told the Feds?

The day had flown by, but time had also dragged like a ball and chain attached to my ankle.

As I sat up and swung my legs over the side of the bed, I

was glad Cynthia had taken Mae with her to visit her sister and their children. I'd insisted on the trip the second I'd been notified that I was expected to speak to the FBI. The peace and quiet of my massive house were a welcome reprieve from the cacophony of thoughts whirling through my head.

One of the plus sides of homeschooling was that we were in charge of Mae's schedule. More importantly—and the entire reason for my decision—homeschooling kept her shielded from the public and the media. The less she appeared on the news, the better. The last thing I needed was for one of the Passarellis to spot her in some stupid TMZ article and put two and two together.

Raising Gianna's child as my own adopted daughter was risky, but it was the best way to keep the secret close. Besides, I was Mae's biological father, so the decision made sense.

In a couple of years, I planned to take her to Europe where one of the finest plastic surgeons in the world would change her appearance enough to put us in the clear. That had been the plan, anyway.

But now?

Refusing to think about that question, I pushed to my feet and pulled the cell off the wireless charger, unlocking the phone.

Twenty-one missed call notifications, forty unread text messages, and god only knew how many emails.

What in the hell was happening? Had Armageddon started while I was sleeping?

No, I didn't think I'd receive this many notifications for the end of the world.

Clenching my jaw, I mentally steeled myself and opened the newest text message from my wife. I quickly scrolled through the thread, my stomach clenching as I noted the words *news*, *kidnapping*, and *censure*.

I tapped a button in the top corner to dial Cynthia's number. I wasn't going to read through all this shit.

Hell of a day to sleep in an extra hour.

My wife picked up after the first ring. "Stan, what the hell is going on?" She was out of breath, as if she'd just sprinted to another room to take my call.

"I was hoping you could tell me that. I just woke up."

I caught the faint creak of a door before she replied. "You're all over the news. The story broke a couple hours ago."

A block of ice expanded in my chest, and I had to force my words through clenched teeth. "What story?"

"The kidnapping. They didn't say the girl's name. She's just being referred to as Jane Doe, but they're saying you had something to do with her being kidnapped and raped. The Senate Majority Leader is calling for a full investigation, and the party is threatening to censure you."

Fuck me.

My racing brain could hardly comprehend the information she'd just spat at me. I had to break down the situation and deal with one facet at a time, starting with the source of the story.

Michelle Timmer.

Cynthia didn't need to ask me if the headlines were true. She was aware of some of my darker predilections, but she had plenty of her own, so we'd always been on even footing. It was an unspoken rule between us that if she threw me to the wolves, I'd bury her. Figuratively or literally, either way was fine with me.

Right now, however, I was counting on her loyalty.

I scrubbed a hand over my face. "Has anyone tried to contact you?"

"Not yet. The story is still brand-new. Give it some time,

and I'm sure one network or another will figure out where I am."

"You can leave Mae with your sister and go lay low at the penthouse. You should leave soon." Though I was confident Cynthia wouldn't rat me out, I didn't want to take the chance. The woman would rip out her hair if she was forced to share a space with a nine-year-old without the aid of a nanny or housekeeper, so it was best she went alone. I'd rather have Cynthia remain hidden while I figured out a way to end this dog-and-pony show.

If there was a way to end it.

"All right. I'll tell them there's been a family emergency. I'll figure it out." She paused, but even with her more than a hundred miles away, the air was thick. She wanted to say something, but she was biting her tongue.

"Spit it out, Cynthia." I forced the words through gritted teeth.

"I can't help but wonder if your son had something to do with this. I told you he's been acting extremely odd lately."

I'd already gleaned that the news stories had to do with Michelle Timmer, and I was certain there was no earthly way Josh could have known about her.

Still, Cynthia's suggestion prickled the hairs on the back of my neck. If I wasn't about to be forced to contend with the press hounding me, I'd pay my son a visit and ask him a few pointed questions.

"It's a little too late for that." I fought back the bile rising in my throat. "But for whatever it's worth, I doubt Josh had anything to do with this. When I talked to him last, he mentioned he'd broken up with his girlfriend, which is why he's been acting odd."

Besides, I had no idea how Josh could have known enough to feed a story to some blood-sucking reporter.

"Well," Cynthia cleared her throat with a sharp cough that

seemed to dig into my brain, "it's something to keep in mind for when this calms down, and we're doing damage control. I'll leave for the penthouse soon but try to keep me updated. If I'm accosted by a reporter somewhere along the way, I'd like to make sure we have our stories straight."

"I will."

After we said our goodbyes, I disconnected the call and let out a sigh I'd been holding for the duration of our conversation. Ignoring the plethora of notifications on my phone, I snatched a remote off the nightstand and turned on the television. I bounced around a few channels playing commercials before I landed on a national news network. If what Cynthia had said was true, then the story had already gone beyond the local Chicago outlets.

Swallowing to return some moisture to my suddenly dry mouth, I took a seat at the foot of the bed. The anchor was rambling on about cryptocurrency, but I didn't miss the text scrolling along the bottom of the screen.

Illinois Senator Stan Young accused of aiding in the kidnapping, unlawful captivity, and assault of an unknown woman.

A rush of anger burned away the nervous energy wreaking havoc on me.

I was the only one mentioned in the ticker. Just *me*. No Brian Kolthoff or Joseph Larson—the two men who'd inflicted far more harm on Michelle than I had.

Just. Me.

As a commercial started, I dialed Brian's number. With each ring, my ire was slowly replaced with the cold creep of dread.

My call went to voicemail, but I hung up without leaving a message. Maybe he was in the shower, or maybe he was still sleeping. I'd wait a little while and try him again, though my gut told me I wouldn't have any luck. This situation was devolving too quickly for me to salvage, and if

Brian wasn't willing to speak to me, it could only mean one thing.

No, that was ridiculous. *I* was the one with the political power. I held the winning cards in my hand, and Brian wouldn't turn tail and rat me out. If he was banking on Michelle Timmer to bury me, then he was in for an unpleasant surprise.

Aside from one little smack across the face, I hadn't touched that bitch. Joseph was the one who'd lured her to Kolthoff's yacht, drugged her, and taken her belowdecks to a prison cell. Brian was the one who'd beaten her to within an inch of her life. As far as Michelle's situation was concerned, I'd been a fucking saint.

All the more reason for Brian to turn on me.

I shook off the paranoid thoughts and returned my attention to the news.

"We've been covering a breaking news story regarding Illinois Senator Stan Young." The anchor's ruby-red lips curved into the slightest frown, her expression dire. *"According to an article published early this morning by National Horizon reporter Zack Hartman, Senator Young stands accused of kidnapping and assaulting a woman. Her identity remains anonymous, but we have been able to verify that Mr. Hartman's sources were accurate."*

Zack Hartman? The name was vaguely familiar, but he wasn't any of the political reporters I knew. Why in the hell had he taken point on this?

Better yet, who were the man's sources? Was there a leak in the FBI?

Maybe, but maybe Hartman had been keeping an eye on me for longer than I'd realized. If he'd known where to look, he'd have been able to uncover some of the basics about the case. FBI or not, pending investigations weren't always kept a closely guarded secret.

It didn't help that Michelle's sister was an FBI agent. I really needed my contact to get more information on her.

"We'll have an interview with Mr. Hartman coming up in about a half hour, but for now, we go to our Chicago affiliate reporter, Kristi Stevens. Kristi?"

When the image on the screen changed, the blood in my veins ran cold, my muscles tensing like I'd been thrown into the vacuum of space, and my body was about to turn inside-out.

Kristi Stevens was standing in front of my fucking house.

"Thank you, Rhonda." She gestured to the front porch. "I'm standing here in front of Senator Young's home. I tried earlier to knock on the door, but I was turned away by the senator's security team."

I scoffed. At least someone was doing their job today. For a beat, I wondered why no one had come to wake me with the news that there was an army of reporters almost literally on my front doorstep. However, two years ago, my head of security had walked in on a scene I'd have preferred he didn't see.

I'd caught a lucky break since the man was my most trusted and most discrete guard, but I hadn't wanted to take any chances in the future. Everyone in my household was under strict orders not to interrupt me when the bedroom door was closed, even if the world was ending.

Was it ending?

Rubbing my eyes, I heaved another sigh as the reporter rehashed a few of the details of Hartman's article.

Neither Brian Kolthoff nor Joseph Larson was mentioned. I couldn't tell if it was simply because their names didn't conjure up the same sensational headlines as mine or if Hartman's source had conveniently left them out.

Honestly, I suspected the former. I'd always known being

in the spotlight would make my life a hundred times more difficult than Brian or Joseph's if things went south.

Sure enough, here I was.

I tried another call to Brian, but for the second time, he didn't answer. Then a third, and a fourth, all while ignoring three incoming calls from my colleagues in the Senate.

If I couldn't get ahold of Brian to help me with damage control, then I'd have to take matters into my own hands.

My attention darted back to the television as the scene switched over to a familiar parking garage in downtown Chicago—the garage adjacent to the headquarters of Happy Harvest Farms.

The camera panned over to an Audi I recognized as Josh's, and I held my breath.

Pushing his aviator sunglasses to the top of his head, Josh flashed the press an irritable glance and turned to march toward a nearby set of double doors.

"Mr. Young, are you aware of the breaking news about your father's role in kidnapping a woman and holding her against her will? Could I get a statement from you?" The query came from a petite woman in front of the camera.

"No comment." Josh flung open the door and disappeared behind the tinted glass.

When the reporter hurried over and tugged on the handle, the door didn't budge. She shook her head at the camera, and the feed switched back to the blonde with the red lipstick.

So much for Cynthia's theory that he was behind the article. I'd recognized the genuine surprise and annoyance on my son's face.

Without my allies and with the press hounding me and my family like rabid dogs, I needed to put some distance between me and Chicago. Maybe once I was out of this suffocating mess, I could clear my head and figure a way out of the situation.

I also needed to make sure the headlines accurately reflected who'd been responsible for Michelle Timmer's kidnapping, and I didn't want to do that in a place where Brian could easily reach me.

Turning off the television, I rose to my feet. A handful of my most trusted security personnel and I had secretly planned for a day like today. I'd had a secret exit built more than a decade ago, right after I'd moved here. I hadn't quite expected things to go *this* awry, but I was glad for the foresight nonetheless.

Once I was out of here, I'd start digging my way out of this hole.

If I couldn't dig my way out of it, I'd buy my way out.

One way or another, there was no way I was taking the fall for any of Brian or Joseph's indiscretions.

If they thought they could turn on me to save their own asses, I'd show them just how wrong they were.

18

Leaning against the breakroom table to blow on her scalding mug of coffee, Amelia observed the media circus in front of Stan Young's palatial estate with a grim sense of satisfaction. Stan was a rat caught in a maze, and his only way out was a fall from grace so steep he'd be lucky if he survived.

She could only think of a few other men more deserving.

The night before, Zane had run through his idea to notify Zack Hartman of the developing case. After she and Zane had met Hartman during their investigation of a serial killer who'd murdered a federal judge and her family, they'd earned a rapport with the man. Hartman wasn't some nosy tabloid writer searching for his next scandal—he and the *National Horizon* provided their readers with the most accurate reports possible.

Zane had reasoned the case would eventually make its way to the media, so they might as well let it out on their own terms. To ensure Zane wasn't going rogue, he'd cleared the strategy with Spencer and SAC Keaton.

By getting ahead of the curve, they'd ensured Stan

couldn't pay to have the story swept under the same giant rug that housed countless other scandals. More importantly, they'd told part of Michelle's story before Stan or Brian had a chance to drag her through the mud.

Amelia knew it was coming. It was the only move Stan had to redeem himself in the eyes of the press.

Although they thought they knew the reporter, Amelia and Zane had been somewhat shocked that Zack wanted his name on the story. He wasn't a fame-seeking reporter hoping to make his own headlines. But by keeping his name attached, he had argued that he'd be able to help keep the story focused on the elements Zane and Amelia wanted.

It took guts. By insisting on the byline credit, Zack had placed a large target on his back. Zane admired the man's resolve.

As the news broadcast switched over to a commercial, Amelia took a swig of her bitter coffee and started back toward the incident room. Nudging open the door, she slipped inside and set the mug next to her open laptop.

Zane's gaze shifted to hers, one eyebrow quirked up in a curious expression. "So, how bad is it so far?"

"It's a circus, just like we were hoping. They even tried to talk to Josh Young, which I feel a little bad about. But I'm sure he can handle himself. No one's talked to Stan yet, though."

Scratching the side of his unshaven face, Zane leaned back in his chair. "Well, the zoo in front of his house should make it a little difficult to skip town at least."

Uncertainty prickled the back of Amelia's neck like an insect. "Maybe, but..." She left the thought unfinished as her cell buzzed in the pocket of her black slacks. Lifting a finger to Zane, she pulled out the device.

Her gaze settling on the text message, excitement zinged through Amelia's veins. She leapt to her feet and shoved her cell in Zane's face. "It's the lab. They've finished the analysis of the DNA I gave them. Of Josh, Mae, and Alex."

Zane pushed himself out of his office chair. "This could be huge. Let's go."

With all the anticipation pinging around in Amelia's brain, with all the what-ifs that were shrouded by faint clouds of doubt, she only managed to respond with a nod.

They made it down to the lab in record time. An analyst met them at the tall glass door and introduced herself as Henrietta Esparza. She was an inch or two taller than Amelia's five-eight, and her long, dark brown hair was pulled away from her face in a ponytail.

As Amelia followed Henrietta to a standing desk at the end of a lab table, she fought to rein in her anticipation. If they had proof that Stan Young was Mae's biological father and Gianna Passarelli was the girl's mother, a little bit of basic math would be all they needed to obtain a warrant for Stan Young's arrest. They'd start by charging him with kidnapping and rape. But that was only the tip of the legal iceberg for the senator.

These results could be the evidence Amelia's brother had died trying to obtain, and it was within Amelia's grasp.

Henrietta's calm voice pulled Amelia out of her thoughts as the woman opened an image of the DNA analysis. Mentally, Amelia had always compared the visualization of DNA to a bizarre, elongated barcode.

Henrietta zoomed in on the image. "This should just take a minute. These results can look confusing sometimes, so I wanted to take a moment to make sure you knew what you were looking at."

Zane smiled. "We appreciate it."

Returning the pleasant expression, the analyst gestured back to the monitor. "All right, well, first off, I can confirm that there are several common markers between these three samples. Person A, which was the sample we obtained from the green toothbrush, shares the same paternal link as Person B, which was the pink toothbrush."

Just as Amelia had suspected. Josh and Mae were biological siblings, and Stan Young was their father. "And what about Person C, the coffee cup?"

Henrietta moved the mouse cursor to one of the barcodes. "He's related to B, but not A. I'll spare you all the technical jargon. Based on the pattern of mitochondrial DNA and a few other markers, the analysis confirms Person C is Person B's uncle."

There it was, indisputable scientific proof. Alex Passarelli was Mae Young's uncle, meaning the only person who could possibly be Mae's mother was Gianna Passarelli. Nine years plus nine months, give or take, would put Gianna at age thirteen or fourteen when she'd gotten pregnant.

Amelia's stomach turned while anger seared through her. Though Stan Young had arguably been the least involved in Michelle Timmer's suffering, the senator was just as twisted as Joseph and Brian. Maybe even more so.

Stan Young, a sitting United States senator, had kidnapped, raped, and impregnated a thirteen-year-old girl. The evidence indicating the crime was unorthodox, but it was irrefutable.

Henrietta sent a copy of the analysis to Amelia and Zane, and as much as Amelia wanted to fly out the door to slap a pair of handcuffs on Stan's wrists, they had to take a moment to ensure all their ducks were in a row. Arresting a billionaire senator for kidnapping and rape wasn't an everyday occurrence. The process of dealing with the rich and powerful was anything but straightforward, especially when they didn't have a living victim.

Amelia would play the game if it meant she could lock Stan Young in a cell and throw away the key.

A niggling doubt in the back of her head insisted that putting Stan in prison wouldn't be enough. Putting Brian and Joseph in prison wouldn't be enough.

But what could she do other than her job? She already knew the U.S. Attorney wouldn't be able to press for life in prison without parole—not unless they uncovered a few *literal* skeletons in the men's closets. Simone Julliard would charge them with every single crime they'd committed to maximize their time behind bars. But the legal system set limits on the time criminals could be charged for certain offenses.

Cross that bridge when we get to it. Uncertainty is the name of the game when you're dealing with men like these. Do your best and worry about the rest when the time comes.

The time *would* come. Her battle against Joseph, Brian, and Stan didn't end when the men were in prison. She'd have to continue fighting them while they exhausted appeals, while their expensive lawyers threw motion after motion at the court.

If that's what it took to make sure none of those sick bastards ever hurt another person again, then so be it.

If she had to, Amelia would devote the rest of her life to keeping the trio locked in a cage.

19

Stretching both arms above his head, Zane held back a yawn as he observed his half-full coffee mug. The breakroom sludge just wasn't getting the job done today. Glancing to his watch, then to the empty incident room, he sighed. Nearly three hours after he and Amelia had received the results from the lab's DNA analysis, and he was the only one still in the office.

"Holding down the fort," he muttered to himself.

Well, technically, he wasn't the *only* person from their team who was still in the building. Assistant U.S. Attorney Cassandra Halcott was around here somewhere. She wouldn't have a problem if he took fifteen to go down the street for a real cup of coffee, would she?

As long as he got one for her, he doubted she'd mind.

Unfortunately, even though the evidence of Stan Young's involvement in Gianna Passarelli's disappearance was solid, arresting a sitting U.S. senator wasn't quite so simple. Especially when that senator also happened to be a billionaire whose family owned one of the country's largest agricultural empires.

Before any of them had even thought to get near Stan, Cassandra had personally visited a judge to secure a warrant for Stan's arrest, as well as warrants to search all his properties—and there were plenty of them. No one knew what had become of Gianna Passarelli, and they could only assume she'd been killed. However, Cassandra had argued that they needed to search high and low to be certain.

To Zane's relief, the judge had agreed. Stan Young was facing two charges for kidnapping—one for Michelle and one for Gianna—sexual assault of an underaged person, unlawful captivity, and a pending charge of premeditated murder. Now, if Stan had kept Gianna alive, it was in his best interest to provide her whereabouts so the murder charge would be dropped.

Not that he would. Zane had dealt with dirty politicians during his time in the CIA, and he already knew how Stan's song and dance would go. He'd deny any wrongdoing to start. Then, gradually, as new evidence surfaced, he'd admit to one small kernel of wrongdoing at a time.

Before Amelia and Spencer had left for Stan Young's Chicago residence, the unspoken sentiment in the room was that Gianna Passarelli was long dead. None of them were under the illusion they'd find the poor girl ten years after her disappearance.

Proving that Stan Young had killed Gianna would be an uphill battle, but it was one they were all glad to undertake. At the absolute least, they'd destroy his public image and decimate a significant portion of what made him so powerful —his political livelihood.

After today, Stan Young would never step foot through the doors of the U.S. Capitol again. The senate majority leader was already calling for Stan's head on a platter. Anything to save face for their political party.

Zane blinked away those thoughts, stretched again, and

pushed his chair away from the table to stand. He'd shoved one arm through his coat sleeve when his laptop and phone *pinged* at the same time.

On any other day, any *normal* day, he'd have checked the message when he returned from the much-needed coffee run. Considering all that had happened and all that likely was yet to happen, he decided he'd be a little more proactive.

Shaking the wireless mouse to bring the screen of his laptop to life, Zane hunched over the table as he pulled up his inbox. When his gaze settled on the name of the sender, the warmth of anticipation provided a renewed sense of energy.

The body of the email was succinct, just like all Nate's messages had been so far. Coordinates, a date, and the recording timeframe were all he'd written. Zane's previous requests to Nate had taken more time, but for the newest videos, Zane had been prepared with a date, time, and even the name of the vessel.

"July eleventh, fifteen-hundred-hours to July twelfth at the same time." He didn't bother to take off his coat as he sat. The combination of curiosity and eagerness planted his ass firmly in the chair as he loaded the video.

Nate had been searching for Kolthoff-owned yachts docked anywhere near Chicago around the time of Michelle's disappearance, but her statement had given them enough specifics to focus the search to a pinpoint.

She'd arrived at Kolthoff's yacht at six in the evening, so Zane fast-forwarded to four p.m., zoomed in on the vessel in question, and played the footage at three-times normal speed.

For a solid twenty minutes, Kolthoff lounged on the deck with a cocktail in hand. He didn't move from the chaise until another man emerged. Since Zane didn't recognize the guy, he took a screenshot and sent the image to the printer down the hall.

Kolthoff disappeared, and when he re-emerged, he was clad in a tailored suit and tie. A couple younger men scrambled around the deck to arrange furniture and prepare the bar, presumably getting ready for the so-called fundraiser Michelle had attended.

Zane figured the workers were unwitting staff, but he took stills of their faces just the same.

The surveillance video was a veritable gold mine.

As the footage rolled and the first pair of visitors arrived, Zane vaguely recognized the man as a foreign politician. An ambassador to Denmark if he remembered correctly. The man had occupied the position since before Zane had left the CIA, and the Agency had long suspected his corruption. He just hadn't been quite enough of a risk for the Agency to deal with him—his predilections trended more toward sexual deviancy than terroristic threats to national security.

Not a big enough fish for the CIA, but I'm sure the Bureau will be more than a little interested in what the hell he's doing with Brian Kolthoff.

After the ambassador, Stan Young and his wife, Cynthia, strolled onto the deck.

Zane chuckled to himself and sent the still to the printer. "Gotcha, Senator."

Another eight people arrived after Stan, and Zane made sure to capture clear photos of their faces. Once they'd taken down Brian and Stan, he intended to make sure they followed up on the rest of the partygoers from the night of Michelle's kidnapping. The fact they had attended an event with Kolthoff wasn't necessarily indicative of skeletons in their closets, but in Zane's opinion, it sure as hell warranted a closer look.

Joseph and Michelle were the second-to-last couple to arrive on the luxurious yacht, and once Zane had printed still shots of all the partygoers, he focused on Michelle's movements. Any time she interacted with someone, even if it was just the bartender, Zane took a still.

The night wore on, and a handful of attendees departed. While Brian and Joseph were conversing near the rail lining the deck, Michelle ordered a drink. Joseph just so happened to choose that precise moment to stroll over to Michelle and drape an arm around her shoulder. Though the view of Michelle's cocktail was obscured by her and Joseph's bodies, Zane's gut insisted this was the moment Michelle had been drugged.

Less than five minutes after Michelle took her first sip, she was passed out with her face tucked into the inside of one elbow.

A combination of disgust and anger rose in the back of Zane's throat as he printed a photo of Michelle's unconscious form. Brian and Joseph left her like that for close to twenty minutes before they returned. Laughing like they were a couple hyenas about to drag their next meal back to their den, the men pulled Michelle from her barstool and hauled her into the cabin through the nearest door.

Knowing what Michelle would endure over the next nearly eight months saddened Zane as the door swung shut behind them.

As much as he wished he could crawl through the screen like the woman from *The Ring*, Zane would settle for the next best alternative—taking away Brian, Joseph, and Stan's freedom.

20

For the second time in the past forty-eight hours, Amelia entered the drab interview room on Spencer Corsaw's heels. Since they'd dealt with Brian Kolthoff during his initial interview, they were the first on deck to talk to the man now that he'd been officially arrested.

Amelia cast a quick glance at the two-way mirror. Behind the reflective glass, Cassandra Halcott and Zane both stood watch. Journey Russo was staying at Michelle's safe house, along with Dean Steelman and Sherry Cowen. Knowing Michelle was in the agents' capable hands had put Amelia at ease from the first day Michelle had been transferred to the secret location.

A search warrant for Stan Young's palatial estate was currently being executed, along with similar warrants for any other properties they could find in his name. Though the senator hadn't been found at any of the locations, Amelia hoped they'd caught him off-guard enough that he wouldn't be able to destroy valuable evidence. As far as locating Stan went, she'd trust the experts they'd enlisted at the U.S. Marshals' fugitive recovery team.

With Stan's vast wealth, his opportunities to slip out of the country undetected were plentiful. Considering the severity of the crimes with which he'd been charged—including the pending charge of the premeditated murder of Gianna Passarelli—the Bureau had pulled out all the stops. Senator Stan Young was now a proud member of the no-fly list, and private airports had been strictly advised to deny him access to a plane.

Whether or not he'd manage to bribe his way past the order remained to be seen, but Amelia wasn't sure he'd have such an easy time. Most folks didn't take kindly to a man accused of raping a thirteen-year-old girl.

Amelia made a mental note to text Alex to let him know the results. She'd promised him as much, and she would hold up her end of their deal.

For the time being, the entire focus of Amelia and her colleagues had shifted to Brian Kolthoff. When she and Spencer had knocked on the man's door, he'd been in the middle of throwing articles of clothing into a suitcase.

At the thought, Amelia offered Kolthoff a smile laced with venom. "Sorry for interrupting that little vacation you had planned. Where was it you said you were going again?"

Brian's jaw clenched, but he didn't speak. Instead, his lawyer held up a hand. "You have no right to arrest my client. The video evidence here is circumstantial at best, and there's no—"

Crack.

Brian and his lawyer both jerked their attention to Spencer as he slammed the door closed. "Oh, sorry. What was that you were saying, Mr. Byrd? There's no what, again?"

A faint flush crept to the lawyer's cheeks. "My client has been arrested for kidnapping, sexual assault, and sex trafficking. The evidence doesn't substantiate any of these claims."

"Actually." Amelia dropped down to sit across from

Brian and pinned him with a withering stare. "There is. See, Mr. Byrd, your client downplayed his affiliation with Joseph Larson, and he lied about never having met Michelle Timmer before. That would be bad enough all on its own, but as it so happens, your client not only met Michelle Timmer, but he met her on the night she disappeared."

Before either of the two men could speak, Spencer slapped a manila folder down in the center of the table. Without a word, he flipped it open to reveal a photo of a redhead passed out at a bar on the deck of a yacht. In the next image, the camera was zoomed out to display the vessel's name.

"The *Equilibrium*. Huh." Spencer turned a curious glance to Amelia. "Why does that sound so familiar?"

Amelia lifted a shoulder. "I'm not sure. Do you suppose it's the name of a yacht owned by a certain lobbyist in this room?"

If Brian Kolthoff tightened his jaw any more, Amelia suspected he'd break one of his porcelain veneers. "That woman could be anyone. You can't even see her face!"

Harvey snapped out a hand to grab Brian's wrist. The message was clear…stop talking.

Chuckling low in his throat, Spencer flipped to the next image. In this one, a pair of men stood beside the passed-out redhead—Joseph Larson and Brian Kolthoff, both dressed to the nines, with Joseph smirking like he'd just shot the world's last white rhino. "Keep digging yourself into that hole, Mr. Kolthoff."

Harvey leaned in closer, his eyebrows furrowed. "Where did you get these photos, Agents?"

Amelia had suspected the question would be brought up sooner rather than later. They couldn't exactly tell Kolthoff and his lawyer they'd obtained footage from an advanced

CIA surveillance system—the Agency would lose their minds.

Fortunately, as with most aspects of the Central Intelligence Agency, they weren't required to divulge the truth. Harvey could file motions until he was blue in the face, and he'd come away with nothing every time.

Spencer flashed the pair a knowing smile and turned to the next photo. "That's classified, Mr. Byrd. We're not at liberty to discuss the origins of this footage, but we've already made sure to include the video as evidence. You'll be able to review it along with the rest of the case."

Ignoring the petulant glare Harvey directed toward her and Spencer, Amelia pointed to the newest still. "You can clearly see Michelle's face now, and Mr. Byrd, you can also clearly see your client carrying her. Aided by Joseph Larson, of course." She folded her hands atop the table. "I'm curious if this is your client's definition of never having met someone before? I'm not really sure what to call this interaction if it doesn't constitute *meeting* someone."

The lawyer snapped up a hand as soon as Kolthoff opened his mouth. "Don't answer that, Brian. My client has interacted with thousands of people over the past seven months, redheaded women included. You can't honestly expect him to remember one drunk from a fundraiser in July, can you?"

Amelia and Spencer spared a brief glance at each other.

"Yes, actually, we do," Spencer deadpanned. "Unless your client's starting to go senile at age fifty-three."

Though Amelia wanted to laugh in Harvey and Brian's faces, she kept her expression calm. "Is this really your excuse? You're claiming your client forgot he'd hauled Michelle's unconscious body into the cabin of his yacht?"

Harvey's irritation was so plainly visible Amelia could practically hear the four-letter words rolling around in his balding head. "My client is an important man in D.C., as I'm sure you're aware. He doesn't make it a point to learn the name and likeness of everyone who gets drunk at his parties."

Anger unfurled its tendrils in Amelia's chest, but she pushed the rage aside in favor of cold indifference. "First of all, Mr. Byrd, Michelle Timmer wasn't just *drunk*. She was drugged. I think that's pretty obvious in these photos, and especially on the video. Second of all, it sure is convenient that your client just so happened to forget about the only woman to attend one of his parties and go *missing* on that same night. And finally, you may recall your client denied there even being a fundraiser on that night. Yet here we are, with you labeling that very event a fundraiser."

Brian glared at Harvey as the smallest hint of a crack in the lawyer's armor appeared as he withered on his client's death stare.

Harvey collected himself and crossed his arms. "Do you have any idea how many parties Mr. Kolthoff throws in a given year? It should come as no surprise that he doesn't remember the *purpose* of one of them. Fundraiser or friendly get-together, they're all the same to someone as important as my client. And he isn't responsible for what happens to someone after one of his events. If Michelle Timmer disappeared that night, then it didn't have anything to do with my client. If anything, that video shows he was helping Ms. Timmer before someone could take advantage of her."

The irony of the lawyer's rebuttal was like another log on the fire of Amelia's fury. Despite her desire to reach across the table and throttle Brian and his smarmy lawyer, she simply folded her hands on the table. "Riddle me this, then. Why is it this surveillance video never shows Michelle *leaving*?"

Harvey let out a derisive snort. "You can't possibly know that for certain."

"We can, actually." Spencer shuffled back to the zoomed-out image of Kolthoff's yacht. "There's only one way on or off this vessel, Counselor. In the remaining twenty hours the *Equilibrium* is docked here, Michelle Timmer doesn't leave."

Brian started to open his mouth again, but Harvey shot him a death glare. "I provided you with Mr. Kolthoff's account of events, Agents. We have nothing more to say here."

Amelia had expected no less from a defense attorney who charged as much as Harvey Byrd. Like the answer to the question about the video, she and Spencer had come prepared with a rebuttal.

"Suit yourselves." Shoving to his feet, Spencer jerked a thumb at the two-way mirror. "Just so you're both aware, an Assistant U.S. Attorney is on the other side of this glass. She'll be taking this interview, along with all the evidence we've collected so far, to the U.S. Attorney herself. Both the other men involved in kidnapping Michelle Timmer are MIA, so it looks like it's going to be your client's head on the chopping block."

Amelia took her cue. "I'm not sure if either of you have met Simone Julliard, but she's not the type to let something like this go. Her vow to the Northern District of Illinois was to clean up Washington, and well," she paused for a drawn-out shrug, "your client happens to be a prominent lobbyist in D.C. He's exactly the type of person Simone Julliard will want to make an example out of."

It might have been Amelia's imagination, but she could have sworn Brian Kolthoff paled.

"My client did nothing wrong. This evidence is nothing more than a farce being used to try to demonize my client simply because he's wealthy. It's a witch hunt."

Spencer let out a derisive snort. "Far from it."

Amelia followed Spencer's lead and rose to her feet. "One

more thing before we go. The U.S. Attorney will be pushing for remand at arraignment in the morning." She met Kolthoff's pale green eyes and smiled. "Just something to think about while you spend the night in holding."

The implication hung in the air like humidity on an August morning.

If Brian was remanded to custody until his trial, he'd be subjected to all the enemies he'd made during his various forays into the criminal underworld. The D'Amato family, the Russians, the cartels—anyone he'd pissed off over the last few decades.

A man as wealthy and powerful as Brian Kolthoff didn't ascend to his position without making his fair share of enemies. Once Brian was behind bars, his amassed wealth wouldn't be able to protect him from a homemade prison shank.

Even with Joseph Larson and Stan Young in the wind, Amelia was finally confident their investigation was trending in the right direction. She couldn't be certain just how deep the three miscreants' loyalty to one another ran, but she sure as hell intended to find out.

All they had to do now was *find* the other two. As with most aspects of dealing with Joseph Larson, the solution was never straightforward. Though Amelia and her colleagues were on the right path, she had to keep her wits about her. Had to be prepared for the unexpected.

Until all three of those pricks were dead or behind bars, she'd remain wary.

This time would be different.

21

Though Amelia had remained at work until nearly ten at night, she was back in the building bright and early the following day. Whenever a case picked up steam like this one had, she often contemplated how much it would cost to rent a room *in* the field office. Considering Chicago's godawful traffic, sleeping in the FBI building would be efficient if nothing else.

As Amelia and Zane settled into their spots in the incident room, Amelia took a moment to savor the rich, buttery flavor of her salted caramel latte. She and Zane had a long day ahead of them, and she suspected the early morning would be one of their only quiet moments.

After Kolthoff's arraignment, they'd be joined by Cassandra Halcott and possibly even Simone Julliard, depending on whether or not Kolthoff was remanded to custody. From there, they'd combine notes, making sure the U.S. Attorney was caught up on all the evidence gathered so far. The prosecutors would take over Kolthoff's case, and Zane, Amelia, and Spencer would get to work helping the U.S. Marshals locate Joseph Larson and Stan Young.

It was a bizarre junction in the investigation, one where they had a great deal of work on their plates, but their hands were also tied by the fact that Joseph and Stan were in the wind. Amelia wanted to watch Brian Kolthoff hang for what he'd done to Michelle and god only knew how many other women, but she wouldn't be able to rest until the entire band of merry shitheads was locked away.

Amelia and Zane started their morning by parsing through the evidence that had been collected from the search of Brian Kolthoff's numerous properties, including his veritable fleet of boats. The sheer manpower required to comb through so many different locations would cost taxpayers a small fortune.

It better be worth it.

Spencer soon joined them, and Amelia kept one eye on the clock as the time for Kolthoff's arraignment drew nearer. Unsurprisingly, Harvey Byrd had squeezed Brian in for one of the earliest time slots. It was almost eight now, and they'd have their answer in an hour or so.

"What've we got so far?" Spencer's tired voice pulled Amelia out of her reverie.

Shaking off the thoughts, as well as a few lingering cobwebs of sleep, she turned her laptop so the SSA could view the screen. She pointed to an image of the second-lowest deck of Kolthoff's mega-yacht, the *Equilibrium*. Four closed metal doors lined a drab hallway on either side, as well as a ninth door at the end of the corridor. To Amelia, the scene resembled a prison so strongly she'd had to double-check she was actually sifting through images of a luxury yacht and not a federal penitentiary.

Spencer's eyebrows creased. "Is that a prison?"

Amelia couldn't help but chuckle. "My thoughts exactly. We went through this same section during the Leila Jackson case, but there wasn't anything in these...*cells*. When we asked Kolthoff what the hell they were for, he claimed he used them for guests."

"Guests?" Spencer echoed incredulously. "The man's a billionaire, and he makes his *guests* sleep in a prison cell?"

This time, it was Zane's turn to snort a laugh. "That's what we said eight months ago. Believe me, the CSU out in Florida went through that yacht with a fine-toothed comb. They didn't find anything. Not a single speck out of place, no signs of blood, absolutely nothing. Those rooms were as sterile as a hospital."

Amelia lifted a finger and pointed to the screen. "He didn't have as much warning to clean this time, or the people he gave the job to were just bad at it."

One of Spencer's dark eyebrows quirked up. "So, you're saying our people in Virginia Beach found something?"

"They did." Amelia clicked an arrow to bring up the next image, a photo of an eight-by-ten room that was just as listless as the hall. A neatly made bed rested against one wall, and on the other side of the space was a stainless-steel sink and toilet. When she clicked over to the next photo, Spencer sucked in a sharp breath through his teeth.

The cramped room was as dark as a moonless night—or it would have been if it wasn't for the glowing pool on the floor beside the bed. More of the glowing substance spattered the frame of the flimsy bed, as well as the wall.

"That's blood?" Spencer's question was more a statement of fact than a genuine query.

"Human blood." Amelia tempered the sense of disgust and anger that threatened to rise in the back of her throat. "The CSU scraped a little bit of it out from behind one of the screws in the frame of the bed. They were able to tell that it was human blood, but we're waiting to see if a DNA sample is viable."

Nodding his understanding, Spencer rubbed the dark

stubble on his chin. "Could it be Michelle's blood? I know Kolthoff almost beat her to death at one point."

"I was thinking the same thing. The tech left a note saying they couldn't quite tell how old the blood was, but it was definitely dried. There's been a little more found in a few of the other rooms, but not anything to indicate a wound quite this severe."

Truthfully, Amelia almost hoped the blood belonged to a different missing woman. If evidence on board the *Equilibrium* could point them to a cold case, they'd not only be able to bring peace to another family, they'd be able to increase the severity of the charges against Brian Kolthoff.

There were a few more peculiar pieces of evidence on board the *Equilibrium*, and Amelia had sent some of the photos to Journey so Michelle could tell them if she'd been held on the yacht. If so, she could help them locate her specific cell. They'd have the crime scene techs focus on the room in order to dig up any hint Michelle had occupied the space. Considering the poor woman had been held captive for several months, Amelia was confident the techs would find *some*thing.

Physical evidence would be the final nail in Brian Kolthoff's coffin.

As Amelia and Spencer were starting on the results from the search of Kolthoff's high-rise condo in D.C., Zane's cell buzzed against the table.

Without announcing the identity of his caller, he swiped the screen and raised the phone to his ear. "Palmer."

When Amelia noticed both she and Spencer were staring at Zane, she almost laughed aloud. In that moment, they gave off the same vibe as a couple kids waiting for their father to tell them whether or not they could attend a sleepover.

Zane either didn't mind or didn't notice, his expression calm and unreadable, even to Amelia. "Uh-huh. All right.

Yeah, I'll do that. Thanks for calling so quickly." As he disconnected the call, a knowing smile crept to his face. He turned to face Amelia and Spencer, their anticipation hanging in the air like a piñata filled with candy.

"Well?" Spencer crossed his arms and leaned back in his chair. "Share with the class, Palmer."

Zane chuckled. "Good news, for once. Thanks in part to all that blood the CSU found on his big boat, the judge agreed to remand Brian Kolthoff until his trial. His lawyer's plea for bail was rejected."

Amelia fought the urge to throw a victorious fist in the air. "That *is* good news. And honestly, how kick-ass is that? Those CSU techs must have busted their butts to get the blood evidence so quickly."

Zane's grin widened as he lifted a finger. "But wait, there's more."

"All right, Billy Mays. This isn't an OxiClean commercial." Spencer's comment earned another laugh from Zane.

"Sorry." Zane waved a dismissive hand. "The *other* news is that Kolthoff wants to talk. He wants to make a deal. The U.S. Attorney personally handled Kolthoff's arraignment, but she's not quite sure what kind of information Kolthoff's willing to cough up just yet."

Spencer's amused expression quickly darkened. "If that prick wants anything from us, he'd better cough up everything."

Amelia was inclined to agree with the surly SSA. "I assume that means we need to head to MCC?" Metropolitan Correction Center Chicago was located in the heart of downtown, and it was hard to miss the towering, triangular building. As much as Amelia dreaded the agonizing commute at the height of rush hour, she figured the delay would give Kolthoff plenty of time to jog his memory.

"Yeah, Julliard said she wants you two since you've been

interviewing him so far. I think she just called me because I was the last person to message her about the progress of our warrants."

Smacking an open palm against the table, Spencer shoved to his feet. "All right. Storm and I will go deal with Kolthoff. Palmer, I'm going to put Journey on this case with you. Unofficially. She can work remotely from the safe house since just about everything that needs doing right now is digital. If we need more manpower, I can pull Agent Bhatti and Agent Alvarez in to help. They're between cases right now."

Zane stretched his arms above his head and nodded. Amelia could tell the desk work was starting to give him a taste of cabin fever, but Zane would never complain about his role as long as it was necessary for them to move forward in the investigation.

They said their goodbyes, and Amelia followed Spencer out to a black SUV in the parking garage. She loathed driving in Chicago traffic, so she went straight for the passenger's side.

Unsurprisingly, the trip to MCC Chicago was long and agonizing. Nearly an hour after departing the field office, she and Spencer walked through the doors of the imposing building. They handed over their weapons, went through a security checkpoint, and followed a black-clad corrections officer to a closed door.

As the guard pulled open the door to usher Amelia and Spencer through, Amelia bit the inside of her cheek to stifle an inane laugh. To one side of the bolted-down table, Brian Kolthoff sat with his wrists cuffed through a ring welded onto the stainless-steel surface. His brown hair was disheveled, and he'd traded his expensive suit for an orange shirt and pants. In place of his usual designer dress shoes were the same white canvas slip-ons given to every new inmate.

On the opposite side of the table, Simone Julliard tapped a ballpoint pen against a yellow notepad. Her shrewd brown eyes shifted toward Amelia and Spencer as the guard closed the door behind them. Most interviews with prisoners occurred in an area where the corrections officers could visually supervise, but Brian Kolthoff wasn't an average inmate. If he was honest about providing information in exchange for a reduced sentence, then they needed to be discrete.

Who knew what types of disgusting secrets were lodged inside Brian's head? Amelia doubted they'd ever learn them all, but she'd damn well try.

Offering Kolthoff a pleasant smile, Amelia took a seat beside the U.S. Attorney. "Nice to see you both again so soon. I have to say, Mr. Kolthoff, orange is a great color for you. It really brings out your…eyes."

To Amelia's immense satisfaction, a moment of amusement passed over Simone Julliard's face. Brian Kolthoff remained silent, his expression impassive. *Mostly* impassive. Though the air of self-satisfaction still oozed from his pores like an alien spewing toxic gas, Amelia noted the jerky movements of his eyes. His knuckles were white where he clasped his hands together.

He was nervous. For the first time in god only knew how long, he wasn't in control. He wasn't sure he could weasel his way out of his current predicament, at least not in the manner to which he'd become accustomed.

Arms crossed, Spencer leaned against a wall directly behind Amelia. "Agent Storm has a point. But I'm sure you know we aren't here to give you fashion advice. Ms. Julliard says you have a few things to tell us."

Amelia wasn't keen on the idea of Brian being released

from prison at any point in the near future, but she was still a realist. If the asshole didn't cooperate, then they'd be forced to drag the case to trial. While the evidence so far—especially if traces of Michelle's captivity were discovered on the *Equilibrium*—granted them a solid leg to stand on in a courtroom, Brian had more money than God. He could afford the best lawyers. Hell, there was even the possibility he could pay off a judge or a member of the jury.

Not to mention the trauma Michelle Timmer would experience by being dragged through the mud by Brian's pricey attorneys.

If the man could provide them with information that would lead to more of his twisted accomplices being put behind bars, then they had to take the opportunity.

Harvey Byrd cleared his throat. "We're willing to make a deal. My client has information he'll share with the prosecution if his charges are reduced."

Simone Julliard clicked her pen. "How reduced, Counselor?" Her penetrating gaze shifted to Kolthoff, a frown tugging at the corner of her mouth. "Because I'd like to tell you right now that your client *will* see jail time."

The defense attorney held up his hands. "I understand. We'd like to discuss *where* my client will serve that time. And he'd like protective custody. Mr. Kolthoff is a powerful man, but his money cannot protect him from jailhouse thugs. Don't forget the two other men involved in Michelle Timmer's kidnapping are currently in hiding."

Anticipation buzzed beneath Amelia's skin. Would Brian give up Stan and Joseph, or did he intend to be cute and offer up two unknown men? Amelia wouldn't put the maneuver past him. "For the record, Mr. Byrd, who are these two men?"

Harvey and Brian exchanged a quick glance, Brian offering his lawyer a slight nod. As Harvey returned his gaze to Amelia, Spencer, and Simone, he threaded his fingers together. "Former special agent Joseph Larson and Senator Stan Young. You'll understand my client's reluctance to bring this up beforehand. Stan Young and Joseph Larson are both dangerous in their own ways."

If Harvey had uttered any other names or if Kolthoff had thought to offer them crumbs instead of a main course, Amelia suspected Simone Julliard would have walked out of the room.

With a smile that didn't reach her eyes, the U.S. Attorney tapped her pen in a steady rhythm. "All right. Mr. Kolthoff, why don't you tell us what you've got, and we'll go from there? I'm sure you'll understand my reluctance to draw up a legal agreement beforehand."

Harvey's mouth twitched with a faint scowl. "With all due respect, Ms. Julliard, my client isn't comfortable providing incriminating information about Joseph Larson and Stan Young without some form of written assurance."

Simone Julliard dropped her pen and glanced at Amelia and Spencer. "Well, in that case, I think we're done here."

Even as trepidation swept through Amelia's veins, she managed a casual shrug. "As soon as our crime scene techs in Virginia Beach locate Michelle Timmer's holding cell, it'll only be a matter of time before we have physical proof that your client held her captive against her will."

"Plus." Spencer made a show of weighing his hands. "Joseph Larson is pretty well sunk at this point. Once we find him, all we've got to do is lock him up and throw away the key. As for Stan Young, well." The SSA offered them a wolfish grin. "Let's just say he's got his own problems to worry about, with or without the Michelle Timmer case. In fact, the more I think about it, the more I'm not so sure we really need your client's help dealing with those two at all."

Pink tinged Harvey's cheeks. "This isn't—"

"I can tell you where they are."

At Brian Kolthoff's sudden interruption, Harvey shot his client an angry glare. Brian's pale green eyes flashed, and Harvey's throat bobbed. Amelia could tell the lawyer knew he was playing with fire by attempting to call the shots on Brian's behalf.

Resting her elbows on the table, she met Brian's stare without flinching. "You know where they are? How?"

Kolthoff sneered. "I know more about those pricks than anyone else on the planet. Make me a deal, and I'll lead you straight to them."

The offer was tantalizing, but Amelia trusted Brian Kolthoff as far as she could throw him. "Why are you suddenly so eager to sell out the two men who've been your accomplices for all these years?"

Metal clattered as Kolthoff flattened his palms. Hatred sparked in his gaze, but the rage wasn't directed at Amelia. For a beat, she suspected she'd caught a rare glimpse of the sadistic creature—the real Brian Kolthoff—who lurked beneath the countless masks he donned in front of others.

His words came out as a hiss. "Because they'd do the same to me, and I'd rather sink them before they get the chance."

Amelia wouldn't have bought a display of anxiety, remorse, or fear from this man, but she believed his hatred. A kernel of doubt remained, but the sentiment wasn't enough to convince her Kolthoff was lying. Not completely.

She'd never imagined the day would come when she'd share a common goal with this sick bastard, but here they were.

They both wanted to rid the world of Joseph Larson and Stan Young. The only difference was that Amelia would do her damnedest to bring Brian down in flames alongside them.

22

The skeletal branches of old maples and oaks crisscrossed my view of the moon's eerie glint on the rippling surface of a sprawling lake. In the darkness of the kitchen, I was afforded a clear view of the backyard and the partially frozen water beyond. Thanks to the warmer weather of the past couple days, much of the ice on the relatively shallow lake had thawed and broken into chunks that floated like driftwood. This was one of the few residences I'd kept hidden from any form of public records.

The most sentimental of them all.

I'd grown up in a house on this very piece of land. After all the suffering I'd endured at my mother's hands here, most people would assume I'd never want to come within a hundred miles of this place. Those people would be wrong.

Instead of running from it, I'd bought the property through the privacy of a shell company before promptly bulldozing the old structure down. I'd even gone so far as ordering the construction crew to fill the cellar with cement. No one would ever enter that space again.

Ever.

Once every single piece of that old house had been taken away, I'd built this one. Fresh...modern...new. My mother would have hated it, which made me love it all the more.

I'd brought Josh out here when he was a kid, but I doubted he remembered much about the trips. I didn't come here as much as I thought I would in the beginning. Maybe my mother's ghost still lingered in the trees and dirt. In the view.

Shaking off the thought, I leaned against the breakfast bar and sipped my pricey glass of scotch, my gaze fixed on the calm scene beyond the French doors. The potent liquor burned a familiar trail down my throat before settling in to warm my stomach.

If memory served, I'd paid almost ten grand for the booze. For the longest time, it had simply sat atop the liquor shelf. I'd viewed it as a symbol of my wealth and power, a reminder that I could drop the same amount of money on a bottle of booze that most people spent on a down payment for a car.

But when the world was ending, such displays were useless. Material possessions were worthless when the end nipped at my heels.

As far as I was concerned, that's what this was. The end of the world.

For most of the day, I'd monitored the news in hopes the story about Michelle Timmer would die down, but I'd had no such luck. Instead, the blaze started by some chump reporter named Zack Hartman had grown into an inferno.

Now, in addition to Michelle, the news stories had begun to mention Gianna Passarelli.

How? How in the hell had Michelle's statement devolved so quickly into the disappearance of Gianna Passarelli? I'd taken Gianna more than a decade ago, and there were zero ties between her and Michelle.

My mind shot back to Cynthia's near constant suspicion of my son. I'd never put much weight behind Cynthia's paranoia, but should I have listened more closely? Should I have heeded her advice and maintained a shorter leash on Josh?

What could my son possibly know, anyway?

Nothing. He doesn't know anything. For all I know right now, Cynthia was the one to turn me in. Or maybe Joseph. No one has seen him in the last week. Who knows what he's up to?

With a groan, I rubbed my temple. Letting my thoughts run in circles wouldn't solve anything. All it would do was give me a headache.

Earlier in the day, before I'd taken off to the Wisconsin lake house, I'd tried to get ahold of Brian Kolthoff more times than I could count. After the first ten attempts, everything went straight to voicemail. I'd shot him a total of nine texts, and all had remained unanswered when I'd left home. I hadn't brought my cell along so that my location couldn't be tracked, but I doubted Brian had even bothered to try to call me before he was arrested.

I shouldn't have been surprised. All this time, I'd assured myself I held enough sway over Brian and Joseph to keep them in line, but I'd never been more wrong about anything in my life.

By now, I could only assume Brian had rolled over to the Feds about Michelle Timmer. If he hadn't yet, he soon would. As for Joseph Larson, I didn't have the first clue what had become of him. For all I knew, he'd crossed the Pacific Ocean to live with a tribe in Papua New Guinea. I'd never been adept at predicting Joseph Larson's next move, and I'd never understood the bizarre bond between him and Brian.

I sighed into my scotch. A trio of my most trusted security guards had accompanied me out to this rural piece of land, but if the Feds froze my assets, I'd soon be paying them with the reserves of cash I'd stashed in the basement here. It was a respectable sum, but nowhere near the amount I was used to having at my fingertips.

My throat burned as I polished off the remainder of the scotch, setting the glass on the granite bar at my back. Irritation sparked to life in my chest as I twisted my wedding ring.

Cynthia had left Mae with her sister, but I had no idea where the girl might be now. I'd cut off any contact with family in case the Feds could use it to track me. With the way everything was shaping up for me so far, Cynthia had probably already spilled her guts, and I could only hope Mae was still in the care of Cynthia's sister.

Just as I was about to let out a slew of four-letter words, a movement near the lake startled me.

What the hell was that? Something on the water? Or am I losing my grip on reality?

I stood perfectly still and scrutinized the water. A persistent breeze rattled the limbs of the trees and sent faint ripples along the surface of the lake, but the motion of the water wasn't what had caught my attention.

I'd spotted *something*. I was certain of it. I just had to…

A shadowy figure darted out from behind a maple near the shore, and I sucked in a sharp breath as adrenaline flooded my veins.

Someone was here.

Was it the FBI?

No, they wouldn't skulk around in the backyard. They'd show up at the front door with a warrant and a battering ram.

I silently cursed my luck, but I didn't pause to give consideration to the identity of whoever might be out there. If they weren't the Feds, then there was only one way to deal with them.

Spinning on my heel, I cast one paranoid glance over my shoulder before I hurried to the living area where my head of security was playing solitaire on the coffee table. Millard

Kaufman was built like a fire hydrant—broad shoulders, a barrel chest, and equally muscular legs. He'd worked for me since before the Gianna Passarelli fiasco, and I trusted him more than my own wife.

Not that my trust was typical. I wasn't even sure if a normal person would call it trust. More like leverage.

I'd made sure to reward his loyalty with periodic trips to Brian Kolthoff's yacht. Millard's tastes were much younger than mine or Brian's, and we'd kept his predilection a secret from Joseph Larson. I wasn't sure what in the hell it was about Larson, but the former Fed drew the line at prepubescent girls. If he'd known about Millard, I was almost certain he'd have killed him years ago.

Millard and one of his buddies—another of my most trusted who I'd brought to the lake house—had been eyeballing Mae for too long for my liking. I hadn't been looking forward to the day when I'd have to confront the men about the situation, but apparently, I no longer had to worry about it.

Millard's head snapped to the side as he met my gaze. Before I could even speak, he was on his feet, a matte black Glock in his hand.

I gestured toward the backyard. "There's someone out back. I saw them run out from behind a tree. The nearest neighbors are more than five miles away on the other side of the lake, so I sincerely doubt it's them."

"All right. I'll take Andrews and head out to investigate."

My muscles tensed like a cornered animal. "There's someone out there. I know I saw him."

The beast of a man nodded. "I understand, sir. We'll clear the perimeter and report back as soon as we're done."

Despite the competent security personnel around me, I couldn't rid myself of the sinking feeling I was an unwitting victim in a horror film.

❄

ALEX PULLED his eye away from the night-vision scope of his rifle and turned to where Gabriel was crouched beside him. The two of them had taken cover behind a massive stump at the edge of a thicket of trees. Down a gently sloping hill to their right, water lapped at a rocky shore. Aside from the sound of the water and a couple night birds who'd flown north early, the night was still.

"How many?" Gabriel's question was barely a whisper.

"Two just came outside, which leaves us with one more indoors, plus Young himself. Christian is leading them past where Angelo and Nico are hidden by the dock."

"Good. We wait for their signal, then we go in through the front, yeah?"

"Yeah." Alex returned his gaze to the rifle's optic.

After Stan Young had slipped through the fingers of the media and law enforcement, Alex had seized his opportunity. Earlier in the day, he'd received Amelia's text message confirming the results of the DNA analysis.

She'd confirmed that the corrupt senator had abducted Alex's baby sister ten years ago, raped her, and stolen her child to raise as his own.

Hatred roiled in Alex's gut. There was no way in hell he'd let the Feds get to Stan Young before he could. Right now, while the senator was at his most vulnerable, Alex and his men would strike. If Alex allowed Stan to be taken in by the Bureau, the cretin would still have ample opportunity to slither away from the consequences of his actions. And once he'd skated on kidnapping and murder charges, he'd be even more difficult to get to.

As far as Alex was concerned, it was now or never.

Having been in regular communication with Josh Young ever since the awkward kidnapping, Alex had enlisted Josh's help locating any of Stan's potential hideouts. The first two Alex had checked had been teeming with FBI personnel, but as the saying went, the third time was a charm.

At first, Alex had been surprised Josh would so willingly hand his own father over to the reaper. But when he'd asked Josh for his reasoning, the man's answer had been simple.

"Some men deserve to die."

Alex couldn't argue with him.

A still silence settled over him and Gabriel as they both kept their attention on the pair of security guards who'd begun to sweep the perimeter of the house.

Under normal circumstances, Alex would've sought a method to neutralize the guards without killing them—he'd have his guys load the men up with tranquilizer darts and stuff them in a garage or knock them out and tie them up in the boathouse next to the dock.

Like any other aspect of dealing with Stan Young, the senator's security personnel were far from normal. During the surveillance they'd conducted earlier in the evening, Alex had identified all three men. Two of them had close ties to the Leóne family, and the other was a pervert Alex had wanted dead for years.

No time like the present.

The larger of the two guards, Millard Kaufman, led the way as he and his partner, Johnny Andrews, drew nearer to the dock. From where he was concealed behind the boathouse, Alex's cousin Christian raised his own rifle and took aim.

Soundlessly, Millard crumpled into a graceless heap, his brains splattering the browned grass. Before Andrews could even finish opening his mouth to yell, Alex squeezed his finger on the trigger. The powerful rifle jerked, but Alex had tucked the stock tightly against his shoulder so the effect of the recoil was minimized.

In the blink of an eye, the world was populated by two fewer child molesters.

Snatching the spent shell casings, Alex shouldered the rifle, drew his handgun, and started for the front of the house, Gabriel on his heels. Their group had decided against utilizing radio communication in case the men inside had the ability to spy on them. Besides, the plan was simple, and Alex had worked with the four others more times than he could count.

Ninety seconds after the guards outside had been neutralized, Alex and Gabriel would kick down the front door while Christian, Angelo, and Nico took the back of the house. With only Stan and a single guard remaining, they'd stand no chance against Alex's highly trained men.

As Alex and Gabriel slipped onto the front porch, one of them to either side of the wooden door, Alex glanced down at his watch. When it was time, he held up a gloved hand and counted down on his fingers.

Five.

Four.

Three.

Two.

One.

The instant he balled his hand into a fist, Gabriel stepped in front of the door and brought his booted foot down on the wooden surface. With a raucous *crack*, the latch ripped away from the frame, and the door swung inward. At the same time, the shattering of glass drifted through the house, and Alex knew that Christian and the others had successfully breached the back door.

Silenced handgun leading the way, Alex stepped over the threshold and into a dim foyer. He swung his arms to each corner of the space as Gabriel closed the door behind them.

Satisfied the foyer was empty, Alex poked his head

through an open doorway leading to the living room. The glow of a floor lamp in the corner was the only source of illumination, but it was all Alex needed to spot Stan Young ducking down behind the couch.

A man beyond Alex's field of view swore, but his words were cut short by the quiet *pop* of a silenced handgun.

"Third guard is down." Alex recognized the speaker as Angelo, and he permitted himself a moment of grim satisfaction at the knowledge that all Stan's security had been neutralized.

Aiming his handgun at the section of the couch where the corrupt senator had hidden, Alex took the first step into the living room. He and his guys had donned bullet suppression vests for their excursion, and knowing Stan Young's lack of combat experience, Alex doubted the man could land a headshot from across the room. Especially not before Alex could pull his own trigger.

"Young's behind the couch, probably hidden from you by that bookshelf."

Angelo snorted as his shadowy figure came into view from the kitchen. "Come out, come out, Mr. Young. Trust me, you don't want us to come over there and pull you out."

"What do you want?" Petulance laced the senator's words, but his voice quavered just enough to tell Alex how frighted the man was.

Good.

"Cut the shit." Alex spat out the order like it was laced with poison. "You know who I am. I *know* you do. I'll give you three guesses what I want, how about that?"

Young didn't respond, and anger curdled in Alex's stomach.

As Christian and Nico emerged, Angelo lifted an eyebrow at Alex. "You want us to go in and drag him out?"

Alex nodded, maintaining his aim in the senator's direction.

In the next couple seconds, all Alex caught was a glimmer of movement as Stan Young rose to his feet, a chrome handgun leveled in Angelo's direction.

Adrenaline surged through Alex's body, both freezing and burning all at once. Time slowed to a crawl, like a frame-by-frame playback of a video recording.

Though Alex's intent had been to pry a confession from Stan bit by agonizing bit, he wouldn't risk his men's safety for his own selfish gain. He'd already decided he'd make his best effort to deal with Stan non-fatally if he tried anything, but if it came to it, he wouldn't think twice to put a bullet in Stan's head.

Taking aim at the senator's arm, Alex squeezed the trigger.

Young howled in pain as the power of the gunshot forced his arm to the side. Alex and all his guys had affixed their weapons with silencers, so when a sharp *pop* rang throughout the space, he knew with certainty that Stan had fired the shot.

Fortunately, Alex was faster. By putting a bullet through Young's right forearm, Alex had forced his aim to go wide.

The clatter of Young's weapon falling to the hardwood floor was markedly less intense than the deafening retort of the handgun.

Angelo and Nico were on the disgraced senator in an instant. Young yelped in pain as Nico jerked his arms behind his back. A popping sound indicated Young's shoulder had dislocated from his arm. The man's childlike squirms abruptly ceased.

Nico gave the arm another jerk. "Hey, we warned you!"

Stan Young was practically limp in Nico's grasp. Alex stepped toward the captive senator, knowing Nico had the situation under control. Clasping the wrist of Young's still-working arm, Nico jammed his index and middle fingers into the jagged red gunshot wound on Young's forearm.

Young's yelp from a moment ago was almost cute compared to the bloodcurdling scream he let loose.

Nico wiped his bloody glove on Young's shirt. "This'll go a lot easier if you cooperate."

Any remaining fight left Stan Young's posture. Alex wasn't sure if the man was actually giving up or if he was attempting to lure them into complacency. Young had lived a privileged life, but Alex still couldn't be sure of the man's breaking point.

Christian dragged over a chair from the dining area, none-too-gently shoving Young down to sit before he bound both the man's wrists to the wooden arms.

Teeth clamped together, Stan Young grated out curses with every movement of his wounded arm. A bone jutted forward below the wrecked shoulder, and crimson darkened the sleeve of his white button-down, the stain growing with each beat of his heart.

Christian and the others appeared satisfied with their handiwork, and they backed toward the nearby breakfast bar.

Switching on an overhead light, Alex picked his way across the living room. "Well, you're still able to move your fingers a little, so it looks like that bullet just went through muscle. I think if I'd hit you a little lower, it might have done some lasting nerve damage, though."

Stan Young tilted his head backward until his gaze was pointed toward the ceiling. Sweat dripping from his head pooled on the floor behind his chair. "Where are my men? Other than the one you killed."

His tone told Alex he was less worried about the welfare

of his security personnel and more hopeful about whether someone was coming to save his ass.

Alex holstered his handgun and drew forth a hunting knife. "They're dead."

Young's eyes flashed with anger as he leveled his glare at Alex. "Those men had families. They had—"

"If it wasn't for you, they'd have had rap sheets a mile long." Alex paused, pretending to be interested in his blade. "They'd all have been thrown on the sex offender registry ages ago if you weren't covering for them. Trust me, Senator. I did my homework. Was that why you kept them around? Did their perversions make you feel less self-conscious about your own?"

Even as Young squared his jaw, Alex didn't miss the hint of fear that crossed his face. "I don't know what you're talking about."

Alex let out a derisive chuckle. "No, of course not." He twirled the hunting knife in one gloved hand. Young's gray eyes followed the movement, and to Alex's satisfaction, the senator strained against his binds. Finally, the man seemed to understand the nature of his predicament.

The senator's Adam's apple bobbed. "What do you want from me? Money? I'll give you however much you're after. Just give me a number, and it's yours. I won't go to the cops or the Feds. I'll just leave, and you'll never hear from me again."

With a roll of his eyes, Alex hunched in front of Young to bring them eye-level with one another. "Not a chance, Senator. I've got plenty of my own money. I don't need whatever pittance you've got access to while the Feds have all your accounts monitored or frozen."

Though brief, Young grasped the chair tighter with the more operational of his two arms. "I can get you more. Like I said, whatever you—"

Since Alex couldn't snap his fingers while wearing his leather gloves, he clapped his hands to interrupt the senator instead. "I already said I don't give a shit about your money. Pay attention, *stronzo.*"

Young didn't react to being called an asshole.

"Then what do you want?" If Young had intended for the question to come across as authoritative, he'd failed miserably. With each verbal exchange, he more closely resembled a cornered animal—terrified but too stupid to admit it.

Abruptly, Alex gestured to Christian. The two men moved out of earshot of Young. "I want to record this bastard confessing to everything he did. Do you have the video camera?"

Christian tapped his coat pocket and nodded at his boss and friend.

"Good. Start recording when I begin questioning him again. I'll make sure he tells the world every sick thing he did to my innocent Gigi."

Christian's determined stare invigorated Alex's resolve.

Alex positioned himself in front of Young's battered body. "*Senator* Young." The sarcasm dripped through each syllable of the title.

Stan Young blinked defiantly at Alex. "What? And what's all this?" Stan nodded toward Christian's camera.

"Don't concern yourself with my associate. I want the truth. About you, about you and my mother, but mostly," Alex narrowed his eyes dangerously as he leaned closer, "the truth about what you did to my sister." Alex glanced at Christian, whose face was partially concealed by the small recorder. "Everyone is going to know what you've done."

In an instant, all the color drained from Young's face. Though the man typically appeared far younger than his fifty-five years, he seemed to have suddenly aged by two decades.

When Young didn't respond, Alex rose to his full height and closed the short distance between them. He didn't bother to give Young another warning before he snatched the man's pinky finger and severed it with one clean movement.

Young howled in pain, but Alex threw a fist into the soft flesh of his stomach, knocking the wind from his lungs. "Shut up!"

Hanging his head, Young wheezed, but he didn't emit another scream. "You…won't get…away…"

"Won't get away with this?" Alex let as much mocking derision into the words as possible. "Or are you just saying we won't get away at all? Because either way, you're sorely mistaken. Last time I checked, *I* wasn't the one who was plastered all over the news for abducting and assaulting an FBI forensic analyst. Sure, I might be a fucking gangster, but I can't hold a candle to you."

From where he leaned against the back of the couch, Gabriel snorted. "If you put together every misdeed all five of us have done and compare it to yours, Senator, you'd *still* be in the lead."

Alex offered his lieutenant an appreciative nod. "He's right. There's not a single D'Amato who's kidnapped, raped, and murdered a thirteen-year-old girl. If they did, I'd find them and put them down like a rabid dog, no matter who they were."

Gabriel snorted. "That's an insult to rabid dogs."

Alex couldn't help a chuckle. Leave it to Gabriel to crack jokes at Young's expense right after Alex had sliced off one of the man's fingers.

Then again, even though Alex and Gabriel weren't blood relatives, he'd looked after Gianna like she was his sister too. Sometimes, Alex forgot how much losing Gianna had impacted Gabriel and a few of his other men.

This isn't just for me, or even just for Gianna. This is for all of us.

Wiping the blood-stained hunting knife on Young's pant leg, Alex clucked his tongue. Embers of rage burned low in Alex's chest, but he'd learned to control the ire long ago. "My lieutenant has a point, but let's not dwell on it."

Light glinted off the sheen of sweat on Young's forehead. Blood *drip-drip-dripped* from the bullet wound and the site of his severed finger, forming a crimson pool beneath the arm of the chair.

Stan's jaw tightened, his chest heaving. "What do you want me to say?"

"I told you." Alex started to reach for Young's ring finger. He was growing tired of the senator's repeated denial, and if the guy kept at it for much longer, Alex would be forced to get creative.

Young sucked in a sharp breath, his eyes popping open wide as he tried in vain to pull away his hand. "No, no, no. Please, you don't have to do this, please, no."

Gritting his teeth, Alex tugged on the man's ring finger until he suspected he might dislocate it. "Is that what my sister said to you before you raped her?"

Like a spell had been cast, Young went still.

When the senator didn't speak, Alex slowly pressed the knife to his finger. A bead of crimson formed along the sharp blade, the blood trickling along the metal as Alex slowly sliced through Young's skin and into the tissue beneath.

Screams of pain were followed by pleas for mercy. "Noooo! Stop! Pleeeeeese!"

In the darkened recesses of Alex's mind, Young's words echoed in Gianna's voice.

Anger slithered through Alex's veins like a poison, slowly eating away at his rational thoughts until he risked granting full control to his baser instincts.

Leaving a nasty gash in the side of Young's ring finger, Alex inhaled deeply. The tang of iron and sweat rushed up to greet him, but he ignored the scent. He counted to four and exhaled. Stan Young would not be the one who made him lose control.

Once Alex was satisfied he'd channeled his rage, he yanked on Young's finger and slammed the blade down at the knuckle. The instant Young opened his mouth to let loose a shriek, Alex backhanded him with the hilt of the knife.

"Shut up! If you don't stop sniveling, I'm going to dislocate your other shoulder."

"P-please." Young's chest heaved as he gasped for air. "Please, it's not what you think. It's not...please, please."

"The truth, Young." Alex's words were as cold as a Siberian winter. He grabbed Stan's hair and forced his head higher. "Look into the camera and tell the world what you did to my sister after you raped her and stole her child?"

"Okay." The disgraced senator licked his split lip. "The truth is...I loved her. Your mother, and your sister. I loved them both so much. I...I thought Gianna was my second chance." The words spilled from his mouth like an avalanche after getting started. "I'd love her, give her everything I'd wanted to give to your mother. There was so much I wanted to do with her. We were going to have our own family, me and her. Even if we had to run away and disappear, but..."

His face screwed up in anger, and Alex's fingers twitched with the renewed desire to break his nose. "But what?"

Young's upper lip peeled back in a sneer. "She was just like your mother. She thought she was too good for me, and she tried to leave...just like Sofia did. Only this time, I was ready for it. I caught her, and I...I had to do something to make sure she knew she was mine. I didn't expect her to get pregnant. Didn't plan for it, didn't know how to deal with it."

An uneasy numbness had begun to push out the persistent burn of Alex's anger. He could hardly imagine the hell his little sister had endured at this man's hand, but he wanted to know. He *needed* to know. "What next?" He forced the words past his lips.

Stan Young's gaze was fixed on a distant point in the living room, his face pinched with an emotion Alex didn't care to decipher. "I took care of her. Made sure she was healthy so the baby would be healthy too. It was a...complicated birth, but she and Mae both pulled through. I'd settled them both in a property I own out in Maryland, not far from D.C. I figured she'd stay there with Mae, and I'd be able to visit when I was working in the Senate."

For a beat, hope that Gianna might still be alive flickered like a small candle in a storm. Alex had given up his wishful thinking that he'd find Gianna physically unharmed, and he snuffed the glimmer of optimism as soon as it formed.

Fortunately, Alex didn't have to prod Young to speak again. "It worked okay for a little while. Five months. But then..." his faraway expression twisted with ire, "she tried to run. Tried to take Mae with her. Millard caught her, and he brought her back to me. I did what I had to do. I couldn't risk her trying to escape every time I was back in Chicago. It wasn't going to work."

The temperature of the room seemed to drop by fifteen degrees. Each of Alex's men wore a dark look, but they didn't move from their posts. Angelo kept watch through the closed curtains of the living room window while Christian stood guard at the breakfast bar, and Nico stood near the broken French doors. They were still wary, but Alex could tell Young's recollection had affected them as well.

Gianna hadn't deserved any of Stan Young's depravity. She'd only been *thirteen*, for god's sake. Alex had been certain Young had taken her due to his alliance with the Leóne family or out of retaliation for some perceived slight, but the truth...

The truth was darker and far more twisted.

Alex understood revenge. Though he operated under his own code of honor, he could grasp why an enemy would seek out one of his family's weak points in retaliation for the death of one of their own.

But this? Stan's claim that he'd loved Gianna?

It was beyond Alex's realm of comprehension. Stan was even more fucked up than Alex had realized.

Now, far too little and far too late, Stan Young would pay.

But first, he needed a true confession from Young. One that didn't include Alex's name.

He nodded for the video camera to be readied, knowing his men would center the frame to only include Young's face and not the mess happening below his neck. The people who listened didn't need to be distracted by blood or misplaced bones.

"Now, I want you to tell the camera this same story, using full names...and excluding mine." Alex leaned close to the senator's face. "And you better get it right the first time."

The moment after the senator finished his confession and the camera was turned off, Alex stepped forward and slammed the blade of the hunting knife into Young's knee with a sickening wet crack.

Young howled like a wild animal caught in a hunter's trap. "W-wh-what the...? What a-are you...d-doing? I thought, I thought—"

"You thought wrong!" Alex steadied his breathing as best as he could, even though his stomach roiled from knowing all that had happened to his precious sister. "Get me something to gag him with. We've got a long way to go, and I'm sick of listening to him talk."

A faint smirk crept to Christian's face as he strolled

around the breakfast bar to rummage through kitchen drawers.

"Wait, wait, what are you doing? I told you the truth! Wait…stop! Please! I have a family!" Stan Young panted, blood draining from his knuckles where he clasped the chair.

"A family?" Alex guffawed, accepting a gray towel from Christian's gloved hand. "No, Mr. Young, you don't. The Feds have a warrant out for your wife's arrest, and Mae is with her aunt, uncle, and cousins. And Josh…" He chuckled darkly. "Josh might be one of the few people on this planet who hates you as much as I do."

Young's eyes widened, a pitiable look of surprise on his pallid face. "My…son? He betrayed me?" The senator spat out a string of curses. "That worthless piece of shit. I knew he was—"

With a swift step forward, Gabriel leered at Stan. "Are you talking shit about my new friend? I think you are."

Alex shrugged noncommittally. "Like I said, I'm sick of him talking."

Stan started to speak, and Alex seized the opportunity to jam the towel in his mouth, stifling whatever nonsense he'd been about to spew.

Yanking the knife free of Stan's leg and the carnage that used to be his knee, Alex waved the blade in front of his face as he strained against the zip-ties.

He could kill Young now, clean the house, and leave, but Stan had earned worse than a couple missing fingers, dislocated shoulder, and a severed quadriceps tendon.

As Josh had said, some men deserved to die.

But others deserved much, much worse.

23

At the creak of a door, Amelia pulled her gaze away from the man and woman on the other side of the two-way mirror. Holding a manila folder, Agent Journey Russo stepped over the threshold. With Spencer and Zane out in the field searching for Joseph Larson, Amelia and Journey had volunteered to question their newest detainee, Cynthia Young.

To no one's surprise, Cynthia had immediately demanded a lawyer. The man didn't have a reputation as fearsome as Harvey Byrd's, but an hour of his time likely cost more than three months of Amelia's rent.

Upon her first interaction with Cynthia, Amelia could tell there was something...*off* about her. Like she was missing a vital piece of her humanity—the portion that made a person fit to live in civilized society. Cynthia's brown eyes were shrewd, but there was an emptiness in her gaze that made the hairs on the back of Amelia's neck stand on end.

No wonder she'd been able to stay married to Stan Young for twenty-six years. They're two peas in a pod.

Amelia pushed aside the thoughts as she turned to Journey. "Ready?"

With a slight smile, Journey nodded. "Yep. Let's go see if this...*woman* knows where the hell her husband disappeared to."

Amelia read some of her own distaste for Cynthia in Journey's tone. Any woman who could aid a sex trafficker or rapist was a special breed of twisted in Amelia's book. Women had to look out for one another, not sell one another out to the scum of the earth.

Although, with the ability to hang Simone Julliard's wrath over Cynthia's head, Amelia suspected the woman would be willing to sell out her husband for a little leniency. Amelia and Journey just needed to help her see the proverbial light.

Though Journey had been dedicated to watching over her sister at the FBI safe house, the agent had admitted to a slight case of cabin fever. At Michelle's behest, Journey had left her sister in the capable hands of Agents Cowen and Steelman. According to Journey, Michelle had taken an immediate liking to Sherry, and she'd even hit it off with Dean—the lone man in the safe house—over the past few days. Amelia had warmed at the news, leaving her even more grateful she'd suggested the two Violent Crime agents for Michelle's safe house.

As Amelia followed Journey into the hall, she shook off her contemplation and rolled her shoulders. Kolthoff's leads for Stan Young's whereabouts had been fruitless so far, though the CSU were currently on their way to a Wisconsin lake house. The location hadn't been provided by Brian, though. Josh Young had called Amelia with the address of a rural residence where Stan had taken him as a boy.

If Josh's lead panned out and Brian's were fruitless, then Kolthoff would be up shit creek without a paddle.

Amelia swallowed a laugh and pushed open the door to

the interview room. Flashing a pleasant smile to the lawyer and then to Cynthia, she stepped into the harshly lit space.

"Good morning, Mrs. Young. Sorry to keep you waiting. And you're Cynthia's attorney, Herschel Mahoney, correct?"

With a quiet grunt, the lawyer nodded. "I don't suppose you two agents are finally willing to explain why my client is being held here? Mrs. Young is an important woman, and she can't waste her entire morning entertaining the FBI's witch hunt."

"Witch hunt?" Journey's normally polite tone was laden with condescension. "Oh, no, Counselor. This is far from a witch hunt. We have physical evidence proving your client's husband raped and impregnated a thirteen-year-old girl and then took that child to raise as his own."

The corners of the lawyer's eyes narrowed. "My client had nothing to do with her husband's actions, whatever those may have been."

"Really?" Journey flipped open the folder to a list of phone and text message records. Several lines were highlighted. "See the extensive list of communication between the two? These are your client's interactions with her husband on the same morning the story about Michelle Timmer broke. GPS puts Mrs. Young in the approximate location of her sister's residence, so why did your client abruptly leave to stay at their penthouse?"

Herschel spared little more than a quick glance at the phone records, telling Amelia he'd already come prepared with a rebuttal. "Of course, my client spoke with her husband after that story broke. What wife wouldn't want some sort of explanation from her spouse? Mrs. Young went to the other residence so she could be alone. Away from the media circus."

The haughty note in the lawyer's voice renewed the burn of anger in Amelia's veins. She kept her expression carefully blank as she folded her hands. "And is there a reason your client left her daughter in the care of her sister and brother-in-law?"

To Amelia's surprise, Cynthia waved a dismissive hand. "Mae loves her aunt and uncle. I left her there because I knew she'd prefer to spend time with her cousins than sit in the place alone with me."

The lawyer opened his mouth to speak, but Cynthia cut him off with a glare.

"I don't see why I need to protect my husband, Herschel. He's a grown man. We're talking to the FBI, for crying out loud." Cynthia gestured fervently at Amelia and Journey, and Amelia fought the urge to offer Journey a confused glance.

Try as she might, Amelia couldn't determine if the outburst was rehearsed or if Cynthia had genuinely grown tired of covering for her husband. The woman was about as easy to read as ancient hieroglyphics.

Journey cleared her throat. "What do you mean, 'protect' your husband? Protect him from what? Mrs. Young, if there's information you have that you're not sharing with us—"

"I know. I can be charged with obstruction of justice. I may have dropped out of law school in my second year, but I still remember plenty of it." Cynthia's posture tensed, and she sighed. "I'm sorry. I didn't mean to snap at you. It's been...a stressful twenty-four hours." She turned to her lawyer. "Herschel, I'd prefer to just answer these agents' questions as well as I can. I know I haven't done anything wrong. If Stan has done the things the news says he has, then maybe he deserves what's coming his way."

If Amelia wasn't so damn sure Cynthia's statement was just a slew of pretty words uttered for the sole purpose of saving her own ass, she might have been struck by a pang of sympathy for the woman. However, despite the difficulty reading Cynthia's expressions, Amelia was one-hundred-percent sure she was full of shit. Her only goal right now was to save herself from drowning right alongside her husband.

Beggars can't be choosers. If she's willing to turn on her husband, then we'll take whatever she's got.

As much as Amelia loathed the idea of a woman covering for her sex-trafficking rapist husband, Cynthia was the lesser of two evils. The unpleasant truth was that if Cynthia knew where her husband was hiding, then Amelia and Journey needed her help.

Swallowing her distaste, Amelia scooted forward and fixed her gaze on Cynthia. Precious time was being wasted as long as they sat here going back and forth with Cynthia and Herschel, and Amelia wanted to get to the crux of the matter. Any other information from Cynthia could wait. "Mrs. Young, do you know where your husband is hiding?"

Cynthia brushed a piece of hair from her face and breathed out a long sigh.

Journey appeared to grasp where Amelia was headed with her question, and she turned her focus to Cynthia as well. "It's imperative we find the senator as soon as possible. We're aware of the resources he has available, and if he manages to slip through our grasp, then..." Journey flattened her hands against the table, palms up, and shrugged. "There won't be much we can do to help you if we can't even find your husband. The U.S. Attorney *will* want someone to hang for what Stan has done, and if you're the only one we can find, then they'll pile on every charge they can come up with."

As Cynthia balled her hands into fists, Amelia could tell Journey had located a sore spot. Amelia made a mental note to compliment Journey for her quick thinking. Though she'd begun to feel like a broken record for parroting the threat that the U.S. Attorney would go after anyone left standing, the statement wasn't a lie. Simone Julliard *would* throw the book at whoever she could target.

Cynthia closed her eyes and took a deep breath. When she returned her gaze to Amelia and Journey, a hint of determination had edged out the moment of despair. "I'm aware, Agents. I've seen the news coverage, but I'll be perfectly honest with you. I don't know much of anything about what my husband and his friends like Brian Kolthoff like to get up to. Those two have been friends for a long time, and I know Brian is always a significant contributor to Stan's political campaigns. But personally? I hardly know anything about the man. That being said, I *can* help you find Stan."

Funny, Brian Kolthoff said the same thing about Joseph Larson, but Zane and Spencer didn't find anything at the address he provided.

If Cynthia decided to lead them on a wild goose chase, Amelia would make it her personal mission to ensure the woman saw jail time. "Do you know where he is?"

"I have a couple locations he might have gone to, but I think," she paused to hold up her hands, "I *think* I know which one he went to."

Journey pulled a small notepad and pen from her blazer. "If this pans out, we'll make sure the U.S. Attorney is aware that you've been cooperative."

Cynthia managed a slight nod as she scrawled out three different addresses, circling the first twice. "I'm pretty sure this is where he went." She pointed to the circled address. "But if he's not there, check these other two locations. None of them are registered in his name. They're all affiliated with shell corporations to hide the fact that he's the owner. He thinks I don't know about them."

With a few parting words and a reminder for Cynthia to stay in the city, Amelia and Journey headed to Tactical. Four agents joined them, leading the way in a black SUV. Amelia had already called the county sheriff's department, but she'd asked them to keep an eye on the location until she, Journey, and the tactical team arrived.

The drive to the Wisconsin lake house wasn't as painstaking as Amelia had feared, and she and Journey used the time to send local law enforcement to the other two properties. A shot of disdain weighed down Amelia's gut when both sheriff's departments reported the houses were empty.

And then there was one.

By the time they pulled up to a rustic, ranch-style cabin on the edge of a large lake, Amelia was a ball of nervous energy. The sun's rays shimmered along the water and scattered chunks of floating ice behind the house, but Amelia's attention didn't linger on the scenery for long. As she pulled to a stop behind the armored SUV of the tactical team, her gaze shot straight to the front door.

From a distance, she couldn't quite make out the details, but the appearance of the door was...*off*. It hung from the hinges at a slight, awkward angle, and she could have sworn the damn thing was ajar.

As Emily Wilson—the senior agent of the little squad—and the three other tactical agents piled out of the SUV, their rifles pointed toward the house, Amelia realized she wasn't the only one who'd made note of the oddity.

Service weapon in hand, Amelia hopped out of the car. Journey was at her side as she approached Emily and the others. The four stood with the SUV between them and the house, as if they fully expected a hidden gunman to open fire.

Emily's brown eyes shifted to Amelia and Journey as they trotted up to the vehicle.

A mixture of adrenaline and anticipation surged through Amelia's bloodstream. "You see the door? It looks like someone broke it and then tried to close it."

"Yeah, we saw it." She gestured to a detached two-car

garage. "Garage is closed, so we can't be sure if anyone's here. I haven't seen any movement in the windows, even as we were driving up."

Journey pressed her lips together as she studied the house. "Why would Stan Young break down his own door?"

Try as she might, Amelia couldn't come up with an answer to the agent's question. "We should go in as soon as possible, just in case there is someone in there. We don't want to give them any more time."

Wilson nodded her agreement. "Call the guy sitting in the sheriff's department car and let him know what we've found so far. We'll split into pairs. Sanford, you and Castaneda circle around to the back. Browning and I will take the front. This place isn't very big, so we should be able to clear the house quickly. Then, we'll fan out and clear the rest of the premises. Agents Russo and Storm will standby out here and get ahold of additional backup from the local sheriff's department."

Amelia's knee-jerk reaction was to protest, but she bit her tongue. Right now, Emily Wilson was in charge, and Amelia wasn't about to mess with her team's dynamic. From her ten years of military experience, Amelia knew better than most how one new person could interrupt the usual flow of a close-knit unit.

Besides, there was only one road leading out of the wooded area—two if she counted the lake itself. Fortunately, the slight incline of their post near the driveway provided them an expansive view of the water. They'd have plenty of time to notify the authorities, and a boat wouldn't get far. Navigating the bobbing blocks of ice would slow any getaway by water. If the escapee chose to make a break for the road, Amelia and Journey would be right here waiting for them.

In the tense moments following Wilson and her team's

departure from the relative cover of the SUV, Amelia strained her eyes to make out any hints of movement inside the cabin. Windows lit up as the tactical team turned on lights, and every few seconds, one of them shouted, "Clear!"

To Amelia's relief, no gunshots shattered the quiet afternoon. Her attention jerked to the shape of a man trotting toward the boathouse, but before she could signal an alarm, she recognized him as one of Emily's team.

"Agent Storm, Journey, you need to see this!" Emily Wilson's voice carried over to Amelia from the front door.

The wary tone of Emily's announcement rose the hairs on the back of Amelia's neck. She exchanged a fervent glance with Journey, and they hurried toward the front door. As they grew nearer, Amelia could make out the stony expression on Emily's face. However, the agent's rifle was slung across her back, a clear indication that they weren't in immediate danger.

Oddly enough, the relaxed stance only piqued Amelia's morbid curiosity. "What is it?"

Holding open the door, Agent Wilson jerked her head in the direction of the living room. "A body."

Amelia's stomach flip-flopped as she stepped over the threshold. She'd barely made it inside when the first traces of iron and decay wafted beneath her nose. Blinking repeatedly as her vision adjusted to the low light, Amelia chose her steps carefully as she made her way out of the foyer.

Right away, her attention was drawn to a person who sat slumped in a wooden chair. Both his wrists were bound to the arms, and his head lolled over the back.

She didn't need to advance any closer to confirm the battered corpse's identity. His face was bruised and swollen, but not to the point where she couldn't recognize Stan Young.

"Holy shit." A litany of questions raced through her head

at the sight of the senator's body, but one was louder than all the rest.

Who?

Who had killed Stan Young? Who had even known he was out here? The only reason the FBI had made it to the location was because his wife had provided it to Amelia and Journey.

A stone sank in her stomach as one man's name buzzed in the back of her skull.

Joseph Larson.

Swallowing the sudden rush of unease, Amelia gestured to the front door. "All right, let's keep everyone out of the house and call in the CSU."

In tandem, Emily and Journey nodded their agreement.

Amelia had come out to Wisconsin in hopes she could find answers from Stan Young, but now, she would only be left with more questions.

24

As Zane pulled to a stop at the intersection a block away from the towering monolith that was MCC Chicago, his gaze was quickly drawn to the flashing red and blue lights in front of the prison. For the first chunk of the day, Zane and Spencer had wasted their time chasing down a supposed lead given to them by Brian Kolthoff.

Kolthoff had assured them the property down in rural Illinois was one of Joseph Larson's, but when Zane and Spencer had arrived, they'd been greeted with a whole lot of nothing. Even the melting snow around the wooded cabin had appeared untouched.

Though the property was owned by a shell corporation that reeked of criminal involvement, none of them—Spencer, Zane, a couple guys from Tactical, and a handful of crime scene techs—had found any indication of Joseph Larson's presence, past or recent. Whether Kolthoff had purposefully fed them bad intel to waste their time or had simply not realized Joseph wouldn't be there remained to be seen. Zane had every intention of shaking the answer out of Kolthoff once he and Spencer were in an interview room with the man.

To Zane's side, Spencer leaned forward in his seat, his eyes glued to the squad cars in front of MCC Chicago. "Something's going on over there."

The light turned green, and Zane barely tapped the gas as traffic crawled away from the intersection at a snail's pace. "It's a prison. Lots of things happen there."

Spencer snorted. "Thanks, Agent Smartass."

Though Spencer didn't elaborate out loud, Zane caught the meaning that underscored his observation. A handful of squad cars and a crime scene van weren't an everyday occurrence, even at a prison as large as MCC Chicago.

Unease nibbled at the back of Zane's mind as he and Spencer fell silent.

More than seven hundred inmates were kept here at any given time. The odds that this had anything to do with Brian Kolthoff were tiny.

Despite the mathematical reasoning, Zane's concern persisted. He didn't necessarily care whether Kolthoff lived or died, but right now, the prick was their best source of information about Joseph Larson—even if he *had* led them on a wild goose chase.

Zane didn't bother to break the tense silence as he flashed his badge to the guard at an adjacent parking garage, hunted for a stall, and stalked toward a staircase that would take him and Spencer back to ground level. The faint squawk of police radios grew louder as they emerged from the stairwell and neared the prison's front entrance.

Though Zane was prepared to go through the motions of waiting to be buzzed into the building and passing through a security checkpoint, he'd only just approached the exterior set of double doors when the warden emerged.

Amelia and Zane had first been introduced to Donovan Gillem during the Carlo Enrico case. Carlo had been about to give them information about a corrupt detective in the

Chicago P.D., but the detective had managed to have Carlo killed before he could provide anything useful.

Gillem beckoned Zane and Spencer into the drab lobby. "Agents, I was just about to call you when I heard you'd pulled up. I've notified the U.S. Attorney already, and you were next on my list." The warden's brown eyes darted back and forth between the officers stationed outside. "I'm afraid the news isn't good, unfortunately."

A sick sense of déjà vu washed over Zane as he and Spencer followed Gillem to a security checkpoint on the far side of the room. "News about Brian Kolthoff?"

The warden nodded. "Yeah. He was found dead about an hour ago. I locked the prison down, which is why I didn't get ahold of you two right away. It was part of our usual procedure."

"Right, of course." Spencer's expression remained unchanged as he tucked away his service weapon and keys in a locker. His lack of a reaction told Zane both their minds had gone to the same place when they'd driven by the hubbub in front of the building.

In what Zane figured was record time, they passed through a metal detector and boarded a large elevator. Without any prying ears nearby, Zane turned his full attention to the warden. "What have you got so far on Kolthoff's murder?" Even though Gillem hadn't specifically stated Brian Kolthoff had been murdered, Zane's gut had already filled in the blanks.

Gillem glanced around the elevator like a spy was going to stick their head through the ceiling at any moment. "We have a suspect in custody already. Bloody clothes were found in his cell, stuffed under the mattress. It was like he didn't even try to hide them."

Zane fought to keep his eyebrows from shooting up his

forehead in surprise. "A suspect already? What about a motive? Was it a fight, or was it premeditated?"

"Premeditated. Kolthoff was killed in his cell. We're pulling all the security footage from the last twenty-four hours." Gillem paused in his rundown as the elevator car came to a halt. Silver doors slid open, revealing another hallway colored in various shades of utilitarian beige.

They were in a prison, sure, but would it have killed the designers of the place to add a little color?

Biting the inside of his cheek to stifle a laugh at the inane thought, Zane followed Spencer and the warden. Their footsteps echoed against the shining tile floor as they passed a visitors' waiting area. Zane glanced at the narrow window in the door, but unsurprisingly, the room was empty.

After a couple more turns, they arrived at a short corridor with two doors on either side, as well as a set of double doors at the end.

Gillem paused in front of the first room on their right, trepidation alight in his caramel-colored eyes. "The CSU is working on Kolthoff's cell, and the M.E. had just gotten here right before you two showed up. As you can imagine, it's a little crowded in there right now, which is why we're here instead."

Spencer lifted an eyebrow. "What about the suspect? Where is he being held?"

A weary sigh escaped Gillem. "He's in solitary confinement right now. His name is Maxim Severov, and I've already sent you both his file. It'll be about fifteen or twenty minutes before my guys get him up here, so you'll have the time to do a little research."

Zane's jaw clenched at the mention of the suspect's name. He'd known Brian Kolthoff had loose ties to the Russian mob —at least, he'd *thought* the ties were loose.

He cleared his throat. "Maxim Severov, that's Russian. I assume he has ties to the Russian mob?"

"He does." Donovan shifted his weight from one foot to another as if the topic unnerved him.

It *should* unnerve him. Zane had dealt with the Russians for the majority of his tenure at the CIA, and he was well-versed in its members' volatility.

Fighting back a sudden onslaught of memories, Zane absentmindedly rubbed at the site of an old tattoo on his shoulder. One nautical star on each shoulder symbolized a position of authority in the Russian mob, and one star on each knee was a way to tell the world the wearer would bow to no man. Zane's time undercover had resulted in both sets of tattoos.

Wonder what Maxim Severov would say if he saw them.

Zane fought to blank his thoughts. Any brush with the Russians always came with the baggage of traumatic memories, but this wasn't the time to indulge his PTSD-ridden brain.

Though Zane's gut told him they wouldn't get a single shred of information from a loyal Russian soldier, he joined Spencer in the interview room as Gillem departed. One wall of the space was comprised of metal bars overlayed with mesh to close the gaps but allow the guards a relatively unobstructed view of the room.

Zane leaned against the wall as Spencer took a seat at the stainless-steel table bolted to the floor. There was no way in hell Zane could sit still while he waited to interview a full-fledged Russian mobster.

As the warden had recommended, Zane opened Maxim Severov's file on his phone. "Maxim Severov, age twenty-eight, born in Saint Petersburg, Russia. There isn't much here about his younger years, probably because he spent them in

Russia. He and his mother and two sisters came to the United States when Maxim was eight, but they were deported three years later. He didn't come back to the States again until he was nineteen, but that time, he came here legally."

Spencer drummed his fingers on the table. "How long has he been in Chicago?"

"On and off since he was twenty. He lived in Oregon for about a year, then moved to Illinois. Became a permanent resident at twenty-three, supposedly working at a warehouse unloading consumer goods from cargo ships. He didn't get arrested until a few years ago when he beat some guy half to death on Navy Pier."

A crease formed in the center of Spencer's forehead. "Is that why he's in here?"

"Nope." Zane scrolled down to the charge that had landed Maxim in MCC Chicago. "He's in here for first-degree murder. While he was out on bail for the assault charge, he shot and killed a drug dealer who'd been suspected of colluding with one of the Mexican cartels."

He and Spencer ran through the details of the case, as well as what little was known about Kolthoff's murder. Though the medical examiner required an autopsy to confirm an official cause of death, there were already a few gruesome details of Kolthoff's final moments noted in the file Donovan Gillem had sent to Zane.

First and foremost, Kolthoff's tongue had been excised. Based on the amount of blood in his mouth and on his face, the M.E. concluded he'd still been alive when the cuts were made. The perpetrator had also cut Brian's throat, but the wound appeared too shallow to be a quick death. Instead, Dr. Sabrina Ackerly suspected Brian Kolthoff had died from a combination of two things—blood loss and choking on the blood from his severed tongue. Either way she painted it, the man's last moments alive had been marked by intense suffering.

By the time Zane and Spencer finished reading through the M.E.'s preliminary notes, a trio of guards appeared on the other side of the metal bars. The tallest of the three corrections officers clutched the bicep of a shorter, orange clad man whose wrists and ankles were shackled. Maxim Severov.

After an obnoxious buzz sounded overhead, the door beside the bars clattered open. In silence, Zane and Spencer waited as the CO led Maxim to a chair, fastened his wrists to a ring welded onto the table, and then strode over to stand next to the closed door.

With a prisoner who'd just killed a man hours ago, Zane realized the futility in requesting that the hulking guard meander out of earshot.

Not that we'll have to worry about him overhearing anything. This guy isn't going to talk. There's no way in hell.

Loyalty was the crux of every criminal organization, but the Russians operated on an entirely different level. The Russians didn't request loyalty—they demanded it. And if any man, woman, or child sought to betray them, the snitch not only paid with their life, but they also paid for the misdeed with the lives of their friends and family.

Invisible spider legs skittered down Zane's back. He'd witnessed firsthand how brutally the Russians dealt with traitors. If they'd ever caught him, he wasn't sure he wanted to know what they'd have done.

Zane gave himself a mental shake.

Not the time. You've got a job to do.

"Afternoon, Mr. Severov." He used his own voice to ground himself. "I'm Special Agent Palmer, and this is Supervisory Special Agent Corsaw. We're here to ask you a few questions about the man you killed earlier today."

For how much Maxim reacted, his expression might as well have been carved from marble. For a beat, Zane wasn't even sure he spoke English.

When Maxim didn't respond, Zane continued. "Brian Kolthoff was a powerful man with a lot of powerful allies. You don't seem too concerned that any of them are going to come for you, though, do you?"

Maxim lifted a shoulder in a shrug. "No. I'm not worried." Like his expression, Maxim's voice was devoid of any discernable human emotion.

Spencer leaned back in his chair and crossed his arms. "We were told you didn't ask for a lawyer. You do realize you have the right to legal counsel, whether or not you can afford it?"

Finally, a ghost of a smile crept to Maxim's face. "I don't need a lawyer."

Zane narrowed his eyes at Maxim. It was time to switch tactics. He hoped his abrupt switch to Russian wouldn't give Spencer too much mental whiplash. "Why don't you need a lawyer? And why aren't you worried about Brian Kolthoff's allies seeking revenge? Is it because you didn't kill him?"

Blinking a few times in rapid succession, Maxim shot Zane a puzzled glance. Clearly, the language change had caught him off-guard. "You speak Russian?" he asked in the same language.

Zane fought the urge to roll his eyes. "Yes. My mother was born in Moscow back when Russia was still the USSR."

The statement was a big fat lie. Despite her Nordic ancestry, Anne Palmer was as American as apple pie and baseball. However, Zane hadn't missed the hammer and sickle tattoo peeking out from beneath Maxim's short-sleeved shirt. Perhaps believing he was speaking to a child of the Soviet Union would loosen his tongue.

Maxim suddenly offered Zane a wide, unnerving smile.

"Nice to meet you, brother. But I'm afraid you won't like the answers I have for your questions."

No, I probably won't.

Zane strode over to the table and took a seat next to Spencer. "Try me."

Scooting forward in his chair, Maxim looked to Spencer, then to Zane. When he spoke, he stuck to Russian. "I killed Brian Kolthoff. I didn't like him. The news said he was a rapist, and there was this look in his eyes…like he was a man born without a soul."

Well, Maxim wasn't wrong. "So, you're telling me you killed Brian Kolthoff because you don't like rapists?"

"Yes."

"And you expect me to believe that?"

To Zane's continued surprise, Maxim threw back his head and laughed. "I don't care if you believe it or not. It's the truth. You know what I'm in prison for, right? First-degree murder. I killed that man for the same reason." He offered a noncommittal shrug. "I figured I'll be in here for the rest of my life, so why not do everyone a favor and take out another rapist?"

As much as Zane wanted to follow Maxim's lead and laugh in his face, he refrained. "You cut out his tongue while he was still alive, and I'm assuming you held him down so he could choke on his own blood. Is that just something you happen to do to rapists?"

Another shrug. "They deserve worse, but I do what I can in the time I have. With all due respect, Agents, I don't have more to say on the matter. I'd like to return to my cell." He turned in his chair as much as he was able since he was shackled to the table and nodded to the guard.

Maxim's tactic was a classic method to deflect the real reason for a hired murder. If Maxim provided a suitable motivation, he could cling to the story during grueling interrogations. Admitting to the crime took away a massive chunk of the state's bargaining ability—why would Maxim want to make a deal to give up his associates when he'd already confessed to the murder?

Zane held back a resigned sigh. Donovan Gillem's skepticism had been right on the money. Maxim Severov would never reveal the true reason for brutally murdering Brian Kolthoff, though Zane strongly suspected Maxim had been ordered to carry out the hit so the Russians wouldn't have to worry about Kolthoff ratting them out alongside Stan Young and Joseph Larson.

The world was a better place without Brian Kolthoff, but to Zane's dismay, Kolthoff had been their best chance at locating Joseph. If Larson disappeared into the woodwork now, god only knew whether or not they'd ever find him.

Michelle wouldn't be safe until they located the former agent, and Zane wouldn't stop worrying about Amelia's welfare too until Larson was locked up or dead.

25

Sighing into her coffee, Amelia scrolled absentmindedly through old emails in her inbox. Golden, late-morning sunshine spilled in through the dining room window of her apartment, the glow sliced horizontally by the partially open blinds. In the center of the pool of light, Hup lay on her side, her green eyes drifting closed, popping open, and then shutting again.

Even though Amelia and Zane both had a heap of paperwork to slog through over the weekend, SAC Keaton had been kind enough to allow them to do most of it from home. Amelia couldn't speak for Zane, but to her, the time away from the FBI office was desperately needed.

In fact, she and Zane had been at the apartment so seldom over the last couple weeks that Amelia's fridge and cupboards were sorely understocked. Zane had volunteered to run to the store to pick up food for the next couple days until they had a chance to go grocery shopping for real.

Amelia sipped her coffee, focusing on the warmth of the brew instead of the bitter flavor. She'd been out of coffee creamer for the last few days but hadn't even noticed until this morning. Her and Zane's frequent trips for lattes had spoiled her, leaving her unaccustomed to black coffee.

Oh well. It's caffeine, and it'll get the job done.

Though she'd hoped to wake with an update from the CSU waiting in her email inbox, Amelia had been disappointed to learn that forensics had found next to nothing at the scene of Stan Young's murder. The corrupt senator had been dead for approximately twelve hours when they'd found him, and he'd suffered numerous injuries before he was killed by a gunshot to the back of the head.

In layman's terms, he'd been tortured. Several of his fingers had been cut off, his knee was a ruined mess, he'd taken a gunshot to the arm from a nine-millimeter, he'd suffered a dislocated shoulder and broken jaw, and he'd been stabbed in the gut and damn near eviscerated. The CSU had recovered the bullets from Young's arm and head, but so far, ballistics wasn't a match to any firearms or crimes on record.

If Stan Young's mutilated corpse wasn't enough, the crime scene techs had also located the blood of three additional people on the property.

Not just blood. They found brain matter on the grass in the backyard.

Amelia's current theory was that the blood belonged to whatever security personnel Stan had brought with him to Wisconsin. Their bodies hadn't yet been found, but there *was* a massive lake right behind the house. The lead crime scene investigator had advised Amelia they'd be calling in divers to search for the missing corpses. Since the lake was relatively shallow, there was hope the search would be quick.

Of course, her first question was why the killer—or killers, potentially—would have left Young's body on display but go through the trouble to hide the corpses of anyone else who'd been on the property.

Was the person who'd tortured and killed Stan even

responsible for the three additional murders? Or had Stan killed them?

Glancing back to her inbox, Amelia shook off the questions. All she was accomplishing right now was mentally running in circles. When Zane got home, they could bounce theories off one another while they dealt with the tedium of paperwork. Currently, Amelia's favored theory was that word of Brian Kolthoff's betrayal had made its way to Joseph Larson, and Larson had gone after Stan Young to preemptively shut him up.

Which brought her to Brian Kolthoff's murder.

With a groan, Amelia tilted her head back until she was staring at the ceiling. Zane had told her all about his interview with Maxim Severov, including his speculation about Maxim's standing in the Russian mob. Unlike Brian Kolthoff, Maxim's loyalty was unquestionable.

Amelia turned to Hup to find the cat's lazy gaze fixed on her. "What do we do, Hup? Do we charge Maxim Severov, or do we petition to add him to the pool of candidates for a Nobel Peace Prize?"

The calico yawned, and Amelia followed suit.

"Stop that. You know it's contagious. I'm sitting at the dining table, so I don't fall asleep again, but you're over there rubbing it in. Must be nice to be a pampered house cat."

As if in agreement, Hup closed her eyes. Though Amelia wanted nothing more than to mimic her lazy house cat and crawl into bed, she slugged down a few gulps of coffee. Just as she returned the mug to the table, her laptop *dinged* to advise her she'd received a new email.

Hopeful the notification was a breakthrough from forensics, Amelia quickly scrolled to the newest message. As she noted the sender's identity—or lack thereof, since she'd never seen the username before in her life—her optimism faded. The username was a nonsensical jumble of letters and numbers, and the subject was clickbait if she'd ever witnessed it.

Read this NOW. If you don't, you will never see Joanna alive again.

Joanna? Her beloved sister-in-law?

Dread surged through Amelia as the blinking cursor hovered over the message icon.

This was no scam. But would it unleash holy hell on her work computer? Perhaps it was a decoy email to gain access to the FBI through the back door.

The more she stared at the subject line, the more threatening the statement became.

If you don't, you will never see Joanna alive again.

Amelia grabbed her phone and dialed the Chicago Field Office's IT department. After forwarding them the email, they confirmed it was legit…and time sensitive.

The tech department declaring the email "safe" didn't mean it wasn't dangerous in other ways.

Joseph Larson was behind this. That much was certain.

She clicked on the approved email and waited. As the screen loaded, time slowed to a crawl. There was no text in the body of the email, only a video. The still of the thumbnail was grainy and a little dim, but Amelia would recognize that woman anywhere.

"Joanna." She croaked the statement. The voice didn't even sound like hers.

Over the past few months, Amelia hadn't spent nearly as much time with her sister-in-law as she'd have liked. As much as she wanted to facilitate get-togethers so Zane could get to know her little family better, their jobs had been especially demanding lately. Amelia hadn't dwelled on the lack of family time—she'd been certain Joanna would still be there when Amelia and Zane caught a lull between cases.

She'd be there, wouldn't she?

Pain lanced through Amelia's chest, and she could have sworn the sensation was her heart breaking into tiny pieces.

Pulling her gaze away from the image of Joanna, Amelia realized with a start that she'd been holding her breath. She inhaled deeply, squeezed her eyes closed, and rubbed the bridge of her nose. Good lord, she hadn't even started the video, and she was already losing it.

Knock that shit off, Storm. Joanna is in trouble and needs your help. Pull it together so you can deliver an ass-kicking to the person responsible. Larson.

The mental pep talk gave her a sense of renewed determination. Leaning closer to the laptop, she maximized the video and pressed play.

Joanna's tear-streaked face immediately came into view. The background was a plain, beige wall, and there were no windows visible. No décor, nothing to indicate where the video had been filmed.

Amelia scrutinized Joanna's face next, and aside from a red mark on her cheek, she appeared physically unharmed. The camera panned out to reveal Joanna's wrists bound tightly to the arms of a wooden chair. Peeking out from under one rolled up sleeve was her sister-in-law's tiger lily tattoo that matched Amelia's.

Glancing to a point behind the camera, Joanna licked her lips. Strands of her dark auburn hair were matted to her pale cheeks with tears, terror plainly visible in her eyes.

"A-Amelia, it's me. Joanna." She shot another tentative look to whoever was holding the camera. *"I'm going to give you a location, and I need you to come to it at one p.m. today. You need to come alone. If..."* Her voice cracked, but she swallowed and lifted her chin. *"If you try coming here with anyone else, I will be k-killed."*

Joanna's words were wooden, almost like she was a kid

being forced to read an unfamiliar passage in front of the entire class. Whoever was behind the camera had fed her the lines.

You know who's behind that damn camera. Joseph Larson. He's the only one who's still alive to retaliate.

The conclusion wasn't necessarily correct, but there was certainly a measure of truth to it.

However, Joanna's captor could be a goon hired by Cynthia Young. What if Stan's will had stiffed his widow, and she was pissed that the entire Young empire was being passed down to Josh? It wouldn't be a stretch to think she'd lash out at the person she felt was responsible.

Why Amelia, though? Why not Spencer, Zane, SAC Keaton, Simone Julliard…the list went on.

In her gut, Amelia already knew who'd filmed Joanna's plea.

As Joanna rattled off a series of coordinates, Amelia typed the numbers into a notepad. For good measure, she listened to her sister-in-law give the location two more times.

"Please, Amelia. Help me." Joanna's voice had become a squeak, and Amelia got the distinct impression Joanna hadn't wanted to beg for help. Though she wasn't law enforcement and had no military experience, Joanna was still a proud, strong woman. Joseph had *forced* her to beg and plead.

Because he also had her children?

The video suddenly cut out, and an onslaught of white-hot rage seared through every fiber of Amelia's being like molten rock.

Was Joseph holding her niece and nephew too? Was that why Joanna was begging? Was he using them to force Joanna to comply? Amelia needed to make some phone calls to see if she could find the kids.

Part of her wanted to take off for the location right now.

She could fish out the biggest damn firearm she owned, throw on some Kevlar, and hurry out to where Joseph was waiting with her kidnapped sister-in-law. The video hadn't alluded to what Joseph expected to gain, but Amelia already knew.

Joseph wanted Amelia. More than likely, he intended for Amelia to trade herself for Joanna. Or maybe he just wanted Amelia at the location so he could kill them both.

And the kids?

Closing her eyes, Amelia forced herself to take a few deep breaths to slow the rage and concern eating her alive. She needed to think.

If Amelia showed up early, she could take Joseph by surprise…

As she punched the coordinates into an online mapping service, her stomach clenched. The location was in the middle of rural Illinois, and if she wanted to arrive by one p.m., she had to leave within the next forty-five minutes.

Dragging in a deep breath, Amelia gave herself a mental shake. What the hell was she thinking? Was she *really* about to heed Joseph's warning that she come alone? Had she really been about to go full cowboy and drive down to southern Illinois by herself, without warning SAC Keaton, without warning *Zane*?

"Dammit, Amelia. Get ahold of yourself. Stop acting like you're some newly enlisted eighteen-year-old trying to prove herself to her buddies. You're a thirty-year-old woman, and you're an FBI agent, for god's sake."

She had no earthly idea how her friends and colleagues would circumvent Joseph's order that she come to the rural location alone, but she was certain of one thing.

There was no way she'd heed Joseph's request. Doing so was a death warrant not just for her but for Joanna and possibly the kids. Joseph wouldn't let Joanna live after she'd heard his voice and possibly even seen his face.

The metallic *click-clack* of the deadbolt ripped her from the horror of her situation.

Zane was home, and it was time for Amelia to act.

26

The old floorboards of the farmhouse creaked and groaned beneath Joseph Larson's feet as he paced back and forth. Early afternoon sunlight flooded through the picture window at his side, casting a shadowy version of himself along the dining table and chairs.

Five chairs, not the usual six. He'd dragged the sixth chair into the living room and had bound Joanna Storm's wrists and ankles to it before slapping her across the face to wake her. Christ, the woman was almost as stubborn as her sister-in-law. No wonder she and Amelia got along so well.

A tendril of rage threatened to unfurl in Joseph's chest, but he wouldn't allow it. Not right now. He needed to keep a clear head in case Amelia got the bright idea to send the location to the county sheriff's department. Amelia ought to realize by now that Joseph wasn't playing a game with her, and that he *would* kill her precious sister-in-law if he so much as thought he saw a cop car closing in.

She won't do it. She won't risk Joanna's life by calling in the sheriff's department.

If she intended to break Joseph's rule about coming alone,

she'd bring the FBI tactical team with her. Not a handful of sheriff's deputies.

Part of him wished she would. He had a high-powered rifle stashed in the kitchen, and from his vantage point on top of a gentle hill, he'd be able to pick plenty of them off before they even got close.

That was his plan...to take as many people down as he could before any of them could take him out. He was trapped, he knew. He had no means of escaping the country, and he refused to spend the rest of his life in prison.

No way.

Pausing mid-step, Joseph shot a glare at his captive. Through the arched doorway of the dining area, the majority of the living room was visible, including where he'd situated Joanna beneath a bare wall. After recording the video for Amelia, he'd duct-taped Joanna's mouth so he wouldn't have to listen to her either plead or threaten him.

To his surprise and amusement, Joanna's eyes narrowed slightly before she looked away.

I'll enjoy killing you in front of your sister-in-law. Too bad the bitch's brats were away when I paid my visit. What I couldn't get Amelia to do if she thought the two ankle-biters' lives were on the line.

If he had more time, he'd do more than just kill Joanna. But in spite of his insistence Amelia come alone, he'd be prepared for a worst-case scenario. As much as he wanted to watch Amelia suffer, he wanted her dead even more.

The mental imagery of Amelia's expression when he put a bullet through Joanna's head brought an involuntary smile to Joseph's face. He'd make her suffer before he killed her, and he'd savor every sweet second of her misery.

It was what she deserved. He'd already heard that Brian Kolthoff and Stan Young were dead on the police scanner. By now, Cynthia had undoubtedly rolled over on her husband.

Joseph wasn't sure where Stan's kid, Josh, played into their collective downfall, but he wouldn't be surprised if Josh was celebrating by rolling around in a pile of cash.

With Stan dead, the entire multibillion-dollar Young empire would probably go to his son. Since Stan seemed to barely tolerate his wife, Cynthia would likely receive a relative pittance. Stan had always mused that it'd be enough to keep her out of Josh's hair.

What about Mae Young? Aside from the initial article that broke about Gianna Passarelli, there'd been little mention of Mae in the news. More than likely, she was in the care of Josh or another relative. Joseph suspected Cynthia wouldn't want her—provided, of course, Cynthia was even in a position to abandon the girl. Maybe Mae's life would be better off far away from the twisted Young dynasty.

Mae…the physical manifestation of every event that had led to Stan's downfall. All Stan's effort, all the money he'd thrown to bribe cops, all the people Joseph had killed to cover up Gianna Passarelli's kidnapping, it was all for naught.

Joseph should have cut his losses ages ago and left Chicago, but he couldn't have predicted a wild card like Amelia Storm. Her desire to unearth the truth about her brother's murder had spiraled out of control in record time.

There was no way Joseph was leaving this world without making sure Amelia paid first. She wouldn't just pay with her own blood, either. First, he'd take away something she loved.

GRAVEL CRUNCHED beneath Amelia's boots as she stepped out of the car. The midday sun beat down on the rural Illinois landscape, the warmth of the day melting any remaining snow. Though she wished she could enjoy the warmer temperature and the sensation that spring was just on the horizon, there was nothing joyous about this afternoon. Once upon a time, the farmhouse might have hosted family get-togethers bursting with raucous laughter, but those days were long gone.

As she peered up at the single-story farmhouse, her stomach attempted to tie itself in knots. The gold feather pendant tucked beneath her scarf doubled as a microphone that would relay audio back to where Amelia's colleagues waited at a safe distance.

Or so she'd hoped. By now, she was all but certain the signal had been jammed. Joseph was a piece of shit, but he wasn't stupid. He'd realize she would come prepared with some form of communication to the outside world, and he'd make damn sure she couldn't utilize it.

A potent cocktail of hatred and anger coursed through her veins.

Time to do this.

Service weapon in hand, she forced one foot in front of the other. Her backup plan rested in the pocket of her canvas jacket—a digital voice recorder. She'd pressed play before even getting out of the car, and she knew from the steep price tag that the device would capture crystal clear audio even through the fabric of her coat.

However, the recorder had one major pitfall...it wasn't connected to the internet, nor was anyone listening on the other end. Amelia had to make it out alive if she wanted it to be of any use. If she died inside, Joseph would no doubt search her body and find the device. Odds were, he'd have plenty of time to break the thing before backup arrived.

As she made her way up the slight incline toward the covered porch, she understood why Joseph had chosen the location. Even with a thicket of trees just past the backyard, the hill provided a vantage point for miles in each direction.

If Amelia's fellow agents had been stupid enough to tail her closely, Joseph would have spotted them with ease.

Fortunately, the FBI's vast resources had afforded them a comprehensive satellite view of the house and the land surrounding it. Their diligence left Amelia's backup farther away than she'd have liked, but she was grateful to know she wasn't alone.

Zane, Spencer, and a couple tactical agents would soon begin creeping toward the house. By their best estimate, they'd reach the doors approximately fifteen minutes after Amelia went inside.

Amelia's job? Well, it seemed simple. She had to keep Joseph Larson distracted long enough for the team to get to the house.

Easier said than done.

If Amelia was the only one here—if Joanna was safe at home—then Amelia was confident she'd be able to stall Joseph long enough for the takedown. But with Joanna's life at stake, things were different.

Provided Joanna wasn't already dead.

An icy knife stabbed Amelia. No, she couldn't think like that. Joanna was here because of Amelia, and Amelia would get her away from this godforsaken place, even if she died in the process.

Joanna was a kind soul, a fantastic mother who'd raised her two children alone after Trevor's death, and someone who had never hurt another living thing. Even though Joanna hated spiders, she'd recruit one of her kids to scoop up the wayward arachnids and release them outside. She even refused to kill house flies.

Thoughts of her tenderhearted sister-in-law filled Amelia with renewed purpose. Hailey and Nolan, Amelia's niece and nephew, had already lost their father. They couldn't lose their mother, not while Amelia was still breathing.

Thank god Amelia had confirmed the children were safe. It was a blessing they'd been at a neighbor's house when Joseph had captured Joanna. Their lives had been warped enough without witnessing their mother being kidnapped.

Straining to make out any movement through the curtains that shadowed the front windows of the house, Amelia strode toward the porch. Though she was walking at a normal pace, her movements seemed sluggish, like she was in the middle of navigating an awful dream and not reality.

She and the others had planned as well as they could, but Amelia was certain they hadn't had enough time to cover every possibility. Plus, Joseph had been an FBI agent for most of his adult life. He knew how they operated.

So, we'll have to operate differently.

Amelia squared her shoulders as she reached the heavy wooden door. In the shade of the porch, a chill settled in her skin, but the goose bumps were driven away by adrenaline. Her first inclination was to try to shove open the front door so she could barge in to confront Joseph.

She quickly dismissed the idea. Joseph was no doubt jumpy, and he'd shoot first and ask questions later if she took him by surprise. Tightening her grasp on the Glock nine-mil, Amelia lifted her other hand and pounded against the door with the side of a closed fist.

Several seconds stretched into a small eternity as Amelia waited for an answer, a multitude of disastrous scenarios racing through her mind's eye. She pictured Joseph and Joanna both dead as the result of a struggle, or even a murder-suicide. Maybe Joseph had only wanted Amelia to come here so she could witness firsthand what he'd done to her sister-in-law.

"It's unlocked."

The muffled words rushed up to greet Amelia, shattering

the unpleasant reverie and depositing her in a marginally less unpleasant reality.

If there had been any doubt in her mind about who had lured her here today, it was squashed the instant he spoke. She'd hoped never to hear Joseph Larson's voice again unless he was being cross-examined at his own trial, but here she was.

In the middle of nowhere, her backup too many minutes away, armed with nothing more than her service weapon and a backup twenty-two around her ankle.

Lifting her chin, Amelia turned the door handle and stepped inside.

27

As Amelia stepped past an undecorated foyer, details of the house came into focus as her eyes adjusted to the lower light. With her glare fixed down the sight of her service weapon, she stepped through a wide doorway into a living room. Drawn curtains blocked out some of the daylight, but the sun's rays pierced through a slight gap in the fabric. A sectional couch faced a fireplace, above which was a television mounted to the wall.

In the reflection of the television, Amelia spotted movement—one person was seated, and another stood at their side.

Blood thundering in her ears like the rapid beat of a war drum, she whipped her aim around to the far end of the room.

Not fast enough. She could've been The Flash, and she wouldn't have been fast enough.

With the barrel of his own handgun jammed into Joanna's temple, Joseph ducked down behind her. Poor Joanna. Amelia's sister-in-law looked petrified but otherwise uninjured. Thank god. If Joseph harmed one hair on her head, she would...

She would what?

Joseph was versed in Amelia's history as a sniper in the military, and she could tell he wasn't willing to take any chances. She'd told him at least once that sniper school hadn't taught her to make distance shots with a Glock, but if he'd remained out in the open, she'd have been tempted to try.

Even then, she wasn't stupid. She wouldn't risk Joanna's life by crossing her fingers and hoping her aim was accurate enough to land a perfect shot between Joseph Larson's eyes.

"Drop your weapon, Storm." Joseph's command was cold and level, but the way he spoke from between clenched teeth told Amelia he was fighting anger.

High emotion could be good for her, could lead Joseph to make a mistake she desperately needed. On the other hand, Joseph's rage also had the potential to render him unpredictable.

Swallowing the urge to tell Joseph to go to hell, Amelia gritted her teeth and slowly lowered the Glock to the wooden floor.

"Now, kick it over here. Hands where I can see them." Inch by inch, Joseph rose to his full height behind Amelia's sister-in-law.

Nausea, the result of unfettered ire and worry for Joanna, threatened the back of Amelia's throat, but she complied. Her trusty Glock skittered along the floorboards after she sent it flying with a small kick. For a reason she didn't understand, she was almost compelled to apologize to the handgun. Maybe she was losing her mind.

Amelia held both hands in the air and took a tentative step forward. "What do you want, Joseph?"

Sighing, he knelt to scoop up her service weapon. After

checking it was loaded, he tucked the Glock behind his back and returned his icy blue gaze to Amelia. "I think you've probably figured it out by now. I didn't see the need to spell it out in the video I sent." An unnerving smile twisted at his lips. "I want *you*."

Amelia took another step forward, making sure to keep the movement as subtle as possible. "If it's me you want, then I'm right here. Joanna doesn't have anything to do with this. Let her go, and I'm all yours." Her only hope was to close the distance between her and Joseph so she'd have an opportunity to make a grab for his weapon. That would still leave him with her Glock...

Joseph's perverse smile didn't even falter. "No."

The single syllable slammed into Amelia's chest with the force of a Mack truck. "N-no?" She hated the stammer in her voice, but at the same time, she didn't care if she seemed desperate. With Joanna's life at stake, she *was* desperate. "You said...this wasn't part of it. You were supposed to let her go!"

Rolling his eyes, Joseph brushed a piece of matted hair away from Joanna's tear-streaked cheek. "I didn't say anything, and you know that. All I did was send you a little video of Joanna, and you came running like you thought I was willing to make you a deal. News flash...there is no deal!"

As Joseph pressed the barrel of his handgun harder into Joanna's temple, Amelia swore she stopped breathing. Though Joanna remained perfectly still, a single tear traced a path down her cheek, and her expression morphed into a mask of despair. The sight of her beloved sister-in-law's life threatened by this bastard broke Amelia's heart and stoked her fury all at once.

This wasn't how the exchange was supposed to go. Amelia was supposed to come into the house, free Joanna to get her away from this damn place, and then buy time by indulging whatever bullshit Joseph wanted to discuss.

It's a bump in the road. That's all it is. Think, Amelia. You have to buy time, and you can't let him keep that weapon aimed at Joanna.

Amelia needed to take the heat. She needed Joseph's wrath directed at *her*, not Joanna.

She inched forward again, her gaze locked on Joseph's, her hands still in the air in front of her. "What is this even about anymore, huh? Is it about me, and…and *you*?" She spat the word *you* like it was a foul taste on her tongue. "Or maybe about the lack of me and you, is that it?"

Though slight, Joseph's eyes narrowed. "You just had to keep sticking your nose where it didn't belong. You went too far, and I think you know that."

"*I* went too far? Are you serious?" She let a derisive laugh slip from her lips, confident it would get under Joseph's skin. "*You're* the one who kidnapped Michelle Timmer! You're the one who raped her over and over again while your pal Brian Kolthoff held her captive on his fucking mega yacht!"

Joseph's upper lip peeled back in a snarl. Amelia was playing a dangerous game. At any moment, Joseph could snap and kill Joanna as punishment for Amelia's transgressions, but she was out of options.

"You don't know the first thing about Michelle Timmer. She practically begged for it every time I showed up. She'd always tell me how scared she was of Brian, and she'd plead with me to protect her from the boogeyman." His eyes glittered like glaciers, but to Amelia's tentative relief, his entire focus was on her. The barrel of the handgun had even begun to drift away from Joanna's temple ever so slightly.

Amelia wanted nothing more than to close the ten feet between them, wrap her hands around his throat, and smash his head into the drywall over and over until he lost consciousness. Maybe after she threw Joseph behind bars, Maxim Severov would butcher him just like he'd done to Brian Kolthoff.

She boxed up the urge and pushed it to the back of her mind. If she got herself killed now, Joanna would be dead. Joseph had given her an opening, and she had to take it.

"You're telling me Michelle begged for it, huh? Just like I did when you tried to blackmail me to fuck you after I killed Alton Dalessio?" Amelia was all in, and there was no turning back now. She inched forward without dropping her intense stare. "Because, let me tell you something, Joseph. There's nothing on this planet I'd like *less* than to sleep with you. I'd rather cut off my own hand and strangle myself with it until I die!"

His jaw ticked, his face a mask of fury.

Amelia didn't give him time to reply. "You think you're something special, don't you? You think you're god's gift to women and that, if they don't want you, then there must be something wrong with *them*. You thought your position as a special agent meant you were a cut above all those other creeps and perverts out there, but you're not! All the power, all the money you had, it's gone! You can kill me if you want, but it won't change anything. You'll still be the same pathetic prick who has to force himself on women to validate his own existence. Maybe you're a hero in your own story, but you're a disease in everyone else's!"

"Shut up!" His movements were a blur as he swung the handgun and took aim at Amelia. At the same time, he took three swift steps toward her, covering almost all the distance that remained.

Amelia's celebration of her success at taking the heat away from Joanna was short-lived. Now, she stared down the barrel of a semi-automatic handgun wielded by a man who wanted nothing more than to watch her suffer.

Don't dwell on it. He's close. This might be the only opportunity you get. He screwed up, so capitalize on it.

Opening his mouth to speak, Joseph leveled the gun with her forehead.

Amelia didn't give him time to form the first word of whatever diatribe was rattling around in his head. Joseph was a military combat veteran, taller than Amelia, and built like a brick shithouse, but Amelia still had one advantage —speed.

Side-stepping the handgun, she slammed the heel of her hand into his nose with as much power as she could manage. His head snapped backward, and his grasp on the handgun faltered for just a split second.

The split-second was all Amelia needed.

Clamping both hands down on his wrist, she kept ahold of him as she ducked beneath his arm. A raucous *crack* split the air as Joseph squeezed the trigger, but Amelia didn't even pause. Using the base of Joseph's palm as leverage, along with her new angle at his side, she twisted his wrist until the sickening crack of cartilage vibrated beneath her fingers.

Joseph grunted in pain as his handgun clattered to the floor. In the same breath, Amelia kicked the thing across the room. Joseph still had her service weapon. Would her plan work?

So much adrenaline surged through Amelia's veins that she couldn't honestly tell if Joseph's desperate shot had hit her. She hadn't spotted any blood when she'd glanced down at the fallen handgun, but she tried not to put too much stock in the fleeting glimpse.

This battle was far from won.

Like a coiled snake, Joseph's uninjured arm shot out toward Amelia. Balancing on the balls of her feet, she tried to pivot away from the sudden movement, but he was too fast. Faster than she'd anticipated.

His hand closed around her throat, his fingers digging into the sensitive skin until Amelia worried he might draw blood. Just as Amelia began to claw at the exposed skin of his forearm, he slammed her back into the drywall like she was nothing more than a ragdoll.

All the breath exploded from Amelia's lungs in a *whoosh*, and bright splotches of light danced in her eyes as her head collided with the wall. Still, Joseph's grasp didn't relent. Blood seeped from his busted nose down to his lips, lending him the appearance of a flesh-eating madman.

Amelia tried to drag in a breath of precious air, but all she got was a strangled gagging noise. Squeezing her eyes closed, she sank her nails into Joseph's flesh as deep as they would go. God, she wished she'd had the time for Joanna to give her a manicure earlier in the week. Acrylic nails didn't seem conducive to an FBI agent's day-to-day activities at first, but in a pinch, they could make a huge difference in self-defense.

No matter how hard Amelia tried, she couldn't choke down even a wisp of air. Joseph was speaking, but through the thunder of her pulse, she couldn't make out a single word. Truthfully, she didn't care. Her lungs were on fire, and her limbs felt as if they'd been weighed down with lead.

The outside world was slipping away.

It can't. You can't let it end like this. Fight, dammit!

A new wave of adrenaline, Amelia's last gasp of energy, washed over her in a blinding wave. Ignoring the darkness threatening the edges of her vision, she swung at Joseph's face. Her nails gouged his cheek, but he seemed to hardly notice.

"That's right, babe," he purred, his nostrils flaring. He was enjoying the fight. "Keep your eyes open so I can watch the light go out."

Eyes.

The single word echoed through Amelia's head. Drawing

on her remaining energy reserves, she leaned into Joseph's strangling grip. Her esophagus burned almost as badly as her oxygen-deprived lungs, but she used the pain to keep her focused, to keep her brain from whisking her off to the unconscious world.

Curling her index and middle finger, she jammed both digits into the soft warmth of Joseph's eye socket. As her fingertips caressed the stringy muscles and tendons behind his eye, she only pushed harder.

Joseph's grip on her throat loosened as he howled in pain. Sensing the fleeting moment of opportunity was about to fizzle out of existence, Amelia tucked the fingers of her other hand beneath his palm. As she sucked in a desperate gasp, she coughed and sputtered.

The black spots cleared from her vision, and the pain in her lungs began to recede. The relief wasn't enough to fool her into complacency, but the sensation allowed her to regain her wits.

Spitting out a series of four-letter words, Joseph wrenched her hand away from his face. Amelia's body moved of its own accord as she swiftly moved toward him. Before he could react, she rammed her knee into his balls.

To her dismay, she was still weakened from the near-strangulation, and the blow didn't elicit the crippling response for which she'd hoped. Cursing, Joseph shoved Amelia backward.

Her body met the wall with enough force to rattle a nearby bookshelf, once again forcefully expelling the air from Amelia's lungs. She'd spent the remainder of her energy on her attempt to dig out his eye, and suddenly, her rubbery legs weren't enough to support her weight.

Another coughing fit wracked her bruised body as she slumped to the floor, and she half-expected Joseph to start pummeling her with his fists. In fact, she went as far as to brace herself for the blows.

None came.

"Look at me, you stupid bitch!"

His shout pushed through the haze threatening to obscure her normally clear thoughts. Blinking repeatedly, Amelia pitched forward and tucked her legs beneath her body as if she was preparing to stand.

Joseph read her intentions. "Oh, no. You stay right where you are."

When she finally dared to look up, Amelia refused to show fear as she stared straight into the barrel of her own service weapon. So much could go wrong right now.

"Yeah, I get it." With one hand clamped over his wounded eye, Joseph glared down at her with the other. "I get what you did. It was a good effort, you know that? Piss me off, so I get close to you. It was smart. Well-executed." He paused to cluck his tongue. "But it wasn't enough. You really thought you could overpower me? Thought you'd be able to take me down? Is that it?"

Amelia channeled all her hate, all her anger, all her disgust into her stare. If a dirty look could kill, she was certain Joseph would have been dead ten times over.

He let out a derisive chuckle. "Yeah, that's what you thought. Cute, Amelia. Really cute. Christ, you're just like your brother, you know that?"

She wanted to ask him what in the hell he was talking about or to demand he shut the hell up and kill her so she didn't have to listen to his monologue, but her voice failed her.

A bloody smile slithered to his face. "You don't know, do you? You know by now that Stan hired some Leóne dipshits to kidnap Gianna Passarelli, but you don't know what happened after that, do you? After your brother started to stick his nose in that old case, for god only knew what reasons. Morbid curiosity, maybe. Or maybe he just had the same stupid sense of justice that you do, I'm not sure."

Amelia tried to speak, and though all she wanted to spit out was a bitter *"fuck you,"* she only coughed instead.

Joseph lifted a shoulder noncommittally, but the sadistic glint in his eyes told Amelia he was enjoying every second of his victory. "He got a little too close to the truth, thanks to some informant of his. I still don't know who the hell that was, but after I shot Trevor, they didn't bother with any follow-up. I guess they weren't that committed to putting Stan away, after all."

After he shot Trevor?

Fury like she'd never known twisted inside Amelia, consuming every fiber of her being like it was a black hole. At the same time, a bizarre sense of calm, a feeling of closure, tempered the anger.

For years, she'd been unsure who'd orchestrated her brother's murder, but now she knew. Now *Joanna* knew.

Part of Amelia had suspected Joseph's involvement for weeks, maybe even months.

If he'd intended to surprise her, he'd failed. Nothing about Joseph Larson could surprise her anymore.

Rather than give in to the animalistic urge for violence or permit Joseph to witness a display of weakness, Amelia lifted her chin in defiance.

She had nothing more to say to this man. This twisted son of a bitch who'd wrought so much misery on her and her family.

His mouth curved into a derisive sneer, and he leveled the Glock with Amelia's head.

He squeezed the trigger...*click*. Incredulous, he squeezed again...*click*.

Pulling the hidden twenty-two from her ankle, Amelia

smiled as she leveled the sites over his stone-cold heart. "I beat you."

Amelia had known from the get-go that he would take her service weapon—she'd prepared for it, turning that knowledge into an integral part of her plan. Knowing that she'd be disarmed upon entering the house, she'd loaded her service weapon with blanks. After Joseph took the Glock, she'd had a singular goal...disarm the bastard.

The decision had been a gamble because, even a blank could maim or mortally wound, but the risk had paid off.

From her position on the floor, Amelia aimed the smaller handgun up and eased her finger back on the trigger.

By the time she fired, Joseph had started to turn toward his fallen weapon, but the handgun was at least fifteen feet away at the edge of the sectional.

He didn't make it past the second step.

Bam-bam-bam.

Three rapid shots punched into Joseph's side, and red blossomed over his white dress shirt where the bullets ripped through muscle, organs, and bone.

He collapsed into a heap, a puddle of crimson oozing out from beneath his still form.

Still unsure if she possessed the strength or balance to walk, Amelia scooted over to Joseph's body. She narrowly avoided the growing pool of blood as she pressed her fingers to his throat.

Holding her breath, she waited in uneasy silence until her greatest hope was confirmed.

No pulse.

Amelia smiled at Joanna as she moved to free her from her bindings. To Amelia's amazement, Joanna smiled back.

"He better be dead, or I'll kill him myself." Joanna's voice only trembled a little.

When she was free, Amelia pulled her sister-in-law into her arms, holding her close. "He's dead."

Amelia glanced back at the body of the man who'd done such harm to others. His blood was solid proof of Amelia Storm's revenge...for her brother and herself.

28

W ith one last wave to where Journey Russo and Michelle Timmer filed into line at the airport's security checkpoint, Amelia linked her arm with Zane's as they started off in the direction of the parking garage. Though Amelia was a bit saddened to see Journey and Michelle go, she was glad the two women were headed back to Journey's home in Las Vegas.

As strong as Michelle had been immediately after her escape, the young woman would need a great amount of time to truly recover from her brutal abduction. Amelia hope that being with her sister would help with that process.

Before they left, Journey and Michelle had presented Amelia and the team with the best present in the entire world...a state-of-the-art coffeepot for the breakroom. It was so pretty, Amelia grew misty just looking at it. It brewed a beautiful cup of coffee and even had an attachment that made shots of expresso.

Amelia was truly in love.

Four weeks had passed since Amelia killed Joseph Larson, allowing plenty of time for the FBI to wrap up the investigation into Joseph, Brian, and Stan. All three men were dead, as were the wealth of secrets they'd no doubt possessed, but Amelia would rather dig through the belongings left behind by dead men than deal with any of those three pricks in person.

Already, the Bureau had taken in the United States ambassador to Denmark, as well as some European prince Amelia had never heard of before. Josh Young had publicly denounced his father, though out of concern for his safety, he'd not admitted to his role in Stan's downfall.

Rather than the usual platitudes offered by those in Josh's position, Josh had turned his words into action. He'd donated a sizable chunk of money to the Chicago Police Department to help them work through a backlog of untested rape kits. In addition to the CPD, Josh had given funding to nonprofits who combatted human trafficking, both locally and nationally.

Amelia wasn't sure if *proud* was the right word to describe how she felt when she thought of Josh, but it was close.

She'd been less optimistic about Mae Young's future, certain the poor girl was destined for a shocking lifestyle change in the foster care system. Her concerns hadn't lasted long. Mae had only been with her foster parents for a week when a relative had stepped forward to obtain emergency foster parent privileges.

To Amelia's continued surprise, she'd soon learned Mae's new foster parents were none other than Alex Passarelli and his soon-to-be wife, Liliana D'Amato. The couple had already filed papers to legally adopt the young girl.

Rumors and conspiracy theories swirled in the sludgy depths of the internet about Mae's true parentage, but no one in Chicago was stupid enough to willingly put themselves on Alex's bad side.

"So," Zane prodded Amelia's upper arm with an elbow, "what do you want to do for the rest of the afternoon?"

She pulled herself away from memory lane and turned to flash him a smile. "I'm not sure. I'm not really used to having free time." An idea flashed in her mind, and she took hold of Zane's arm. "Oh, I know! You got Hup that harness, right? Let's see if we can take her for a walk."

The corners of Zane's gray eyes creased as he laughed. "All right. All right, I like this idea. Do you think we could take her to a café somewhere near your place? Kind of like how dog people take their pups with them to get coffee?"

As Amelia pictured her surly cat sitting beside them at a table outside a quaint little café, she joined in Zane's laughter.

For the rest of their walk back to Zane's Acura, he and Amelia brainstormed a few more realistic ways to spend their rare day away from the FBI office. Rather than drag Hup around the block, they decided to go for a walk without the cat, order takeout, and start watching a new show Dean Steelman had recommended.

Over the past few weeks, Amelia and Zane had gotten together for dinner with Dean, Sherry, and Sherry's husband, Teddy. Sherry and Teddy were gracious dinner hosts, and they both loved to entertain. Apparently, they'd just lacked the guests until recently.

Once, Amelia had even convinced Joanna to accompany them, and another time, they'd been joined by Michelle and Journey. After everything Michelle had endured, Amelia was comforted by the sight of her laughing and joking with Dean and Sherry. She was sure Michelle's road had plenty of bumps ahead, but her being able to enjoy a genuine moment with friends was encouraging.

After a painstaking trip out of O'Hare's perpetually disgusting traffic, Amelia and Zane returned to her apartment. Neither of them had made an official announcement, but Amelia figured Zane might as well move in with her considering how often he was here. She'd already given him the spare key, and any time he was gone, the place felt oddly lonely.

Amelia had barely locked the deadbolt when Zane paused at the edge of the foyer to dig his buzzing phone from his back pocket. His gaze flicked up to Amelia's as a crease formed between his eyebrows.

Her good spirits sank as she watched their plans for the day fly out the window. She knew that look.

As if he could read her mind, Zane sighed. "It's work."

Squeezing past him to make her way to the kitchen, Amelia rubbed his shoulder. "I'm shocked."

Chuckling, he swiped the screen and raised the phone to his ear. "Palmer."

His expression changed little as a tinny voice responded.

"And?" He glanced toward Amelia and mouthed *Spencer*.

This time, when Spencer responded, Zane frowned. "Where? All right. Yeah, we'll be there soon."

Dammit.

Amelia kept the protest to herself as Zane bade Spencer farewell and disconnected the call. "What is it? I take it we've got another case?"

Zane pocketed his phone and leaned forward to press his lips to her forehead. "Yeah. Actually, Dean and Sherry need our help."

The End
To be continued...

Thank you for reading.
All of the Amelia Storm Series books can be found on Amazon.

ACKNOWLEDGMENTS

How does one properly thank everyone involved in taking a dream and making it a reality? Here goes.

In addition to our families, whose unending support provided the foundation for us to find the time and energy to put these thoughts on paper, we want to thank the editors who polished our words and made them shine.

Many thanks to our publisher for risking taking on two newbies and giving us the confidence to become bona fide authors.

More than anyone, we want to thank you, our readers, for clicking on a couple of nobodies and sharing your most important asset, your time, with this book. We hope with all our hearts we made it worthwhile.

Much love,
Mary & Amy

ABOUT THE AUTHOR

Mary Stone lives among the majestic Blue Ridge Mountains of East Tennessee with her two dogs, four cats, a couple of energetic boys, and a very patient husband.

As a young girl, she would go to bed every night, wondering what type of creature might be lurking underneath. It wasn't until she was older that she learned that the creatures she needed to most fear were human.

Today, she creates vivid stories with courageous, strong heroines and dastardly villains. She invites you to enter her world of serial killers, FBI agents but never damsels in distress. Her female characters can handle themselves, going toe-to-toe with any male character, protagonist or antagonist.

Discover more about Mary Stone on her website.
www.authormarystone.com

Amy Wilson

Having spent her adult life in the heart of Atlanta, her upbringing near the Great Lakes always seems to slip into her writing. After several years as a vet tech, she has dreams of going back to school to be a veterinarian but it seems another dream of hers has come true first. Writing a novel.

Animals and books have always been her favorite things, in addition to her husband, who wanted her to have it all. He's the reason she has time to write. Their two teenage boys fill the rest of her time and help her take care of the mini zoo that now fills their home with laughter…and yes, the occasional poop.

Connect with Mary Online

facebook.com/authormarystone

goodreads.com/AuthorMaryStone

bookbub.com/profile/3378576590

pinterest.com/MaryStoneAuthor

Printed in Great Britain
by Amazon